LOVE ME LIKE YOU DO

SASHA CLINTON

Copyright © 2016 by Sasha Clinton

All rights reserved.

No part of this book may be reproduced in any form or by any electronic or mechanical means, including information storage and retrieval systems, without written permission from the author, except for the use of brief quotations in a book review.

Edited by Chelsea Kuhel

Cover design by Sasha Clinton

❀ Created with Vellum

CHAPTER ONE

Bad habits came in a variety of shapes and sizes. Picking your nose. A sweet tooth. A porn addiction.

Loving unavailable men. That was Bella's vice. It had also been her mother's, though Mama also indulged in the bottle quite a bit. But in the end, Bella thought it was the heartbreak that had cut her life short more than the drinking. Emptiness and fleeting pleasures. Men who promised nothing but took everything from her.

Because while bad habits looked harmless on the surface, they could destroy the very fabric of your soul. It had happened to her mother. It could happen to her if she wasn't careful.

Bella closed her eyes against the harsh sunlight that skimmed over her eyelids, hearing the ominous rustle of leaves in the cemetery. Her mother's funeral had ended only moments ago. It was an overstatement to call it a 'funeral' since she'd been the only one in attendance. Even the pastor had shaken his head at her in pity. She'd wanted her eulogy to be good, but in the end, there had been none at all.

When Bella thought of her mother, all she recalled were bad memories, bad decisions, bad men, and instability. Growing up, she hadn't experienced any security. They'd moved from home to home as the whims of the men in her mother's life waxed and waned like the moon, as their attraction for her faded and restarted.

Well, it was over now. And she was officially an orphan. She was also officially moving on with her life. And the first step was to get out of the shadow of her rocky childhood by fulfilling her long-held dream of buying a house.

"Isn't there anything cheaper?" Bella asked the real estate agent at the risk of sounding like a broken record. She'd asked him that question hundreds of times already over the two months they'd been working on finding her a home. And she was expecting the same answer this time around.

"Well, it's completely turn-key, no renovation required. And it's in Brooklyn, so it's going to cost this much."

"I suppose…" she trailed off, sparing the designer kitchen with stainless steel appliances and white quartz countertops one last glance. Oh god, how badly she longed to stand there, to cook on that gas hob, to run her fingers over the kitchen island in her own house. "You're right."

The moment she'd stepped into the condo, she'd fallen head over heels in love with the vibe of the house. The building had a beautiful, art deco exterior; the doorman and concierge had smiled at her. The apartment, a one-bedroom, was on the sixteenth floor. The city view from the floor-to-ceiling windows was gorgeous, the most breathtaking sight ever. Even twenty years later, she wouldn't tire of it. Sunlight cascaded in from everywhere, flooding the entire space with natural illumination and giving it an airy, open feel. The interiors in the house were of an extremely high standard, every detail rendered perfect. The bathroom even had golden fittings.

She *had* to have this house. Her chest burned with the desire to own it, to own a piece of security. But she knew better than to expect those wishes to come true.

This was her fifteenth viewing with the agent. Like all the previous houses she'd seen, she'd fallen in love with this one, too. It checked off every item on her list. And it was completely out of her budget. Which was depressing as hell.

She wasn't poor by any means. She was a professor. She made decent money. But not nearly enough to pay back her student loans, cover insurance costs and rent while still be able to save enough for a hefty down payment. She'd ruthlessly cut costs in the last few years, opting to do all the housework herself, buying groceries at cheaper stores, repurposing old clothes instead of splurging on new ones, canceling online subscriptions, dialing back expenditure on luxuries. She'd lived frugally, hoping it'd all pay off when she held the keys to her own dream home.

But that dream seemed to be slipping further and further out of her reach. House prices rose drastically every year in New York City while her savings only increased moderately. A bust in the real estate market was nowhere in sight. Unless a miracle happened, she was afraid she'd die homeless.

"If you had a partner, you could split the cost," the agent suggested. "Not many people can afford a home on a single wage in this city. Why don't you try again after a few years, once you've had time to find someone?"

"I want to do this by myself," Bella emphasized.

Independence was everything to her. Unlike her mother, she wouldn't let her material security be swayed by unstable relationships. Of course, she did plan to find a partner. She wanted to fall in love with someone committed and stable, to experience a healthy companionship. But that was that and this was this. There was no way she was going to let anyone dictate her home situation.

"Can't you borrow money from your parents? If you can get them to loan you even fifty grand extra, we'd be able to put in offers on similar properties. There's a studio in this building for that price."

"I want a one-bedroom," Bella said. "And I don't have parents."

Even if her mother had been alive, she was too broke to lend her money.

"Friends, then."

"I'll see what I can do."

"You need to act fast if you want to get that studio property. The one-bed I showed you in Morningside Heights the other day already sold for fifty grand more than the asking price. Properties get snapped up quickly here. It's a war and you need to be fast to win."

"I know. I'll try to get some extra cash. In the meantime, can you keep looking for cheaper properties?"

The agent sighed, adjusting his brown jacket. "I've told you before. The areas you're interested in have high average property prices."

"But there must be *something*."

The furrowing of the agent's brows told her that he didn't share her optimism. "The market's hot right now. Lots of sales happening."

"Do you think it'll cool down soon?"

"Unlikely." Bella soaked in the glory of the one-bedroom she'd never have for the last time before the agent led her back to the elevator. He gave her a professional nod. "I'll be in touch with you."

"Thanks."

Back in her rental apartment, Bella collapsed onto her sofa. Every outing with the agent ended with her concluding that it was impossible to buy a house in New York. She couldn't afford a house like the one she wanted. She also couldn't afford to lower her expectations because if she was going to live in a house forever, it should be a place she'd be able to love ten years from now. Maybe, if she met her savings goal this year, then she could afford the down payment next year—if the prices didn't shoot up by then. Which they definitely would.

Frustration burned a trail through her throat. There was no way out of this situation.

Because she was self-sabotaging like that, Bella scrolled through Zillow, visually absorbing the picture-perfect condos and townhouses that she would never own, plummeting her already low mood. Every house on here was pretty enough to hurt her eyes and expensive enough to hurt her sanity. One time she'd tried to arrange a viewing through the app, it'd been a scam.

Suddenly, a ping flitted into her ear from her phone, waking her up from her real estate dreams. A notification from Tinder. Someone had matched with her. Bella didn't use dating apps much, since she'd all but vowed to end her string of short-lived, shallow relationships with unavailable men. It was in the aftermath of her mother's death.

If there was one thing she didn't want to turn into, it was a carbon copy of her mother. Since she was focused on finding a stable partner who'd invest just as much as she did emotionally into the relationship, the thought of checking Tinder hadn't crossed her mind. But it was a welcome distraction from her apartment browsing now so she took a chance.

Jamie Star. That was the name of her match. She sensed a familiar ring but couldn't place him. Was he a celebrity? A fellow student at university?

Whoever he was, he wasn't Greek god handsome, or at least he didn't appear that way in his photos. But he was cute. In an artsy sort of way. Of course, he could be a total creep. He could also be abusive, have STDs, be deep in debt, a conman, or all of the above.

His first message was, to say the least, generic. But it was blunt and straightforward. She was beginning to appreciate this style of communication nowadays.

Jamie: I'm not looking for sex. I want a partnership.

Bella scoffed. That was what they all said. Still, his message lit something inside her. A flicker of hope. To be honest, she was looking for a partnership, too. What was the harm in giving this guy a chance? The home buying was stressing her out anyway. She needed a break.

Bella: Tell me more about yourself.

Jamie: I work in television. I like romantic movies and cold days.

Bella: I like romantic movies, too. I work in education.

Jamie: Any hobbies?

Bella: Reading, house hunting, getting revenge on people I hate by baking for them. One of my colleagues got food poisoning after consuming my marble cake, but he couldn't blame me for it because he had no proof. Best day of my life.

Jamie: Woah. What did the bastard do to you?

Bella: He grabbed my butt. Twice. And kept giving me dirty looks during department meetings even though I told him it was sexual harassment.

Jamie: In that case, well done! That's the most creative revenge plot I've heard of. I should try it sometime.

Bella: Shall I send you my recipe?

Jamie: Wouldn't mind. But I've never baked before.

Bella: Trust me, you'll learn fast. But moving on, tell me about your hobbies.

Jamie: Let's see...fucking up the lives of imaginary people, escaping reality, and providing employment to chefs across the city.

Bella: So writing, sleeping, and eating out?

Jamie: Pretty much. And if that doesn't convince you I'm boring, I also watch Netflix.

A self-deprecating guy. She likes that. Bella realized she'd almost forgotten about her disappointment with the condo and her fingers were flying over the keyboard.

Bella: What was the last thing you watched?

Jamie: A Japanese movie about a girl who moves into her father's house after college and refuses to grow up. It was very slice-of-life. Very relatable.

Bella: Haven't seen that one yet. Maybe I should.

Jamie: It was good. But tell me about your house hunting. Not going well?

Bella: Ugh. I messaged you to forget about that. Houses in this city are eye-wateringly expensive. By any chance, do you own a house?

Jamie: I do. But not in this city.

Bella: How did you manage to buy it?

Jamie: I bought it from a friend so I got it at a good price.

Bella: How lucky! Tell me about this house.

Jamie: Seven bedrooms. Ten bathrooms. Ten thousand square feet. Swimming pool, Jacuzzi, and three acres of lawns. Draw your own conclusions.

Bella: Are you showing off right now?

Jamie: Only stating facts. You were the one who asked me to tell you about it.

Bella: You cannot imagine how envious I am of you at this moment.

Jamie: You really want a house? Maybe I can help you. I know some people. Why don't we meet at a coffee shop to talk? My fingers are fatigued from typing on my phone and I don't feel very comfortable chatting online.

Bella considered this for a moment. She didn't like jumping into a face-to-face meeting so quickly, but maybe this Jamie was a shy person, not adept at using technology. And he'd suggested meeting at a coffee shop, not his house or a hotel, which meant his intentions were pure. She had nothing to lose. Plus, he wasn't turned off by her dark humor, which was always a good sign.

Bella: Sure.

She sent him the name of the place they were going to meet at because she was a control freak, didn't trust strangers, and was absolutely not going to leave the decision up to him. He messaged her back with a time. Saturday.

She had no house viewings on that day.

Bella: That works. See you then.

Jamie: Can't wait.

CHAPTER TWO

The last time Jamie had met a woman at a coffee shop was when his ex-girlfriend had begged him to give her money to move to Australia for her modeling career, then promptly spent the cash on drugs, plastic surgery, and new clothes. She'd bled him dry with that one, and though it'd been three years since then, he still didn't trust himself with women or relationships. He could never say no to tears and emotional blackmail, which meant he was emotionally manipulated all the time. No. Hookups were definitely better. But today wasn't about relationships or hookups. It was about business.

Jamie yanked open the glass door of Grumpy Coffee and Bakery. A bell tinkled above his head, and a few of the people huddled around the oak tables briefly glanced up, before realizing that he was just an ordinary man and returning to their conversations. He took a moment to bask in the cool wave of air from the air conditioning, letting the heat and sweat clinging to him dissipate. The aroma of roasted coffee beans mingled in the air alongside the sweet scent of burnt sugar and baked goods.

He scanned the coffee shop but there was no sign of Bella anywhere, so he bought two large double chocolate muffins and a cold brew, then settled into one of the long-legged stools set in front of a wooden table attached to the wall. The seat beside him was empty, but beyond that, a student in an NYU hoodie was drawing on his sketchpad and a woman in a suit was typing furiously on her laptop. The exposed brick wall behind the counter cast their profiles in stark relief.

When five minutes later, there was still no sign of Bella, he began to panic in earnest. The words of his assistant producer swirled around his head.

"You're going to replace Martina with a chick you met on Tinder?"

"They look exactly the same. See?" he'd protested.

He hadn't believed it at first, either. It was the stuff of Hollywood movies. He'd been swiping through Tinder in search of his next hookup when, out of the blue, *her* face had appeared on his screen. It had blown his mind. Her likeness to Martina was uncanny. Jamie had right-swiped immediately, hoping they'd match. If they didn't, he was ready to hire a detective to find her. Because without her, his life was over.

The production of his Netflix show was in a spectacular pickle since Martina, the actress playing the main supporting character, had vanished, leaving behind a note that she didn't want to be found. By that point, they'd already shot six out of ten episodes for the show already, and re-hiring extras, paying all the actors and cameramen for extra time, the scheduling headache, setting up the props again...it'd cost too much money to hire a new actress and reshoot all the previous episodes. They were dangerously close to going over budget already. Plus, it would delay the production time and as it was, they were operating in a time crunch. To be fair, it was his fault for not managing everything properly, but this was his first gig as a producer on a Netflix show and he was too ambitious to let it become his last. There was one thing in life he had control over, and that was his career. And he wasn't about to lose his control over it.

So he needed the Tinder woman. Bella. He needed her and he was prepared to grovel and beg and seduce her if it meant his production could go on.

"You've lost it. She's not even an actress. How are you going to convince her?" Those were the words his assistant had uttered when he'd revealed his grand plan to her—hire Bella, go ahead with shooting the remaining four episodes, remain on schedule. Boom. Everybody wins. His assistant, however, had been completely unimpressed.

"It might be a catfish," she'd said. "That might not even be her real face."

Damn. He hadn't considered that possibility at all.

But Jamie was desperate to succeed and desperation made one willing to cross bridges that were dangerous and unstable. Hence this faux coffee shop date. He checked the contract documents he'd had the lawyer draft last minute, smoothing his fingertips over the bright, white paper.

Money. He was going to convince Bella with money. She'd mentioned that she wanted to buy a house but was struggling with financing it. Well, he was about to pay her enough to make her dreams come true. In return, she'd help him stave off the biggest nightmare of his career.

As he said, win-win.

When the bell tinkled again, Jamie bobbed his face up. The figure at the door was already striding toward him. Hope squealed inside his head like a chorus of angels. The woman was around 5'6—the same as Martina. He'd put her weight at around 150 pounds—also similar to Martina. Her curves were killer. She had a round face with a rounded chin and a tiny, cute nose. Smooth, dark hair rolled over her shoulders in waves that seemed almost black when shadows fell over them. Jamie was overcome by a strong urge to bury his hands in that hair. As she approached, he couldn't take his eyes off her lush lips, painted a sexy red with lipstick. He'd seriously hook up with her if it wouldn't mean the end of his professionalism. She was gorgeous.

Before she could blink, her deep, feminine voice filtered into his ears. A citrusy scent enveloped him. "Sorry. I'm late."

The clearest pair of blue eyes he'd ever encountered appraised him, and he tumbled back, involuntarily. Heat flushed across Bella's collarbone, a streak of red on her skin.

Jamie's eyes widened, then popped. Clasping her shoulders, he bored into her with his focused gaze. "You....you look exactly like your Tinder profile."

"Did you expect a catfish?" she asked, cocking an eyebrow in amusement.

"If I'm being honest, yes," he replied.

"I try to be as real as possible. Honesty is good." She quirked her lip, expecting agreement but Jamie's mind was occupied by the contract and how to convince her to sign it. Now that he'd confirmed with his own eyes that she was real, it was time to roll the dice.

"Let me buy you something to drink first," he said. "What would you like?"

The first step, make her stay by bribing her with food. Then he'd lay out his proposal. He had to admit, now that she was here, looking every inch unattainable and angelic, he was having second thoughts about whether his idea would work out.

"I'll buy it myself," Bella replied with a shrug. "It's my rule for first dates. In case things don't work out between us, I don't want you to have wasted your money on nothing."

Jamie nodded, drinking down his words as she sashayed toward the counter, smiling at the barista whose face lit up instantly. Couldn't blame the guy. She was like a ray of sunshine.

Ordinarily, Jamie would've applauded her independence and consideration for his wallet. But in this situation, it reinforced the fear that if she already had a great job and made loads of money, she'd just turn down his offer. Money was all he had to lure her in. She'd mentioned working in education. That could mean anything from a teacher to an ed-tech startup.

He dropped to the unoccupied stool, chewing his lip. He pulled out a wad of napkins from the silver napkin dispenser and dabbed at the perspiration on his face. Despite the aircon, he was sweating profusely. Things were already slipping out of his control. He hated that, hated when the variables turned out to be wild cards. This Bella was definitely a wild card.

"Maybe it'd have been better to talk over Tinder," Bella's voice shot at him. She was back and making herself comfortable on the empty stool next to his, a cold brew clutched in her hand. "You seem anxious."

She was right; he was three minutes away from a heart attack.

"I've never done this before," Jamie admitted. He placed one hand on the surface of the table, gaze wandering over to her cold brew. "I'm curious; what's your actual job?"

"I'm a professor," she answered. "Can I ask what is yours?"

"TV writer and producer. I'm working on a Netflix series at the moment." He inhaled. His chest swelled under his red T-shirt, and it strained like a tight straitjacket against his broad shoulders. He held his breath for a long beat, building up to the dramatic climax. "I have to tell you something."

She tilted her head at him. There was a softness in her blue irises, an understanding that put him at ease instantly. "Go ahead."

Jamie's knee hit the underside of the table. Smooth. Real smooth. "Look, this is not how I usually roll, but…the reason I wanted to meet you was that I need you. You're special. Your body, your face. It's the exact one I'm looking for. And I can pay you for it…er…I mean the use of it…for you to use it. Fuck, none of this is coming out the way I want it to."

Oh, great. Now he was a bumbling mess. This was what happened when he lost control over people and things and most of all, his own emotions. He made a fool of himself. The incident with his mother had proven that years ago. His love for her had always been out of control, and he'd thought she loved him, too. But she only cared for being desirable, only wanted to be the wife of old Hollywood legend Grant Star. Jamie was simply a way for her to achieve that goal.

Bella rose to her feet, her heels making a loud sound. "That's it. I'm out. It was nice meeting you, Jamie, but I think it's best if we don't continue seeing each other."

"Wait." Panic brought Jamie to his feet, and he grabbed her handbag. She couldn't leave. He couldn't let her leave. "That didn't come out right."

"I'm not a prostitute or an art model. You can't pay for my body," she asserted.

"I'm not looking for a prostitute. Or a nude model—"

"On Tinder, you said you were looking for a partnership. I thought you were serious."

"A business partnership," Jamie clarified.

Bella shook her head. But he could see that her curiosity had been piqued. "What kind of business?"

"Have you ever thought of becoming an actress?"

Usually, when he asked that question to most people, they showed at least a flicker of interest. In the age of social media and celebrity worship, people wanted nothing more than to be the center of attention. Fame, success, riches, being discovered by a producer...this was the stuff of dreams and Hollywood happy endings.

But this Bella simply had to be that *one* woman who was down-to-earth and comfortable in her own skin. At his question, she frowned and jumped back as if he'd asked her to sell her kidneys.

"Never. I don't want to be part of that world again." Her jaw trembled and she turned away, distraught.

Again? There was definitely something he'd missed there.

"Have you been an actress before?" Jamie asked. "Did you have a bad experience? I swear, nobody in my production is going to harass you or ask you for sexual favors—"

"No." She swiveled back on her heel, cold anger flashing in her eyes. What landmine had he stepped on now? "I'm not interested."

"Just hear me out." He inhaled ceremoniously, then held out his business card. His name was engraved in blue letters on the thick ivory paper, followed by the words 'executive producer' and 'screenwriter'. Bella hesitated but snatched the card and examined it closely while Jamie continued to talk. "To tell you the truth, the actress who was originally playing the character vanished midway through the show, and you look exactly like her. That's why I approached you on Tinder. I need you so I can finish the show. Tell me, how can I convince you to take her part?"

"Sorry, but nothing can convince me to go back to LA."

"We're filming in New York," Jamie said, breaking her chain of thoughts.

At this, she paused. Like she was actually going to consider it. But then her mood quickly changed, and she dropped her shoulders. "I have a day job."

He brought his face closer until a faint scent drifted up to her nose. "I'll pay you twice as much as you currently make."

Her lips thinned. "I'm happy with what I make."

He scoffed. "You live in NYC. You can't be happy with what you make. Rent is through the roof. The subway isn't cheap. Food's not cheap. A few extra thousand dollars could buy you a lot."

He was getting somewhere with this. He could feel it in his bones. Bella was hesitating again. She balled her fingers into fists at her side, opening and closing her mouth without saying anything.

All he needed to do was that she couldn't refuse

"Give me five minutes to convince you. Let's sit down. We're both already here." He gestured at the stool she'd vacated not even moments ago.

Bella dug her hands into her hips, crossing her legs and seating herself. "Five minutes. And you need to tell me all the details including what you'll pay me. Don't leave anything out. I'm going to fact-check it later."

Cradling a cold cup of coffee between his palms, Jamie made an effort to hold onto his composure, which was slipping away faster than money at a Vegas casino. He waited for Bella to sit down and then faced her. "You'll have to work five days a week—rehearsals Monday through Thursday, shooting on Fridays." He paused. "Pre-tax, your payment will be about twenty-five grand per episode, and if we get renewed for a second season, you can renegotiate your salary." He speared the table's surface with the tip of his finger. "As a bonus, you get to work alongside great actors like Catherine Martin and eat free lunch every day."

Twenty-five thousand? Did you say twenty-five thousand? Thousand with three zeros? I must be hallucinating."

"Yes, three zeroes."

"How many episodes will I have to do?" she asked.

"Four." He paused, waiting for her to do the mental math in her head. "Not a bad deal, right?"

"And this offer is not fake?" There was an audible question mark at the end of her sentence. Bella tapped the edge of the coffee table, sliding a glance at her iPhone.

Jamie slammed an impatient hand on the table. "I swear it's not."

"Can I verify with another source?" She fidgeted with the hem of her skirt, too excited to stay calm. He tasted success on his tongue. He was so close to getting her to agree. The feeling of being back in control again made his thoughts clearer. Made him straighten his spine and project more confidence.

"Sure, you can call the studio." Jamie pulled out the contract he'd brought along and circled Star Studio's phone number at the bottom with his finger. "Your resemblance to Martina is unbelievable. Once we dye your hair red—"

"Red?" She pulled one leg from the ground, inadvertently kicking Jamie's knees. Okay, that hadn't been entirely inadvertent, because she smiled, showing teeth as sharp as daggers.

"That's non-negotiable," Jamie said, trying to wrestle the situation back in his favor. "Your character has red hair."

"So it's *my* character now? I haven't said yes yet."

"But you will." Jamie was confident. He'd seen the way her lips had parted when he'd mentioned how much he'd pay her. She was poring over the document with great focus, and why would she do that if she had no intention of signing it? The desire, the greed, the way her nails scratched the paper like she wanted to own it, was unmistakable.

"Let me think about it. Give me a few days." Bella drained her cup, tongue darting out her tongue to wipe the coffee residue off her luscious lips. Jamie's heart did a backflip. He pinched himself. He absolutely would not destroy his career over a stupid chemical attraction. Wouldn't give up control to a woman again. The gnawing hunger, the needy heat in his groin would have to starve to death because he wasn't going to feed it.

"I don't have that kind of time," he snapped. "Think you can decide faster?"

"I need time to research." Bella swept her cup of coffee into her arms and glided away to deposit it in the trash. "Learn patience."

She maneuvered to the door of the shop, waving him goodbye. Jamie's muffin sat uneaten and he'd only taken one sip of the coffee but he discarded the items in the trash bin and followed her like a faithful dog, all the way to the end of the block, where their paths split.

"Bella." The words rolled off his tongue like he was born to say them. "See you soon."

"Don't get your hopes up, Jamie." She tipped her head forward, and silently strode away.

CHAPTER THREE

Grant Star's townhouse on the Upper East Side loomed ahead of Jamie, its long, rectangular shadow slanting over the sidewalk and the road. The yellow-brown stone walls were weather-beaten, but not worn. Curtains were drawn in the sitting-room window, and there was no movement through the windows, which was, to put it mildly, unusual in the Star household.

Jamie entered the code on the keypad to the left of the Lion-shaped door knocker. The black door swung unlocked, and a whoosh of freezing air gusted over him.

The grand foyer was empty. Jamie spotted several new elements—Warhol paintings, African tribal masks, and tall Grecian vases holding stalks of artificial pink flowers. As he walked towards the stairs leading up to Grant's home office, his sneakers were stifled by the blue Persian rug in the living room.

Overcrowded with furniture, the living room was different from what it'd been during his childhood. The brand new, modern light fixtures on the wall cast a sophisticated light over the space. The TV had been upgraded to a 50-inch plasma screen, and there was a mini-bar right next to the TV.

For a few nostalgic moments, Jamie recalled playing hide-and-seek and watching *Noddy* with his father. Grant had once been a good father. More than good—he'd been cool, present, attentive—the kind of father every boy longed for.

He'd always called his father Grant, rather than dad, because they'd been so close, more like best friends than father and son. He couldn't pinpoint the day when Grant had gone from being the best dad in the world to an absent one, who only saw him at dinner with a different woman on his arm every week.

Maybe the day when he'd not shown up for Jamie's high school graduation, or maybe even before that. Water under the bridge now. He'd grown used to the new Grant and his stream of stick-thin women with silicone boobs just as he'd grown used to this new house and the constant changes here.

"Grant?" Jamie called, spinning his gaze around.

Unflinching silence circled him. Wasn't Grant home?

"Grant!" he called again, louder this time.

He heard rustling from upstairs. The bedroom door was ajar with twin shadows dancing in front of the door. He approached the doorjamb with trepidation and knocked.

"Grant?"

"Come in."

Every time he heard that tone of voice, it was almost always followed by some unsavory revelation of the carnal kind.

"Are you sure it's okay for me to come in?"

Amused laughter roared out, vibrating over Jamie's toes. "I have nothing to hide, J. You know all my vices."

Throwing the door open, Jamie bustled in, to find a young, hot, naked woman in his father's arms, her tongue deep inside Grant's mouth.

His recoil was only moderate. He'd experienced a few too many reruns of this scenario over the last years. Enough to desensitize him. Now, this was normal. Like most superstars who'd enjoyed too much free-flowing pussy during the height of their careers, Grant Star had never quite gotten over the delusion that he was Molly in male form. At fifty-six, he had a revolving door of women at his disposal, most of whom were connected to the studio in some way or the other. The only difference was he'd updated his repertoire to include some 'Fifty Shades,' if the handcuffs and blindfold were anything to go by.

"Hey, J." Wiping away the moisture on his lips with the back of his palm, Grant's piercing gray eyes crinkled at Jamie. Those were super-star eyes, alright. They were also father eyes.

Jamie gave a smirk of disgust when Grant reached up to stroke the blonde's very enhanced butt. While he may have inherited his father's love for movies, he'd not inherited Grant's penchant for women who had more plastic in their bodies than a Barbie doll.

Keen to preserve the image of Grant he had in his head as a kind and supportive dad, Jamie didn't judge him too harshly for it. Grant had a lot of good in him. He'd helped Jamie get in touch with a number of studios to pitch his TV series, and he'd cheered him on at every step of his career. There were many talented writers out there with better scripts who were struggling because they didn't have a Grant Star to believe in them.

This was why Jamie needed to convince that Bella woman to become an actress. The lead actress on his sitcom, Martina, has gone missing just before the deadline for ABC and she'd made it clear in the letter she'd left behind that she wouldn't be back anytime soon. If he couldn't shoot the show on time, it'd lead to it being canceled. Having a show picked up by a cable network was a one in twenty thousand chance. Literally. Not many ideas got past the rigorous winnowing process carried out by studios and network cable executives. There was no way he was blowing his chance because of a missing actress.

"I can take two," the woman crouched at Grant's side said, winking at Jamie.

"Let's not involve J in this, Sheila." Grant didn't look very happy.

Dropping his gaze to the bottle of Johnnie Walker and tub of ice cubes atop the glass-top coffee table, Jamie grimaced. Scotch whiskey and sex. Surely, that was a combination his father could have come up with.

"I'll come back later," Jamie informed, his back half-facing his father. "It wasn't anything important."

In the interest of preserving his modesty, Grant had pulled the sheets to cover half his chest, but the woman with him didn't see the need for such useless pretensions.

Looking at a naked woman didn't make him uncomfortable or turn him on, but he turned his gaze to Monet's water lilies hanging on the wall, framed in gold. Originals his father had paid a mini-fortune for. It had been Grant's fiftieth birthday gift to himself.

Grant curved his head up. "J, you look dejected. Struggling with a script?"

No, he was struggling with an entire production, he wanted to say. He needed Grant, who had a great deal of experience in this business and had been through some really hellish days, to tell him that it was going to be okay. Jamie respected his father. No shit. Grant Star must be one tough man if he'd kept Star Studios profitable for twenty years. Hollywood had way more budget bleeders than TV.

He wanted to ask if Grant had ever felt like he did right now, tired of working all the time and still feeling uncertain about everything. Of feeling like his life was always slipping out of control. No matter how much he succeeded, how many accolades he accumulated, there was a void inside him that wasn't filled by any amount of money or success. After this production, there'd be another production and another…but he needed more than the next stimulating project, the next award, the next box office hit. Sometimes, he felt a desperate longing for something he couldn't even name. And that was darn frustrating. Not to mention confusing.

Today, too, he'd felt a nameless yearning for that college professor. The longing to press his skin against hers, to hear her utter words he didn't yet know but knew only she could say to him. Jamie sighed. He should see a shrink. Maybe he was going mad after all.

"J?" Grant said, puzzled by his long silence.

"It's nothing," Jamie said, hesitating to demand Grant's time. His critics were right when they called him out for nepotism when they said that he was too dependent on his father to do anything without his help. He was even depending on him for emotional comfort now. He was a grown man, for fuck's sake. "Do you have any free time this week?"

"I don't think so. But if it's something urgent—"

Chopped off midsentence by the housekeeper Diana's loud voice, Grant stilled. Jamie reflexively whipped his body around.

"What is it, Diana?" he shouted to the housekeeper. She knew better than to enter his room, but she did have the loudest voice on the planet, which could stop anyone in their tracks.

"Eve Rosenberg is here to see Grant," she shouted back in her thick southern accent.

"Who's Eve Rosenberg?" Jamie put the question to his father.

Panicked, Grant scanned the entire perimeter of the room, snatching a shirt from under Sheila's derriere. "Vice-President of Legal and Business Affairs at Star Studios. I need to get dressed, and you two have to leave." He tapped Sheila, gesturing at her to get out.

Judging from Grant's extreme reaction, Eve Rosenberg was also a woman who had no problem putting Grant in his place. To be fair, none of the studio's executives let him walk all over them as much as the twenty-something starry-eyed interns and starlets did, but a woman with as much spine as this Eve was a rare species at Star Studios.

Skimming past the living room, where Eve was now sitting and unhappily watching *Real Housewives* re-runs with Diana, Jamie observed that she was older than any woman Jamie had ever seen in his father's vicinity, with the exception of Diana.

That must be why Grant hadn't hit on her yet. To quote Grant, "older women were for men who had no options left." Yeah, he could be a bastard. That was probably why no woman stayed with him long.

Still, Eve was an attractive woman for her age. Her hair might be graying, but it was still thick and shiny with enough brown left. She had small, expressive eyes in an intriguing shade of hazel.

Sheila from upstairs rushed out past him, followed by a put-together Grant who shook Eve's hand.

Jamie decided to follow Sheila out.

Outside the townhouse, it took him time to readjust to the humid heat. Unable to make up his mind about what to do with Bella, Jamie wandered around the entrance of the townhouse, jogging up a few blocks until he was at a subway station.

He needed a desperate dose of something funny and interesting at this moment.

He settled for a Tinder hookup. A real one this time.

Until today, Grant could count the number of times he'd been nervous in his life with one hand. Today was the first time he had to use his other hand to do the counting.

Eve Rosenberg made him nervous. Very nervous. Mostly because she never had any good news for him. All that she ever discussed with him were legal and business problems. But there was something even more disturbing than legal problems that she brought up.

A strange desire. A sexual desire that he would never, ever act on. Though he did have momentary lapses in judgment, he wasn't *that* much of an idiot.

Diana set two cups of Earl Grey on the table with a motherly smile. Diana must be the same age as Eve, but unlike Eve, he didn't even notice Diana. Not as a woman, anyway. She'd worked for him over ten years and he'd always seen her as his household help and nothing else. Household staff didn't have a gender or personality to him.

As a rule, he regarded all women over fifty as moving furniture, a distinction that served him well when it came to keeping his lust away from housekeepers. Gray hair, wrinkles, and sex appeal did not mix. Beyond fifty, a female was practically a relic to him.

Eve was the only exception.

Honestly, he'd never been attracted to a woman her age. Menopausal women had no sex drive, and all he needed was sex—preferably with a tight, hot, and enhanced body.

"Um..." He nodded like a dummy when Eve took a breath between her long explanation.

She picked up the teacup and rested the edge of the porcelain between her thin lips.

Regular trips to the hairdresser were keeping her hair brown, but she must've missed an appointment because there was a shock of gray around her temples. Boy, it must be so depressing to grow old as a woman and watch everything you have fade.

What did he see in her then? Grant wondered.

Eve was so flawed. Her breasts dropped despite the bra she wore, and she had a symphony of lines and spots around her eyes and mouth. Not the image of Hollywood beauty, really. Not the image of any kind of beauty, really.

"Are you with me?" Eve prodded, widening her luscious honey-hued eyes. Such a magnificent color. As unique as the rest of her.

"Have you thought about early retirement?" Grant interrupted, drifting off-topic.

Molding her mouth into a pucker, she gave him a shrug.

Next year, he was going to add an option for free Botox to her benefits package. On second thought, she would most likely shoot that suggestion down on the basis of being sexist or ageist. There was no pleasing a woman like her. Melanie—his first and only wife—had been notoriously easy to please. Diamonds and joints did it for her every time. This one was impressed by nothing.

"I don't believe in quitting early," she said, something fiery flaring in her eyes. "I've got a few more years to go before I hit sixty-five. After that, I'm planning to start my own consulting business. You're more than welcome to hire me as a consultant and keep using my services."

A high chuckle climbed out of his vocal cords. God, she was something. Bustling with plans for the future even at this age. Nothing like the demure, easygoing, submissive women he liked. Entirely too ambitious. Entirely too much like how he'd been in his youth.

"Don't you want to take it easy?" Grant asked, pretending to humor her.

"Post-retirement life is excessively glorified." She made a dreary face. "I want to live and work until my last breath."

He decided to try the tea, but after seeing it, changed his mind. Diana made horrible tea, which was ironic since she had previously lived in England. "Overworking ages your skin faster."

Making a funny sound, she scrunched her face. "What am I going to do with tight skin at my age?"

"What're you going to do with more money, then?"

"It's not about the money..." She became alert. "Actually, while we're on the topic of money, I want to renegotiate my salary for next year and discuss my promotion. Atsushi's retiring next year. I'm the most experienced person in legal. In my seven years at Star Studios, I think I've proven myself enough to warrant a promotion."

"Eve. We've done this before." A tired exhale escaped. Every three years, she got this itch to be promoted. "No."

"Why not? I think I deserve it, Grant. I've seen everybody but me getting promoted since I joined Star Studios. I think it's my turn now."

Grant picked up the teacup, then bothered by the smell, set it down. "You don't have sufficient leadership ability. And you don't put in nearly as many hours as Atsushi does. You want to leave by six on most days. Now, I understand that you have a family and as a woman, that's your first priority. We're proud to promote work-life balance at Star Studios. But I have to be fair here. Atsushi works much harder than you, and there are many people in the organization who work longer than you. President is a demanding role. We need someone committed."

"I'm committed," she mumbled, visibly upset. "And you're not right about me working less than the others. Actually, if you total up the number of hours I've worked over the last three years; I've worked more hours than anybody else. And I've shown plenty of leadership."

She rattled off a number of instances. Grant didn't have to check to know that she was right. However, that didn't mean he could promote her. The board and other senior executives already had a man in mind to be Atsushi's successor. A man who was, no doubt, less qualified than Eve. But he was young, and Star Studios needed young blood at the top.

"Eve, we have plenty of high-caliber candidates for President. I don't want to sound harsh, but I think you're fighting a losing battle here."

She swept her palms over her red cheeks. "So tell me. How do I show more leadership? Do I need to be more proactive in soliciting deals? Do I need to exceed my targets by more than I currently am? Or do I need to have a penis?"

Grant expected her to apologize, to flinch, take back her words, but she continued to stand by and let those words echo. The word penis was definitely not moving his thoughts in any fruitful direction.

"I can see you're passionate about this," he started. *And I want to fuck this passionate woman.* "I'll see what I can do."

"You say the same thing every year. Don't you get tired of saying it again and again without meaning it?" She stamped a sharp heel on the hardwood floor. "And it's not even about me being passionate. There is clearly a culture of discrimination against female employees at the organization. Ninety-five percent of promotions in the last three years went to men. Women are grossly under-represented in the top management. Less than five percent of the board is female. Grant, you've got to change that."

Grant squirmed under his skin. Hadn't this brand of confrontational feminism gone out of fashion in the seventies? Bracing himself for a tough battle, he rolled up his sleeves. Every salary negotiation with Eve always degenerated into something like this.

"We promoted six women to middle-management last year and recruited our second female board member." That was his favorite statistic. Because it was the only one. "We're trying to improve the gender balance at the top. But we can't promote you just because you're a woman. That's not what equality is about."

"I'm not asking you to promote me because I'm a woman," she cried. "I'm asking you to promote me because I'm competent!"

"That's your viewpoint. Unfortunately, not everybody shares it." Grant clapped, to add a sense of finality.

Stationing her hands on her thighs, Eve met him with a pained gaze. If he had his way, he'd lick the honey in her eyes all the way down to the honey between her legs. That was how obsessed she had him after fifteen minutes of argument.

God save him, though, because, in the last year, he hadn't fixated on a woman as much as he'd fixated on her. He wanted her more than he wanted the tight asses of more willing women. Eve was long past her prime, both professionally and sexually, and he still had many, many years to go before he had to settle for less-than-attractive women.

Maybe it's because she's forbidden. Maybe that makes her exciting.

No, he'd never enjoyed the chase. For as long as he could recall, he'd preferred easy women. The hard-to-get ones were generally not worth the effort. Unable to reconcile himself to lusting over an aging divorcee with two daughters, Grant shook his head. "I have to be somewhere in the next half hour. So if you have nothing else to say..."

"I'll see myself out," Eve said, in a clipped voice. Collecting her papers, she stuffed them into her large purse and walked out, head held high.

Proud until the last moment.

Just like him.

CHAPTER FOUR

Bella ascended the stairs to the third floor of the walk-up where she lived, regret rising in her throat with the altitude. A too-cold whoosh of air from the air conditioner slithered under her halter-neck top as she stepped into her studio apartment. Goosebumps sprouted all over her chest at the sudden drop in temperature. Free-falling onto the couch, Bella stared at the empty kitchen, which she needed to clean up before Kat arrived. A bath was pending, too.

I'll do it in five minutes, she told herself.

Looking at her herself in the mirror, she went over her conversation with Jamie again and again in her head. What had she done?

After she'd vowed to never associate with someone in showbiz or become part of that industry, what was she doing giving false hope to this Jamie Star? Giving false hope to herself? Dating Bryan Singer had been enough exposure to the toxic culture of the entertainment industry for her.

It was not a place she'd ever go back to. One million dollars and wild horses couldn't drag her back there. She belonged in her quiet, cozy room in East village, reading Goethe and eating Hershey's; staying away from the spotlight where she could be criticized, picked at, and judged.

The words she'd heard from Bryan's friends in LA still echoed in her ears. She'd probably be hearing their haunting echoes in her mind for as long as she lived.

"Nice ass, Bella. Except, I can't really see it under all the flab."

"Those are your legs? I'm sorry, I seriously thought I'd hit a wall."

Those words had hurt her, but she'd risen above all that through the years. Now, their sting was faint, like the momentary prick of a needle.

She'd tried hard to hold onto her dignity at the coffee shop when he'd lured her with money, tried to remember the past, but her greed for that one-bedroom had won out. Jamie had said four episodes. That meant that she was looking at a total of $100,000. Mind-boggling. She could buy an amazing house with that money. All her worries would be over. She'd have a roof over her head, as well as the pleasure of ticking off the biggest goal on her bucket list.

She'd have the security she'd never had. She could finally claim that she was different from her mother, that she'd made the right choices, prioritized the right things. She'd always belong somewhere unlike the woman who, even in her dying moments, couldn't belong anywhere.

But even now, angry tears fountained up to the rim of her eyes at the thought of Bryan Singer and the way she'd been treated by him. She'd vowed to never let anyone else treat her that way like she was nothing. The morning she'd woken up to find Bryan's photo splashed across tabloids, making out with a model and claiming her as his girlfriend, her entire world had flipped on its axis. It had been the most miserable day of her life, but she'd needed that cold wake-up call.

I need you.

That was what Bryan had said, too. That he needed her. They all needed her, but none of them wanted her.

Bella shook her head. Today was a good day, there was no need to ruin it by rewinding her memory tape. But she couldn't help it. Every handsome guy seemed to carry some part of Bryan in him. Every handsome guy was a trigger.

No, don't think. You'll just become depressed.

Against her will, Bella dragged herself to the bathroom. Skipping in for a quick clean-up, she did quick stretches to open up the clenched muscles in her limbs and stomach and looked at herself in the mirror above the basin. It reflected back her red-rimmed eyes. Her eyeshadow had smudged into a dark puddle around her eyes, and black mascara tears were zig-zagging down her cheeks. Bella stuck her face under water spraying from the shower-head and scrubbed her face.

Age was slowly beginning to leave its imprints on her. She was thirty-four already. And if she didn't buy a house soon, she'd end up with nothing by the time she was forty. She knew the sudden desperation for security was the result of losing her two best friends, who had so far, been her only source of support.

Both of them had found the love of their lives—Ashley had found love twice—and were heading towards that settled, secure phase in life where they might no longer have space for her. Bella wanted to see them happy, but she was feeling incredibly left out these days. Soon, Ashley would have her first child, and she'd feel even more alienated.

Hot water soaked into her skin and hair. If only water could soak away these clawing feelings...

Snap out of it, she scolded herself.

Compared to seven years ago, when she'd been struggling to secure a tenured position, a house, and pay back her student debt, she was in a much better place now. She'd almost paid off her student loans, and she was an assistant professor at NYU.

Bella curled her lazy eyelids for a nap while the water warmed her skin. Heaven.

The buzzer beeped.

Ugh. Sometimes, Kat's extreme punctuality got on her nerves. Seven pm did not mean seven pm. It meant after seven twenty and before eight. Shrugging into a bathrobe, Bella tied it around the front. Her damp hair pitter-pattered all over the hardwood floor, leaving a trail to the door.

"You're early." She made a mildly annoyed-at-your-punctuality face at Kat, who was wearing a dress in an electrifying shade of orange. Thin, toned legs stuck out from under the high hem. Kat's waist had shrunk another inch, which definitely was a sign of overwork.

"No, I'm exactly on time." Kat waved the smart watch strapped over her wrist, looking extra-sulky, even for a Wednesday.

"Why do you look like some pervert grabbed your ass on the subway?" Bella asked.

Kat fiddled with the oven's settings. "Because that happened."

"Shit. You reported it, didn't you?"

"Yeah. I'm trying to forget about it." Tidying up the cans of soup on the countertop, Kat followed her usual stress-relief ritual of going overboard with cleaning. "You need to buy a rice cooker, Bell. And when was the last time you vacuumed around here? I can see dust bunnies under the table."

Bella seized an orange from the fruit bowl. "A month, maybe two."

In reality, it had been three weeks, but a little exaggeration here and there could work in her favor, considering Kat's mood.

"I've told you a million times. If you don't vacuum every week, you'll create more work for yourself in the long run." Kat untangled the cord of the vacuum cleaner, plugged it into the socket, and filled Bella's apartment with a loud, electrical buzz. Its head swept over the dust bunnies, swallowing them and leaving a clean, shiny floor.

Bella smiled. Having Kat over saved her the trouble of hiring a cleaner every time. Yeah, she took advantage of her nice friends sometimes, but so did Kat every time she needed someone to use as bait to get scoops.

"Everybody in the world needs a bestie like you," she said to herself, knowing Kat wouldn't be able to hear her over the droning noise.

"You say something?" Kat bent the head under the table, under the couch, and into the hard-to-get corners of her house that frankly, Bella never bothered with.

"I'll throw something on ASAP. There's juice in the fridge. Help yourself."

Dashing to her room, Bella opted for a no-fuss ensemble of shorts and a tank-top. Fifteen minutes later, Kat stored the vacuum cleaner in the same place she'd taken it from. Such a perfectionist.

"Thanks for cleaning my apartment. I appreciate it."

The microwave beeped in the kitchen, indicating that the quinoa was done.

"I'm doing it for myself, not for you." Restless, Kat hurried to check if the quinoa was cooked. "Five more minutes."

"Are you really okay with what happened on the subway?"

"I'll recover. Ashley's sorry she couldn't make it tonight, but there's good news. The doctor said it's a girl."

"Can they tell so soon?" Bella inquired.

Nodding, Kat's mouth pushed up in a wide grin. "Aren't you excited? I'm so happy for her. She's wanted a baby for so long."

"Yeah, it's great. I'll have to remember to send her a text." Keen to divert from the topic of Ashley's pregnancy, Bella turned to the benign subject of Kat's boyfriend. "How's Alex?"

"Busy. He has to go to Albany next week."

"Still meeting him on weekends?"

"Trying to." Unconsciously, Kat rubbed her wrists. "He wanted to take me to dinner tonight."

"And you said no?"

Kat nodded.

"Are you crazy? Alex is the love of your life. If he says dinner, you go to dinner. Where are your priorities in life, girl?"

Kat tipped her head up. "But...but I promised to help you make dinner, and you bought all the stuff. I couldn't bail last minute."

"I'm not going anywhere. We could've done it another day."

Though Bella was happy that Kat hadn't abandoned her completely, she sometimes worried for Kat. Was she taking away precious time from her that she could be spending with her boyfriend? She didn't want to become someone who held others back from their happiness, who selfishly demanded all their attention for herself. She didn't want to become her mother.

Dating the mayor of New York City was a challenge in itself, but throw in a hectic job and it was a wonder how Kat and Alex were still together. It was their third year together this year, but it was getting tougher for them with every passing year. Next year Alex would be running for re-election, and they'd have to deal with all the stress that something like that brought into a relationship.

Kat sewed her brows together.

"That's not right, Bell. You're as important to me as he is." It could be a trick of the light, but Kat's red hair seemed to glow brighter. And Bella's eyes were definitely teary. "I'm not sacrificing our friendship for Alex's sake. He can deal with spending time alone. He probably has enough work to catch up on."

Laying the heel of her hand on the counter, Bella inclined herself backward. "If you keep rejecting him, he'll leave you."

Just like Bryan had left her. Every time she was unavailable, he'd flirt with another woman, get closer to someone else, and maybe those little moments had added up at the end. That could happen to Kat, too. That could happen to anyone. She knew it wasn't healthy to think this way, but she couldn't help it.

Kat raised her chin confidently. "He can't. He's too hopelessly in love with me." Peeling the outer layers of an onion, she slit it into halves with a swift chop of the knife. "And if he does, I'll still have you, right?"

"You..." She pulled Kat's bony body into a hug. Startled, Kat dropped the knife on the cutting board. "You're too loyal for your own good."

Despite being generally averse to cuddling, Kat didn't rumple her face when Bella smeared tears all over Kat's collarbone.

"I can't make out if you're being sarcastic or nice," Kat teased.

"Of course I'm being nice." Bella gave Kat some breathing room and gave herself some space, too, fanning her eyes.

"Sorry, I got a bit emotional there. My date today...it was odd, to say the least," Bella said.

"Spill. Fast," Kat insisted, the smell of the onions making her eyes red and watery, too.

"I matched with this guy on Tinder. He said he was looking for a partnership, so I thought, why not?" Scratching her chin with a pensive look, Bella sighed. "Guess what happened when I met him face-to-face?"

"He just wanted sex?"

"No, he wanted to give me a job. As an actress."

An alarming look flitted over Kat's face. "A porn actress?"

"A regular actress," Bella said. "It's only for a month or so, and the payment is ridiculous. Hundred grand. I'd be able to afford an apartment at last."

Green eyes burning bright, Kat squared her gaze. "I've told you a million times that you can borrow money from me. I don't mind. I want you to buy the house that you've always dreamed of."

"I told you I wanted to do it myself," Bella said defensively. "If I start taking money from other people, I won't be any different from my mother."

"So this is all about being different from your mother?" Kat clamped her teeth shut. "Bell, the woman's dead and gone. How long will you keep living your life in the shadow of her actions?"

"I'm not doing that." Bella angled her head to the left. "But anyway, back to the topic, I don't think I'm going to accept the acting offer. I don't feel comfortable."

Currently, she was on summer break, which was the perfect opportunity to take a side job. But she was afraid. Afraid of the past catching up to her.

"Okay. So why do you look so depressed?"

"I wanted that money."

"Don't lose hope. There will be other ways to make money. You could teach summer school somewhere abroad. I've heard those pay good money."

Bella grimaced. "Too late for that. It's summer already."

"Okay, so maybe something else." Kat stuck a spoon into the bowl of quinoa salad and spooned some onto two plates.

"Yeah, I hope you're right. I just feel like my dream is slipping out of my reach all the time."

"It isn't," Kat said, "And here's your dinner."

As soon as Bella's tongue touched Kat's quinoa salad, she was in heaven. "It's awesome. I could eat this all day."

"Thanks," Kat said. "Now, shall we watch the movie I told you about?"

"The boring political one?"

"Yeah. That."

Bella groaned. "You know the only reason I let you do this to me is that I love you so much."

CHAPTER FIVE

Jamie hesitated outside the walk-up where Bella Hopkins lived. He'd had his Tinder fuck, and the moment the hormones from the orgasm had faded, his mind had found its way back to his replacement actress. He didn't want to scare her away with his tenacity, but at the same time, he couldn't let her leisurely waste time.

He forged ahead. Since the building had no doorman, and someone had left the door open, he stepped in easily. The wood was chipping off the banister of the staircase and the stairs were worn by the grind of many pairs of shoes. He inhaled mac n cheese, paint, and burned food on the way up. Surely, a college professor could afford a better place. Maybe she was skimping on rent so she could save up to buy her own place in a few years.

He could use that as a bargaining chip. 100k could cover 50% of the down payment for a studio in Morningside Heights. And after running some numbers with Daniel, the studio's accountant, they'd discovered that even at thirty-five grand an episode, she'd still be a bargain, compared to re-shooting the previous episodes.

He reached her apartment. Number 4. Even if, by some stroke of luck, Bella didn't call the cops, she'd definitely kick him out. But his greatest fear was no longer humiliation. It was failing. *Troubled Domesticity* had to get made and it had to air. The world needed this show. American television needed this show. He was willing to go to any length to ensure that the studio's money and his months of labor saw the light of day.

Decisively, he knocked on her door, eyes to the ground. No hesitation. Episode 7 was scheduled to be shot in two days which meant he was time-strapped. Today was his last chance.

The hinges creaked and the knob turned. The visual of Bella's curves accented by shorts and a tank top punched him in the gut before her sarcasm punched him in the head.

"I don't even want to ask how you found my address." Wearing an annoyed expression, Bella folded her arms over her breasts. In these clothes, sans makeup, she looked much younger than she had in the morning. And quite alluring.

He waved, relegating thoughts of her sexiness to the back of his mind. She was just an actress to him. Just an actress.

He jumped straight to the point. Small talk would only waste time and he had none of that. "I came up with a better offer. 35k per episode. If you sign by tomorrow. Think about it. You could buy a house with that. Designer clothes, a new car."

"First of all, who even wants to drive a car in New York?" Pissed off, she stretched her neck. "Second, I have no interest in designer clothes."

He noticed she didn't offer a rebuke for the house. So she wanted that one.

"Then tell me what *do* you want. Give me something to work with here." Jamie inched forward, taking one more small step into her space.

She opened the door wider, and he took the opportunity to move closer to her. Her citrusy scent filled his nose. Momentarily, he found himself wishing to sink deeper into that smell. With his face a slip away from hers, he couldn't prevent his gaze from riding over her throat to her breasts. Disgusted by how low his intellect had sunk, Jamie peeled his attention away from her boobs. He didn't want to become a pervert, although, in the interest of fairness, he had to mention that she had great assets.

"I have to verify who you are. I don't know anything about you. If a random guy you met on Tinder asked you to sign a legal document, would you do it?" Bella said but pulled back.

It was a subtle invitation, and he took it.

Her place was neat, but that was pretty much all it was. Uninspiring, antiquated décor made her lack of interest in interior design obvious—second-hand black leather couches, an IKEA queen bed that was visible through the open door of the bedroom, a couple of bright green chairs, and a coffee table that was likely a hand-me-down from an aunt who'd lived in the eighties. Shelves flooded with crookedly arranged books cast shadows over every wall. A lonely lamp glowed on a desk by the window, where a MacBook lay open, the screen powered off. Papers were spilled all around the silver laptop, books plopped over them.

Her nose turned to her shapeless black couch. Jamie assumed that was where she wanted him to sit. He did.

"I'm not in the habit of gloating, but I've had a pretty successful career so far." Jamie fixed a proud grin on his lips. "You should Google me. That might help you trust me more."

"Don't think I won't do it." She wobbled into her house and snatched her iPhone off the kitchen counter. "How do you spell Star?"

"S-t-a-r."

He peered at the screen. Google turned up one million results with his name.

"Well, let's see what we've got here." She clicked on his Wikipedia, which showed a guy who roughly resembled the one sipping lemon slush opposite her. "Your Wikipedia entry says you were born on June second. So you're a Gemini?"

"Is that important?" Jamie asked, mildly amused.

"Not really. Let's see...you wrote *The Fall, Affairs of the Heart, Unlocking Alice.*"

They were all pretty famous movies. Pop culture staples. She must've watched at least some of them.

"I—" Bella's voice got lodged in her throat before she finished. "You wrote *Love Me Like You Do?*"

He confirmed her statement with a nod. "Not my best, but it was my first, so I was still learning."

"Are you kidding me? I adore that movie. Are you planning a sequel? If so, I'd agree to act in that."

"Can I take that to mean you'll act in my show?" Jamie cupped her hands with his. The touch, coupled with the softness of her skin, sent shivers down his spine. He hoped it had the same effect on her, too.

"Not so fast." She pulled her hands away with an irascible frown and tucked one leg over the other as she sat straighter. "I'm having second thoughts about this. I already have a good job. And…there are people I can't afford to run into again in showbiz."

"If you tell me their names, I'll make sure to send them to sleep with the fishes. I have connections to the mafia."

She coughed, clasped her palms, and exhaled. "You're totally bonkers, aren't you?"

"I prefer the word 'passionate'."

"Passionate," she repeated blankly. "You should look up that word in the dictionary. Because I'm not sure it means what you think it means."

"Who are you talking to, Bell?" Someone else emerged from under the kitchen counter. Around the same age as him, but she looked different from Bella.

This redhead was stick-thin, tall, and belonged on the billboards. The strong cheekbones, the straight bridge of her nose that ended in a sharp tip, and her fashionably full mouth were all features of a perfect face. Photogenic. She could easily be a model. Considering this was NYC, she probably was one.

"You didn't tell me you'd invited someone else." She pierced Bella with a stony look.

"Kat, meet Jamie, my Tinder stalker. Jamie, meet Kat, my best friend and reporter extraordinaire. She has put a good number of men behind the bars with her articles."

"Tinder stalker?" Jamie's jaw dropped. "That's not fair—"

"Should I call the cops?" Kat's voice cut over his.

"If he doesn't disappear in the next fifteen minutes, then you should," Bella said.

Jamie wasn't sure how much of what these women were saying was a joke and how much was serious. He decided he didn't want to take a chance. Producing a thick booklet, he handed it to Bella. "If you sign the contract, I'll get out of your hair this moment. To speed up your decision, I even brought you the script. Your character's called Ambrosia. She has five dialogues per episode. It's not a difficult role. And I'll be getting you an acting coach for free so you can learn your lines."

"Why're you so fixated on her?" Kat asked, hovering over Jamie like an overprotective parent. She had the look of a shark. Jamie was familiar with that look. Grant had that look, too, when he was cutting big deals. "It's not normal. She's not even an actress."

Jamie grunted. Realizing that Ms. Reporter Extraordinaire was someone who had some say in Bella's decisions, Jamie decided to change his tactics. Smiling at her, he supplied her his business card, while Bella explained his situation with Martina.

Laughing, the redhead flipped her shampoo-commercial curls. "I've never heard anything funnier."

"You wouldn't be laughing if you were in my position," Jamie mumbled.

Possessively touching Bella's head, that perfect mouth of hers curved. There was a suppressed warning in there that Jamie didn't miss. "For your sake, I hope you're not playing a prank on her."

"Her boyfriend's the mayor," Bella whispered to him conspiratorially. So long-legs, model-face had connections in high places. That didn't scare him. He hadn't been joking about the mafia connections. You couldn't avoid those when you were in Hollywood.

"I'm serious. And I hope you'll take it seriously, too."

"Whatever," Bella dismissed. "The only reason I'm even talking to you is that you wrote *Love Me Like You Do*."

"You did? Really?" Kat clapped her hands at her throat. "Bella's a huge fan."

"She told me." Jamie couldn't help lighting up when he recalled that.

"Sorry, Jamie, I'm going to leave you alone for a moment." Bella grabbed Kat's arm and pulled her along to the bedroom. From her nervous energy, it looked like she wanted to talk to Kat about something. "We'll be back."

Tapping his fingers, Jamie smiled and waited.

CHAPTER SIX

"So, what's happening?" Kat whispered to Bella after they'd closed the bedroom door. "You're not really considering his offer, are you?"

"I didn't expect him to show up so suddenly." Pinching the back of her cottage cheese thighs, Bella cringed. "Oh, God. Why did I have to pick today to wear these shorts? He's probably judging my cellulite. Men in showbiz are all the same."

"He doesn't look like he cares." Kat threw a glance over Bella's shoulder to the closed door. "So what do you plan to do about the acting thing?"

"He's legit. I Googled him." Bella whispered. "I'm going to send this contract to Andrew so he can get his lawyers to check it out. In the meantime, I'm going to read the script."

"And if there's no problem?"

"Kat, I want you to be completely honest with me." Bella grabbed her friend by the shoulders. "Do you think I can do it? Do you think I can become an actress?"

"Before I answer that, I want you to be honest. Why do you want to do it? And why are you hesitating?"

"Money," Bella said. "And Bryan."

"Singer? You're still thinking about that asshole?"

"I can't help it. I don't want to run into him again."

"He's a singer-songwriter. The chances of meeting him again on an acting set are slim. Unless he's part of the cast?"

Bella studied the script, which included the character names plus the names of the actors playing them. Bryan Singer's name wasn't among them, which was, in hindsight, obvious, because he wasn't an actor.

"Seems like it's safe."

Kat brushed her chin. "He's offering you a good opportunity. You have nothing to do during summer break, anyway. And you'll make more money than what you or I make annually."

"I don't have any talent," Bella retaliated.

"Do you need any to be on-screen these days?"

"You have a point there."

"So do it if you want to and if everything checks out. Or you'll waste all summer getting depressed about real estate prices."

And in a split second, Bella made her decision. They walked back to Jamie, who was still glued on the same spot and scanning her living room.

"Here." Kat thrust a bowl of her leftover quinoa salad at him. A muscle in his jaw twitched, but Jamie took it. He didn't eat any, though. She didn't expect him to.

"So what did you decide?" he quizzed.

Kat crossed her arms. "She'll need to consider—"

"I'll do it," Bella butted in.

"Bella!"

"I can't refuse thirty-five thousand dollars. I need to buy that condo."

"Glad you made the right decision," Jamie chimed in. "This is my office address." Another business card came her way. "We'll sign the contract first thing tomorrow morning, and then you can get started with rehearsals. Bring your lawyer, if you have one."

"I have one." No, she didn't, but she'd get one. "And he's the best in the city. Coincidentally, he specializes in entertainment law."

"Good for you." He clapped his hands together. "Would you like something to drink now? To celebrate our deal? Takeout?"

"Not unless you're planning on making this a date."

He whistled. "Sorry, I don't date. I lied to you on Tinder. But it wasn't a complete lie. I wasn't looking for anything romantic with you, but I was looking for a working partnership."

Bella had expected as much. Jamie had a very flaky, player vibe. He'd fooled her for a bit during their first meeting when he'd bumbled adorably. She'd thought he was one of those sincere, shy guys who just needed a little bit of love to open up. But the confident, cocky side of him that she'd seen today had erased all notions of 'sweet' and 'sincere'.

She could smell the feminine perfume on his clothes. Smudges of red lipstick decorated the back of his collar, and scratches that hadn't been there this morning were stamped around the side of his neck. He must've had sex with a woman this afternoon, right after he'd met her. He was *exactly* like Bryan Singer. Exactly like all the men her mother had wasted her time on throughout her life. The sort of man she would never make the mistake of falling for.

"Well," Bella said, "in that case, you should go before Kat calls the cops."

CHAPTER SEVEN

The company picnic was the one place Grant didn't expect to see Eve.

In the six-plus years, she'd been with Star Studios, she'd made it a ritual to avoid these picnics. No doubt, she saw them as a thinly-veiled excuse to kiss up to the senior management. This year, however, with the possibility of promotion looming, she wouldn't want to miss her chance of scoring a favorable impression. Predictable, that woman. And way too ambitious.

Grant didn't want to strike up a conversation with her. After the argument they'd had at his house, they'd mostly managed to stay out of each other's way. But he couldn't say she was staying out of his mind. Day after day, his attraction to her was growing stronger. She was his obsession now, and he didn't know if he was comfortable with obsessing over something as old as her.

When her tawny eyes met his, he was pulled to her like a moth to the flame.

"Having a good time?" The words rolled off his lemonade-soaked tongue casually. He gave her a dispassionate, social hug.

"Yes," Eve said, with an arm around one of her daughters. "My girls. Carla and Alana."

Eve beamed, showing them off like a proud mama. He'd met Carla and Alana a long time ago, at some other company event when they'd both been incredibly gawky and unsocial. The older one seemed to have outgrown her social awkwardness and looked pretty normal now. She had a moderately fashionable haircut, wore age-appropriate clothes, and could even wield makeup to her advantage. The other one, though. Grant shook his head at her in sympathy. Braces, acne, and out-of-style bangs—high school must be brutal for this kid.

"Mom, I'm gonna go get some food." Alana broke away from their small group of four.

"You want to go, too?" Eve patted Carla's back, who scrunched her lips and frowned at her mother.

"Better than being around you." Carla trailed Alana, like a faithful terrier.

A little embarrassed, Eve shifted her plastic cup filled with Coke to the other hand. "They're so difficult at this age. How did you deal with Jamie when he was this age?"

Grant chuckled, paying attention to the faint blush rising on the apples of her cheeks. "I'm the worst person to get parenting advice from."

"Being a parent is hard," Eve mused, pinning her daughters with an angry glance when they hovered too close to the alcohol. She held her glass over her mouth and Coke lapped against her lips, but she didn't swallow.

"If you want parenting to be easy, you've gotta stop parenting. Just forget about them and do whatever you want. They grow up real fast that way."

Drops of Coke spilled when she tipped her glass involuntarily. "You're right. You suck at giving parenting advice."

The comment didn't affect him. For a woman like her, her capability as a mother might weigh heavily on her self-esteem and how successful she considered herself as a human being, but for him, being a father was just another role he had to play. As any actor knew, no role was worth getting attached to. They didn't define an actor. And how he was as a father didn't define his life or his self-worth.

"Don't worry. They'll be fine. They're beautiful and intelligent, like their mom."

Casually, Eve slugged down more Coca-Cola than she should be slugging in one go. "Keep admiring them from a distance."

Grant smoothed over the awkward moment with a throaty laugh, only too aware of what she meant. She, along with everyone else, viewed him as a cradle-robber. That wasn't far-off, but he had standards, too. Underage girls were strictly off-limits. Even college girls were too young, clingy, and immature. He had no patience to deal with drama, so he stuck to above twenty-five.

"Are they in high school?" he asked, taking small steps away from the crowd, moving toward a shaded area separated from the crowd by the shadows falling from trees. He had no plans for what to do when he got there, but he still went. Eve followed his lead.

"No. Alana's a sophomore at Dartmouth. Engineering." Eve glowed with a proud smile. "Carla's in her senior year of high school, though. She's thinking of majoring in chemistry."

"So they're both going to college. That's great."

"I want them to have the best education they can. It's what I work hard for." There was a trace of longing in her voice. "I'd be happy if Carla could make it to Stanford."

"Isn't that where you went?"

"Best years of my life." Her eyes were glazed. "I was the President of the Feminist Society, and I made so many friends I'm still in touch with. I won't forget my time at college."

Grant cocked his head. "Feminist Society. Shoulda saw that coming."

Eve started strolling towards the hotel, which was part of the beach resort the company picnic was at. Her loose dress fell over her knees, and her hair flapped about her face.

Grant followed her in.

She looked like she was searching for something in the hotel lobby.

"You never went to college." She talked distractedly. "Do you wish you had?"

Grant gave an indifferent shrug. "Nah. I always knew I wasn't the brightest crayon in the box, but at least I had a decent face." He served her one of his charming smiles. "Figured there was no point in wasting my time in college, so I packed my bags for Hollywood instead."

"It was a lucrative decision." Eve dumped her plastic cup in a bin. The lemonade in his hand had lost all its chill, so Grant got rid of it, too.

"I got lucky," he admitted.

He'd never imagined making it this big, although he'd always wanted to. In his heart, he craved attention and status the way an addict craved drugs. He always had.

"So why don't you act anymore? I don't remember your popularity ever dropping, but you just left and decided to run a company one day."

"I felt like I'd reached a different stage in life. I wanted to do something different."

Because as much he loved attention, he loved security and power more. He'd not grown up rich, and being poor again wasn't an appealing thought. Besides, he'd been getting tired of the women in Hollywood. Moving to New York and helping his friend with the then-fledgling Star Studios had sounded like a good idea.

The hem of Eve's dress swished about her knees. "You were a good actor. My mother liked you."

Stunned that she'd said something good about him to his face, Grant gripped her arm when she stopped near an alcove. "You didn't?"

"I liked your work."

Soft orange light made her skin shimmer, snatching away the years from her face. She had a beautiful face, now that he looked at it carefully.

"Are you seeing someone?" Grant asked, startling her.

He expected her to pull one of her annoyed faces and tell him to butt out of her personal life or threaten to sue him for sexual harassment, but she didn't.

"Trying to," she said instead, sarcasm thick in her voice. "You want to recommend someone to me?"

"How about me?"

She coughed out a laugh. "Good one."

His ego took a blow at that one. He'd never had a problem with a woman not taking him seriously. "I mean it. Against all common sense, I'm willing to give you a chance."

Pulling her face into a severe mask, Eve said, "That's because you're drunk."

"On lemonade?" he tossed. "And don't tell me you don't feel anything for me. Your heart's beating as fast as a freight train."

He smoothed a finger at the spot between her breasts, where the pulse of her heart ticked against his skin. She didn't protest, click her tongue, or lecture him on sexual harassment. Instead, her eyes met his quietly.

"I've never been attracted to a misogynist before. Don't think I want to be attracted to one now." Saying so, she breathed hard.

"I'm not a misogynist just because I didn't promote you," Grant argued. "And who knows, maybe your chances will be better if you loosen up a little?"

He'd meant it as a joke. He was trying to poke fun at her ambition, but rage glinted in Eve's eyes like pieces of burning coal. Grant saw the way she closed her fingers into tight fists, dug her heels into the ground. He was certain she'd swivel and walk away like she usually did when he annoyed her and she couldn't see a comeback. Or maybe she'd finally snap and slap him.

But she did the most unexpected thing ever. Gliding her palm up the back of his neck, Eve cupped his face, brought him in for a kiss. It was so unexpected that it blew his mind. Grant slid his hands under her waist. Instead of hitting a tight butt, he hit something soft and squishy. And it felt good. Good enough that he didn't want to remove his hand.

Savoring her slowly, he explored the novelty of a woman who had no lip fillers. When her tongue brushed his lower lip, he gave in to her, suckling, teasing her with his tongue. Her lips parted and she let him into her mouth. Moments of sheer bliss passed, then her tongue came into his mouth, played with his tongue. The kiss grew wilder, hotter, deeper until she jerked away.

"So, will I be getting the promotion I'm due now?" She spat the words, her voice dripping with pure scorn. This couldn't be the woman who'd kissed him just now. It didn't add up. Had she done it just to stick the point in his face?

"You kissed me for a promotion?"

"No. I kissed you because I was angry and thought a kiss would work better than a slap to get my point across. And I wanted to believe that you were a good man. A fair man who could draw the line with his employees." She sighed. "But all you see is pussy, not an employee. You should've pushed me away on principle when I kissed you because I work for you. But you didn't. You waited for me to stop."

He couldn't admit he'd liked it. That'd just add insult to the injury. "I was curious to see where you were going with it."

"Never mind. It's completely my fault. I was out of my mind." She dragged a hand through her neat hair, messing it up. She was blinking rapidly, too. The cool Eve was flustered. He liked that. "I let myself become emotional because I was frustrated. It's completely unacceptable. I'm sorry. I won't ask you for promotion again."

Her piece said, she turned, but Grant stepped in closer, caressing the smooth skin of her bare arm. As soon as he got Eve into bed and fucked her enough to get her out of his system, he would have his normal back. A normal where he wasn't falling for women over fifty. But she caught his hand and detached it from herself.

"Since you're being emotional, why don't you go all the way?" He leaned in and whispered into her ear, "I'm not saying this to you as an employee. We're people, too, you know."

Eve's nails perched on her dress's collar. "I can't be another woman who slept with you to move up. You may not think much of my work ethic, but..." She swallowed, glancing past his shoulder. "I want to set a good example for my daughters."

"Your daughters aren't watching us."

"But they'll know. They'll know if I'm away for too long." She went breathless when he trailed his tongue over the shell of her ear. She jumped back as if he'd thrown hot water on her face.

"Don't back out now. It's only started getting interesting." Plunging his hand under her dress, he unclasped her bra wanting her hard, hot nipples in his mouth. Wanting to suck those buds.

Eve leaned away from him. "I know I was in the wrong here to kiss you first. But just because a woman kisses you, doesn't mean she did it to get something more. So I'd appreciate it if you forget about it. Don't lower the already low opinion I have of you."

Grant chuckled and god, he sounded on edge. "Nobody kisses Grant Star without wanting something more."

From the way she hesitated, he could tell Eve would succumb. They all did, to the allure of Grant Star.

But her expression changed, morphed into disgust.

"That's the part of you that I can't stand. Why do you always assume that everybody has a weaker will than you?" Defying his expectations, she shook her hand away from him. Her eyes froze back into solid amber. "Put my bra back on."

"Come on," he begged. He was stooping so low today. Begging an old woman for sex. Was he really going to become such a pathetic man in his old age?

"Fine. I'll do it myself." Her eyeshadow-dusted lids dropped. "I'm not looking for a one-night stand or anything with you, Grant. Let me make it clear in case you misunderstood. I want a man whom my daughters can respect and I can count on. You can never be that man. And trust me, you don't want to sleep with a woman who comes with two daughters and a lot of rules."

He inhaled sharply when he saw her eyes twinkle. The light was playing games on him. But she looked so ethereal. It made his head spin strangely. A woman shouldn't be allowed to look so magnetic when she was mad at him.

"Are you like this to every man who tries to get close to you?" Grant asked, hesitating before hooking her bra back.

Against his desire to remain in control, he found himself touching the tendrils of curls that flew about the nape of her neck.

Eve's voice lost some of its fury. "I chose the wrong man once."

That regretful note in her voice stuck in his gut like a sharp knife.

"I can do long-term," Grant said.

She was intriguing enough for a few nights at the very least.

Eve bent her hands to her back. "I don't want anything with you. I don't like you much if I'm being honest."

There was no reason for her to regard him with such concern like she was worried he wouldn't understand the alien tongue she was speaking in. He understood commitment and courtship well enough. He'd done it often enough.

"I was married once, too."

And that one marriage had been enough to convince him that he didn't want another. After all, the greatest part of living in the twenty-first century was that sex didn't have to come with responsibility. It came freely.

Eve was still suspicious. "That was years ago."

"Doesn't mean I've forgotten what it means to be faithful." No idea why he was doing this. Maybe to prove something to her. Or himself. "You'll believe me once you start seeing more of me."

"And when did I say I was going to start seeing more of you? Besides us being totally incompatible, there's the fact that you're my boss."

"Bullshit. Star Studios has no rule against having relationships with co-workers. I never let the board go through with that one."

Eve rolled her eyes, trying to be annoyed, but she looked thoroughly amused. "I should go now. Your girlfriend seems to be looking for you."

As she turned, Grant found himself neck-deep in a longing he couldn't understand. He was an impulsive man, though, so he acted on it before he could make sense of it. He called out to Eve. "Meet me on Saturday at seven."

"For what?"

"I don't know yet," Grant admitted. "Maybe revenge for the kiss?"

She must be feeling really guilty for that, for she swallowed, hesitating. When she stepped forward, she burst out, "Where do you want to meet?"

"I'll pick you up." It was a command.

"You know where I live?"

"I'll get it from the system." A perk of being her boss.

A click of silence passed before she squirmed. "I want you to promise me that you won't do anything obnoxious."

"I can't make such promises."

She scoffed. "I keep forgetting who you are. But I'll warn you. I'm not easy."

Regardless, she'd be jumping into bed with him without hesitation. There was a lot he excelled at and seduction was near the top of that list.

And if she didn't give in?

Well, then they were talking real long-term.

CHAPTER EIGHT

Three days later

"Okay. Cut," Bruce screamed, bouncing off the director's chair. "And that's a wrap for today. Good job everyone."

Bella let out all the air in her lungs, then some she'd been holding. It was done. Accomplished. She was officially an actress (part-time, anyway) starting today. The days after she'd signed the contract had been intense. Non-stop acting lessons, rehearsals, and then costume rehearsals. She'd said her lines over and over again until she was dreaming of them. At first, her inhibition had made it hard for her to get into character, but she'd lost her reservations quickly after repeatedly being shouted at by the director and Jamie and disappointing her co-actors too many times.

"So, how did I do?" She made eye contact with Jamie. He'd been on the set the entire time the crew had been shooting, instructing her on what to do, correcting her body language, rewriting lines that weren't funny enough in the middle of the scene, and laughing at funny ones.

Drinking a bottle of Evian, Jamie said, "Better than I thought. Acting might be your life's undiscovered calling, professor."

"I had to do re-do every scene," she informed, not happy that she was so bad at this. She'd seriously underestimated how difficult it was to be an actress.

"So did Catherine. That's the way it is. Everybody makes mistakes on set. You'll get used to it."

As if on cue, Catherine King, veteran actress, and three-time Emmy winner, waved at Bella from three feet away. Not sure what to make of Catherine's friendly gesture, Bella turned her head and bit her lip.

"Hey, Cathy." Jamie motioned her over.

Bella started sweating when Catherine came over and stood beside her.

Even though the older woman played her mother in the show, she didn't look that old. In fact, nobody would ever be able to tell that she was over sixty. Her skin was glass-smooth and youthful, her hair a uniform blonde. It was Botox and hair coloring, but it looked natural on her.

"Hi. I'm Bella," Bella introduced herself nervously, for the tenth time.

"I remember." Catherine brushed her fingers over her temples. "Good work today."

Bella's throat went dry, so she grabbed a bottle of water from a table nearby where there were a few of them.

Jamie's hands crawled into his jeans pocket, and his eyes shot to Catherine. "You did a great job, too. I was worried when we had to change your scene three times."

Catherine shrugged. "I'm glad Martina's role got sorted out. Daniel was really worried about it. You found a good replacement, too."

"She's better looking than Martina, isn't she?" With a flirtatious twist of his lips, he angled his head at Bella.

Bella dunked a gulp of mineral water into her mouth, which ended up spilling onto her clothes and soaking the V-neck T-shirt. Shoot.

A sliver of a laugh came out of Catherine's throat. "Better change out of that."

"Yeah. We just found you. We can't have you falling sick," Jamie added with a click of his fingers.

Bella made a face at him and walked to the dressing room so she could slip into a dry T-shirt. Inside, Rosie, another actress on the show, was fussing with her makeup, her reflection taking over the big mirror on the dresser framed by lights. Rosie was one of her co-stars and for some reason, Bella had a feeling she didn't like her. Even when Bella smiled at her first, she never smiled back or made any attempt to talk to Bella.

"Hi." Bella gave her a friendly wave, which Rosie ignored.

Oh, well. She found her belongings stored inside a locket. Something stuck to her palms as she pulled out her T-shirt from her purse. Gooey and black, she noticed that it was all over her tee, running across it in lengthwise lines.

Holding up her ruined pink tee, she turned to Rosie. "What happened here? Who did this?"

Rosie inched up her shoulders and shrugged. "Oops. Mascara accident."

She made an X with her legs by moving one sleek, bony leg in front of the other.

"But how did mascara get on my T-shirt?" Bella almost knew the answer. This was like LA all over again. Like Bryan all over again. Except ten times more childish. Rosie couldn't be older than twenty. That explained the teenage antics, at least.

"I put it there," Rosie admitted, without an ounce of apology.

Bella's stomach rumbled, and a shiver dashed up to her spine when Rosie latched the door and assembled her features into a dark expression. Coming. It was coming.

"Why?"

Rosie flicked her forehead with her nails.

"Because I want you to leave." Hate sputtered in Rosie's voice. "Go back to whichever Burger King you crawled out from. You don't belong here."

"I don't understand," Bella said.

The atmosphere in the room had tipped towards scary.

You should never have agreed to do this. How can you be so stupid? She's right. You don't belong here. Get out of here.

"Look here. I waitressed for six years, dropped out of high school, made ends meet doing crappy parts just so I could get a good role. So how can somebody as fat and lazy as you just waltz in and steal the most coveted role? You don't deserve to be here. You shouldn't be here. It's not fair." Rosie's anger rose in a crescendo. So did her volume.

"Excuse me?" Shocked, that was the best Bella could muster.

"You can't get anything right in one take, you keep stammering on your lines, nobody in the cast likes you."

Bella dug her nails into the heel of her palms, but there was no avoiding the spiraling unease in her abdomen. All the awful, demeaning words she'd heard from Bryan's friends danced around her, too loud to bury. Six years had passed, but she was still the same Bella who couldn't fit in anywhere.

But one thing had changed.

She'd learned to stand up for herself.

Bella put her foot down—both literally and figuratively. "You're the one who needs to get out. This is completely unacceptable behavior. Do you think you can bully me?"

Completely ignoring her, Rosie whined, "Tell Jamie you can't do the show anymore."

"I can't. I won't." Although, she was sorely tempted to. Every instinct in her body screamed at her to quit, to get away from this place. But Rosie didn't have to know that.

"Do it! I don't want to see your face around anymore!" Rosie screamed.

"You can't tell me what to do." Bella gnashed her teeth. "And grow up already. The world's not fair. If you can't stand me, that's your problem, not mine."

If the world was fair, she wouldn't have an alcoholic mother. She wouldn't be attracting commitment-phobic losers into her life when all she wanted was a good man who would marry her. She wouldn't have to do this weird acting gig to be able to afford a house.

Rosie trembled. "I've worked hard, okay? I worked really hard. I'm supposed to be successful. I'm talented, I'm beautiful, I'm a great actress. I deserve to be a big star. I deserve to be noticed. But why am I not famous yet? Because losers like you keep taking away roles."

"How childish, to blame your problems on others." The whir of the projector faded from the background.

"You're the problem." Bony knuckles were protruding through Rosie's tightly clenched fists.

"No, you are," Bella retorted.

Rosie must have been the prettiest girl in her high school, the star of the school play, the center of her small universe. And now she expected the world to fall into her lap.

"How dare you say that? You're so fat!" Rosie screamed, hurling a crumpled tissue at her.

"That's the best insult you can come up with? Fat?" Sucking in a breath, Bella scratched behind her ear—something she always did before she lied. "Sorry to disappoint you, but I'm very comfortable with my weight."

"Losers always say that." The ugly pout smeared Rosie's red lipstick.

Bella squared her jaw. "Well, I'm not a loser."

Losers didn't have PhDs or tenured positions at prestigious universities. As long as she focused on her accomplishments and not on her appearance, she would come out of this okay. But something slimy wriggled between her ribs. A panic she had never been able to suppress. The past was trying to drag her back to its dark hole, trying to drown her in that well of self-hate. And with all her might, she fought it.

"I'm more beautiful than you. I'm thinner. I deserve to have a better life!" Rosie continued to repeat her tantrums. This was getting so tiring.

Bella waved. She was at the end of her patience. "I'm not interested in listening to this. You can continue this self-pity rant on your own. I'm going."

Quickly grabbing her bag, Bella dashed out of the room fuming.

She'd had it. She'd had it with crazy bitches. She'd had it with being called fat. She'd had it with everything. The entertainment industry was no place for her. If she had an iota of sense, she'd never have pushed herself into this shark tank again. She could have been teaching summer school, or spending her Friday lazily curled up on the sand and getting a tan. Or in France, just vacationing. Why on God's green earth had she decided that becoming an actress was a better idea than sunbathing on a tropical island?

Jamie. It was all his fault. Him and his sweet-talking. Urgh!

Marching towards the exit, Bella wasn't pleased when she saw Jamie's form eagerly approaching her. Ruffled by her encounter with Rosie, Bella didn't trust herself to not snap around him.

"Why're you still wearing that?" Jamie asked, hooking a hand around her shoulder.

Baring her teeth at him, Bella yanked his hand away.

"Because one of your stupid actresses ruined my clothes," she barked out, throwing her messed-up tee at him. It ballooned and fell on his face. "Was this what you meant when you promised me I wouldn't be harassed? Because I'm not inclined to believe you anymore."

He plucked away the T-shirt she'd thrown at him and regarded it with a wary expression. "Rosie, I'm guessing. She's the only one who could spell stupid wrong."

Edging a grin her way, he gave her a completely non-apologetic headshake. That just incensed her. Was this a joke to him? She was being bullied by her co-star, and the best he could do was make fun of Rosie's spelling?

Anger sizzled in her. Promising herself that she wasn't going to stay in this toxic, unsupportive environment for one more minute, she tipped her chin up to Jamie.

"I want to quit." Her body was rigid, unmoving, just like her opinion.

Jamie stared at her evenly. "No."

Bella inched up a shoulder blade. "Yes, yes, yes. I'm quitting. I've had enough of this. My co-star's behaving like a middle school bully. I suck at acting. It doesn't matter how much you pay me. I can't do this to myself."

Jamie dug his shoe into the ground. A loud tap sound resounded.

"I could tell you all the legal reasons that would be a bad idea." He paused. "But maybe you should first tell me why you're shaking so badly. You said something interesting when we met at the coffee shop.

You said you didn't want to be in entertainment again. I'm guessing this has something to do with that."

"It's none of your business," Bella snapped.

"Okay, then how about I get you something dry to wear?" He surveyed the massive dark blot on her front. "There are spare T-shirts in Cathy's room. Come with me."

They walked her to a dressing room, where Catherine was leisurely sipping a smoothie. She didn't mind the intrusion.

Retrieving an oversized black T-shirt for her which said 'Born This Way,' Jamie handed it to her.

It was too goth for her liking, but she wouldn't look too out of place amongst the college students on the subway wearing this. Gratefully grabbing it, Bella borrowed the dressing room from Catherine and rid herself of the wet T-shirt.

When she came out, Jamie regarded her carefully.

"What's on my face?" She slanted her lashes up.

"Nothing," he said, face coloring red. His head toward Cathy. "That color looks good on you."

Bella grunted. "I'm not comfortable with my *boss* complimenting me on my looks if you know what I mean."

Raising his open palms in the air, Jamie dropped an emphatic sigh. "Okay. Noted. But I really hope you stop being so hostile to me someday."

Bella strutted ahead on her heels, exiting the studio. "I'm not hostile. Merely suspicious."

Jamie guffawed. "Merely? Who even uses 'merely' in daily conversations?"

"Me. And a lot of other intellectuals." Wiping away sweat from the crease of her neck, Bella swiveled in the opposite direction.

"Not that way. This is the way out." Jamie tapped her arm.

"I could've figured that out on my own," Bella muttered.

"Okay, I get it. You had a bad day. But being angry won't change anything. How about you follow me and get a first-hand look at how I deal with Rosie? Trust me, you don't want to miss this."

"I don't want to be around that girl again. And unlike her, I'm not so petty and vengeful that I'd want to watch her get scolded."

Jamie blazed on ahead, unaffected by her words. For some reason she couldn't explain, Bella, followed him. "I'm going to have to talk to her either way. You're not the only one on the set unhappy with her behavior. But I'm really sorry this happened to you. I hope you'll give me a chance to make things right and not rashly quit the show."

"I need the money," Bella said after a minute when her temper had cooled. "So you can relax."

"You want to buy a house, don't you? I have a friend who's unloading his condo for cheap because he has to suddenly move. It's a two-bedroom in Prospect Heights. Want to see it?" Jamie asked.

"I don't have millions of dollars to throw on a fancy superstar pad," Bella replied, though she was intrigued by the opportunity. The apartment she'd visited with the agent before, her dream condo, had already sold, and since all the money from acting would only come into her account after four weeks, after all the episodes were shot, she was currently in limbo with her house search.

"He'll sell it to you for cheap if I tell him to," Jamie continued. "He owes me one."

"And you're calling in that favor for me? Why?"

"I broke my promise to you to make your work environment free from harassment, so I'm going to have to make it up in some way, right?" He threw her an apologetic smile. His eyes were so clear, almost like transparent glass when the light from the light fixtures in the corridor hit them.

Bella swallowed hard, hoping it'd kill the butterflies fluttering around in her stomach. No point in getting too excited over something she couldn't have. "How much is the condo?"

"Whatever price you want to pay. Whatever you can afford to pay. I'm guessing around five hundred thousand?"

Bella's jaw dropped. It'd be ridiculous to get a two-bedroom for that much in Prospect Heights. Beyond ridiculous. One bedroom in Prospect Park costs double that. But it'd be a dream come true. Even if the apartment was dingy and terrible, at that price, she could afford to spend a bit on renovation. And she'd get a whole extra bedroom!

Bella croaked out something incoherent.

Jamie released a laugh that wrapped around her like silk. "I'm assuming that's a yes. Since I know you're free this Sunday, why don't we go see it?"

Bella didn't expect to see Jamie again before Sunday. He'd messaged her the address of the apartment and confirmed that his friend would sell it to her at the price she wanted. Bella had taken the opportunity to search the house on Google maps, and she had to say, it was way better than what she'd imagined. If the inside of the apartment matched the outside, then she'd literally be stealing the apartment from the owner, because the price she could pay didn't justify that level of luxury.

Bella groaned when someone buzzed. She wondered who it was. Of course, her choices were narrow—it could only be Kat, Ashley, or the delivery from Amazon.com.

But it was Jamie. She let him in.

"You left the set in a bad mood, so I thought I'd bring you some ice cream and my cheerful presence." He handed her a cup with a swirl of vanilla ice cream. Sprinkled over the ice cream were little bits that looked like cereal.

Being all alone, she didn't mind the company. Better than hyperventilating over her dream house and whether it was fair to buy it so cheap. "Thanks."

"Listen...I'm sorry about what happened. Daniel and I talked to Rosie. She's promised not to do anything malicious again. Depending on her mood, she might or might not apologize to you tomorrow, so I'll apologize on her behalf. Don't take it personally. She's still young."

"I don't care. I think I put her in her place pretty well." Bella sauntered back to the old leather armchair she'd been sitting on, leaving the door open.

Jamie made his way in. He was surprised when he absorbed the faces on her TV screen. "You were watching *Love Me Like You Do?*"

"Yeah. I just put it on. Wanna watch with me?"

His nod was short. "It's been ages since I watched this." His sneakers, with the laces untied, clucked over hardwood.

Bella squeezed herself into the armchair, leaving the couch wide open for him. She didn't want to get too close to him.

"Here it goes."

The screen faded to black. Gradually, pictures started to move.

Jamie folded his hands over his chest. "Um... Frankly, I'm a bit worried. I wrote this so long ago. I have a hunch that I'll be cringing at every dialogue."

Jamie was dampened by a voiceover. Damien's voice, sexy British accent and all rolled in to narrate the opening lines.

What is love? There is no answer to that question. But what I do know for sure is that once you find love, there are no longer any questions.

"Fuck. I didn't really write that. I couldn't have written something that bad." Jamie's face shriveled as the voiceover proceeded. "I swear I'm having doubts about my talent as a writer."

"And I thought I was insecure." Bella sighed, waiting for the first scene. As a few dialogues went by, she remembered something she'd always wondered about. "Why did you decide to call her Maddie? Damien's a cool and romantic name. But Maddie is so ordinary."

"You don't wanna listen to that story." Jamie stole a chip from her, and she slapped his hand. While not OCD like Kat, she didn't want him putting his dirty fingers in her packet of Doritos.

"Now I really want to hear it." Bella pulled her back straight.

"Sorry, no." He didn't let up, though he couldn't focus on the movie.

"How bad can it be?"

"You have no idea."

Huffing, she realized that he was starting to color red. Must be really embarrassing, then.

"So, this part. Why does Damien take pills for no reason? It's not tied into any other scene in the story. It's a loose hanging thread in the plot."

"You haven't watched the movie carefully." Jamie stretched his legs. "Do you remember the first time they made love? Why do you think he fell asleep halfway?"

Bella clapped her hands like she'd struck a vein of inspiration. "So that's why. Wow. I never correlated this to that. You're brilliant."

"You might be the only one who thinks so after watching this movie." Jamie's lips took another dip as another sappy, romantic line played.

"Bad, bad, bad," he muttered under his breath, and she saw something she'd never seen on him before—worry.

"Do I need to call the ambulance or can your ego hang in there for another hour?" Bella teased, reaching for the powdered crumbs of Doritos at the bottom of the packet.

"You'd know if you ever wrote a script…" he mumbled.

Bella continued providing running commentary throughout the movie, picking out her favorite lines and asking him to explain his inspiration behind certain scenes.

"I love this part…this one's my favorite scene. Did you hear what he said? He told her that she was—"

"I wrote the movie. I know." He studied the ticking of the clock impatiently.

Splaying her toes, Bella brushed them over her rug. "There was a similar line in *The Fall*."

Jamie quoted the line, slack-jawed. "Sometimes, I run out of creative juice, too."

"Don't be so hard on yourself." Bella patted him. "Everybody's gotta start somewhere. You started in a better place than most. Think about the millions of writers who're still struggling to get their debut movie made."

Jamie's tongue swept over the ice cream in his hand. "You give a good pep talk."

When the scene between Maddie and her brother came on, she sniffled. "I cry every time I watch this."

He reached over and brushed her hips. It was a feather-light touch, with his face turned away like he didn't want her to notice, but he couldn't stop himself from doing it. Heat sizzled between her legs.

No.

She wasn't supposed to feel anything for Jamie. He was all the wrong things rolled into one person. Plus, she'd just done the math and figured out that he was six years younger. She would not, she would not, she would not ever fall for him, regardless of how deep the movies he wrote were, how his presence put her at ease, how he'd offered to make her biggest dream come.

Soon, tears engulfed her eyes and made her go silent. She looked to Jamie, expecting him to be as touched, shattered, and emotional as her.

He was, but for a totally different reason.

Jamie's expression wasn't hard to read. A frown was etching itself deeper into his mouth.

"Pause the movie. I need a beer." Jamie shot a mopey look at her.

"I don't have any beer." Trying to control her body's response, Bella punched the pause button hard.

"Why not?"

Stroking her upper thigh edgily, she said, "My mother's alcoholism left scars."

He was too observant for that unconscious touch to go unnoticed. "Physical scars?"

"Some."

Jamie pushed his hair back, palm resting on his forehead. "Jesus."

Bella stitched her lips together so she wouldn't say more. Trauma was best left buried.

"Ready for the rest of it?" she asked, threatening to press the resume button.

"Gimme a break." Jamie threw himself flat on her couch. "I've reached the end of my cheesy tolerance for the day."

"Hey, it's not that bad. I like it. There's a fan base for cheesy romantic melodramas." Bella massaged her thighs, which were cramping because the armchair wasn't wide enough to accommodate her gigantic ass. They needed to make size sixteen loveseats. Seriously.

Coming onto his side, Jamie lay his elbow down and focused his gaze on her. "I want to hear about your mother."

"I don't wanna talk about that."

"Come on. Sharing's good."

"Will you drop it?"

Jamie touched the side of his face. "If you tell me about it, I'll tell you why I named that character Maddie."

Now that was one trade she couldn't refuse.

"Um…my mom was abusive sometimes. She was constantly abandoned by men she loved and trusted and so she took it out on me. That's all."

There. She'd blurted out what she'd never shared with anybody except her friends. Her stomach scrunched. The ugly, intense emotions thinking about her childhood brought…she wanted to run away from them. The house. She had to think of her house. It was finally within reach. The end was within sight.

Jamie ran his thumb over his wrist. "What did she do?"

"Threw stuff at me. Shouted and screamed. If I retaliated, she'd hit me. But she didn't hit me much."

"Where was child protective services during all of this?" There was way too much care in the way he studied her. It made her uneasy.

"Nobody knew what was happening. I didn't want anyone to find out. I tried to protect my mother. Don't ask me why. I felt bad for her, I guess, since the men she was with were so crappy. I believed I could heal her…that I could save her and make her stop doing all the destructive things she was doing. I thought that she was just like me, a little lonely and unappreciated. If I was nice to her, I figured she would be able to love again…"

The words dried up as tears spilled uncontrollably from her. It was so unexpected it caught even her off guard. She didn't think she still cared about her mother, about her childhood. Didn't think it affected her so much. Bella pressed the heel of her hand against her cheek to wipe the tears away, but Jamie suddenly stood up, came over, and hugged her. Her cheek whisked over Jamie's T-shirt. Bella felt his hand press the back of her head, then slither down.

"Stop it. I don't want your sympathy," she said. "I'm a grown woman."

But she didn't fight to get away from his embrace. She loved being hugged. She'd always longed to be hugged by her mother like this. Hugged and comforted and cherished.

Jamie's breath caressed her scalp. "It's not sympathy. I'm trying to support you."

She adjusted to the planes of his shoulder. Being wrapped up in him felt like a sanctuary. But she'd never had a sanctuary to heal before, so it was a new and uncomfortable feeling.

"It wasn't as bad as I make it sound. She didn't hit me every day or anything. It was...maybe once or twice a month."

"That's still a lot."

"It didn't seem like a lot." At that time, she'd considered it normal. She hadn't known better. "And it's okay. I survived."

"You're brave." His soothing, encouraging whisper rushed over her back.

"Yeah." Bella forced herself to get back to her usual, cheerful self. The past could swallow her if she let it. "But now I want to hear about Maddie."

Jamie drew a breath, like he was going to protest, but dropped the idea. "Maddie was my first girlfriend. I was madly in love with her. When she broke up with me, I was crushed. I wrote her a movie so to tell her how much I loved her and to ask her to take me back." He snorted. "Not one of my finer moments."

Crossing her fingers, Bella asked, "Did she take you back?"

Jamie exhaled, and even though it was only a harmless exhale, it made his heart press against her ear. His heartbeat bled into her bones, and her heart kicked. "No, she didn't, and the box office hated the movie, too. But at least I got off my lazy butt and wrote a movie. I have her to thank for it."

Pushing her knees up to her chin and circling them with her arms, Bella said, "I'd have taken you back."

Jamie didn't look up at her right away. "I'm glad she was smart enough to let me go. It was better for me in the long run. And for her."

"Do you wish things were different?"

"No. It was just a silly, shallow love. I can't even remember what I liked about her. At eighteen, everything seems ten times more important than it is."

Throwing themselves into watching *Love Me Like You Do* again, time sped by and it was almost another half hour before it ended. Jamie had laughed throughout and she'd cried. Still, watching the movie with him was an experience in itself.

"So, fallen in love me with now that you've watched my masterpiece?" Jamie asked.

There was no hint of flirtation in his tone, but heat wrapped over Bella's body. She'd been so engrossed in the move that she hadn't realized how he'd stood at her side throughout, holding her hand. Now, she couldn't ignore the warmth that flowed through their linked hands. As she became suddenly conscious of their physical proximity, he lifted an eyebrow at her. And it was definitely a flirt eyebrow lift. She should've been able to brush it off easily with some sarcastic quip, but as she stared at him, the uncomfortable knowledge that she was beginning to find him sexy seeped into her. He was...well, pretty handsome. And right now, she couldn't ignore that fact. Something hot and visceral pulsed between them.

She tried to wrench his hand away vehemently, lying to herself, hoping that the sudden buzz, the sudden realization that she saw Jamie Star as more than a stalker/nuisance would disappear if she denied it.

But he didn't let go and she ended up stumbling forward. The armchair tipped, and she crashed onto the floor with Jamie. Only a second later did she realize she'd landed on his lap with her mouth right on...well...his crotch.

"Ah." Her cheek rested there for a total of five seconds before every cell in her body ignited and she remembered that there was something called sex in this world.

And she hadn't been having a whole lot of that recently.

And she'd really like some. Like, right this moment. With him.

Tossing her head up, she caught him blush.

"Are you...um...okay?"

Without letting it get awkward, Bella steadied herself on her feet. A sorry would make this even more awkward, so she brushed her pajamas off like it was no big deal and she was so *not* lusting after him.

"It's no big deal." Jamie was talking to himself in a trance.

Arousal sat just behind his eyes, swelling when his gaze met hers. All further conversation between them disappeared. Sparks crackled. Voices from outside the door drifted into the space created by their silence, drumming in urgency to act.

Jamie's Adam's apple strained against his throat. Hers bobbed up, too, when she swallowed. Static played between them, and when she lifted her head and straddled his body which was still flat on the floor, she knew she could never go back from this.

She leaned into Jamie's face. He lifted his face to hers, too, until their lips were a hair's breadth away from fusing into each other. If this was a movie, this night would end in a passionate kiss and a happily ever after. But it wasn't. This was the cold, hard reality, which had a way of disappointing.

So when she moved her tongue to his lower lip, Jamie pulled away, looking repulsed. Shocked.

Bella blinked. "Is something wrong?"

"I don't want to kiss you," Jamie declared, poker-faced.

Her hands flew up to touch her face. Oh god. What had she done? Had she read the signals wrongly? Had she assumed too much? Was she was so desperate that she was becoming delusional? Had she dreamt up his attraction? Damn. This was what her mother had always done, believed there was a romance where there wasn't, believed there was mutual attraction where there wasn't.

"Uh...well. That's fine, then." Bella lifted the armchair and then herself upright.

Despite the easy shrug she gave, his rejection felt like a slap to her face. A sharp, painful slap. Clenching her fists, she swore not to get emotional. Feelings for men who didn't reciprocate had no place in her life plan. Lust and unrequited love were what had ruined her mother's life, turned it into a dumpster fire.

"Look at the time. I should get going." Drawing to his feet clumsily, Jamie angled his head at the door.

"Mmmm."

Repressing her disappointment, she knelt on the floor until her insecurity started slaying her. It was okay if he didn't want her. It was his choice. She couldn't appeal to everyone.

"Thanks for watching the movie." Jamie's sentences flew past her ears.

Look at him. He's pitying you. He thinks you're a freak.

"Mmmm."

Before leaving, he shot her a backward glance and a restrained smile. "Learn your lines for episode eight, okay?"

"Jamie?" She held his gaze, searching his blue eyes for anything that would tell her that if she pushed a little, he would kiss her. Because she wanted to kiss him. Badly.

"Yeah?" His jaw was artificially tight.

"Will you…" Diffidence choked her voice. What was she thinking? She couldn't ask him why he didn't want to kiss her. That would be beyond desperate. "Nothing. Bye."

"Cool. I'll see you tomorrow."

He sidled through the door, leaving her drowning in emotions she didn't understand.

CHAPTER NINE

When Bella showed up for rehearsals the next day, she was clearly upset. Red lines bulged against the whites of her eyes as she jetted past Jamie, not sparing him anything more than a formal 'good morning'. That, too, without eye contact. She must've cried last night. He'd expected her to.

Suddenly pulling out of that kiss hadn't been his plan, but he couldn't fight his instinct. Couldn't heal the scars that were burrowed deep into his heart. He couldn't tell Bella the truth, either. What would he say?

My mother used my love for her to make me steal money from my father. My girlfriend listened to all my secrets like she cared, then used them to buy her way to a better life. I can no longer kiss a woman without feeling the sting of betrayal against my lips, without drowning in those horrible memories. I feel like puking whenever I kiss a woman. Yeah, I'm fucked up. I can't stand being vulnerable with a woman. Go ahead. Judge me.

No. She wouldn't understand. Nobody understood, not even Grant. His issues were his to live with. Bella was no fragile doll. She could live with a bit of disappointment. She'd probably forget about it soon.

"Hey," Jamie tried in a casual tone, hoping they could go back to the way they'd been, but she pretended not to hear.

She got through the rehearsals perfunctorily, ignoring him throughout, except when he was giving her instructions. The rehearsal dragged on well into the evening because they had to rewrite so many scenes. At the end of it, he found himself back in the writers' room alone, having to change the next episode because of all the stuff they'd rewritten in this one. Opening up his laptop, he'd only made the first correction when the door swung open.

"Shawna, can you get me a—" He realized it wasn't Shawna who'd come in. It was Bella.

"Scarlet wanted me to give you this." She threw down a piece of paper.

"Thanks."

Her hair was in a ponytail. Some exotic fragrance hung around her body, probably a perfume. He'd never smelled perfume on her before. She was tapping her feet restlessly.

"Everything okay?" he asked.

"Why wouldn't it be?" she retorted. God, watching her proud yet fragile expression was like dragging nails over his arms.

Jamie wished he could tell her the truth. But then he'd dig his own grave. It would only make him look pathetic and it'd give her more power over him. Besides, he'd vowed not to share his feelings with chicks who could use it to gain a hold over him as his ex-girlfriend had.

"Listen, about last night...I didn't expect we'd go down that path." He fingered his mussed-up hair. "But I guess stuff happened and...can we forget about it? I don't want it to affect our professional relationship."

Her upper lip trembled. She filled her lungs with a large gulp of air, fighting anger. Or tears. He couldn't tell which one it was. It broke his heart, though, and he recoiled at his strong emotional reaction to this woman's sorrow. Feeling so much for her when he wasn't even sleeping with her was terrifying. Why did he care so much about how she felt? She was only an actress he worked with. Why had he offered to help her buy that apartment, knowing he'd be paying the difference in the market price without telling her? Why did he want to see her happy, see her fulfill her dreams?

"It's okay. I don't need a pity kiss from anyone." Bella's voice quaked with barely suppressed fury.

"It wasn't a pity kiss," Jamie protested. Pity had been the last thing on his mind when he'd touched his forehead to hers. "There was no kiss."

"Yeah, right. Thanks for reminding me." She passed him a blatantly hostile stare.

Now that the kiss was dealt with, he could move on to other things. "I don't know if Scarlet's told you about this, but we're planning a party after we're done with episode ten. It'd be great if you could join us."

"I can't make it. I have to write papers. This is not my full-time job." Bella gravitated towards the colorful post-its on the wall.

"Can you make it to the house tour on Sunday?" Jamie clicked his fingers. "It's still on. But if you're not in the mood—"

"I won't miss that for anything in the world." She kicked her heels, then strode out.

She wasn't sulking on the day of the house viewing. In fact, from the moment Bella arrived at the location, she did nothing but beam like a ray of sunshine. She was wearing a yellow sundress that made her seem like a vibrant, ethereal creature.

"I can't wait to see the house." She tapped her feet excitedly.

Jamie could get used to seeing this side of Bella. Worse, he could get used to making sacrifices just so he could see her face light up with glee more often. At least his ex-girlfriend had asked for the money. What was his excuse with Bella? She hadn't asked him for anything but a kiss. He was losing control again. Throwing away everything he had for the sake of...what? This couldn't be love; he hadn't even kissed her yet. Maybe it was just charity on his part, or some deep sense of guilt for letting her down, though his instinct told him the answer wasn't that simple. And this was the reason why he needed to give up thoughts of sleeping with her, of running his tongue down those sexy curves. Because God only knew how much more obsessive his feelings would become if that were to happen.

Get it together, dude.

The condo was on the fifth floor and when he opened the door, Bella screamed. "You can't be serious! Someone's willing to sell *this* to me at five hundred thousand?"

She took off her shoes, bare toes slapping against the wood floor. Stunning panoramic views of Brooklyn and Manhattan beyond the glass walls framed Bella's body. She skated around the various rooms like a kid in a candy store, checking out every single part of the house with keen interest.

Jamie just followed her around, unable to offer any useful information on the specs of the house, since he hadn't bothered to find out anything from his friend Gage but to watch her expression bloom with happiness whenever something lived up to her expectations. Judging by the number of times she'd grinned, there were a lot of things that were living up to her expectations in this house.

That was no surprise. The condo, with recent upgrades, cost upward of a million dollars. Even he wouldn't be able to complain about it. He just hoped Bella wasn't overly aware of the buying process and she didn't ask him how he'd get the sale approved by the condo's board since they had a minimum sale price for the units to preserve the reputation of the building as a premium apartment block. And that minimum sale price was a helluva lot higher than five hundred thousand.

Bella spent a long time in the kitchen, caressing the granite kitchen counters like they were newborn puppies instead of slabs of stone. Something contorted inside Jamie's stomach, an acidic sensation he recognized only too well, but was unaccustomed to feeling around Bella. Was he jealous of a stone slab? A stone slab. For what?

This was ridiculous. His lust for her should've died after he'd rejected her kiss. Awkwardness could bury even the strongest sexual chemistry. Instead, why did every minute he spent with her make him feel like he was being consumed by a fire stronger than the one he'd put out by rejecting her? Like he was a man freezing to death, and he'd die unless he could grasp her warmth in his hands. His fingertips longed to be buried in those beautiful curves, dig into that soft flesh and—

"Will you stop ogling my butt?" Bella's voice struck him like a whip. "It's ruining my moment of happiness."

"Sorry." There was nothing to do except beg for forgiveness.

Jamie was glad he'd asked his friend Gage to clear out of the house while he showed Bella the place. He didn't know why he'd done that; Gage would've been the better person to show her the house. But he wanted to be the one giving her the tour. She'd probably visit the house a couple more times before signing the contract so she could meet Gage then.

Bella finally left the kitchen, bringing relief to his nerves which were stretched thin with tension. He was far too aware of the shape of her body, the seductive sway of her hips, the moisture of her lip balm on her lips, and the fact that they were very, very alone in this apartment.

"So, what do you think?" Jamie asked, keen to move to a more public place. "Wanna check out the outdoor patio and fitness center?"

Bella let out an erratic breath. "It's everything."

Her expression was everything. Joy and tears and amazement and wonder all rolled into one. He regretted he didn't have a camera to capture it.

Then, suddenly, like a blue sky overcast with gray clouds, Bella's expression went taut with tension. "There's no catch to this, right? I won't share this apartment with anyone."

"It's all yours."

"This is too good to be true. I've seen apartments half this size for twice the price." Bella balled her fists tight like she was afraid of being disappointed. Like she'd been disappointed before. "You're not going to make me pay the rest of the money later, are you?"

"Nothing except the monthly taxes and common charges," Jamie replied.

"I'm not going to believe anything unless I see it in writing."

"Um...sure."

That part, Jamie had still not figured out. The deed would contain the actual sale price of the house, which included the portion he was paying for. He still hadn't managed to come up with an idea of how to disguise that. But if she realized he was paying half the cost, she'd be furious.

"I'm going to buy it. How soon can I get it?"

"In four weeks," Jamie said. "You should come again and meet Gage. He was busy today, but he'll be able to give you all the details."

"Thank you. You've really helped me out with this. I can't tell you how much this means to me." Every oxygen molecule in Jamie's lungs was knocked out the moment Bella raised herself to her tiptoes and hugged him. It was just a friendly thing. She was just overflowing with happiness. But her warmth enveloped him like warm honey, seeped into his cracks, and made him crave its sweetness. "Consider yourself completely forgiven for the Rosie incident and the kiss."

"Yeah. Glad I could help." He tried to brush it off smoothly, but his dick was starting to get hard and his heart was drumming at a mad pace. He'd thought he'd brought his feelings back under control, by they were breaking their shackles again. He couldn't lose control. Not now.

"I grew up without a house," Bella continued. "Buying a place of my own means a lot to me."

"You deserve it," Jamie said, trying to calm himself.

When she pulled away, he should've been relieved. Instead, that emptiness he always felt at random moments, that strange void of dissatisfaction and boredom that accompanied him like a faithful dog, twisted in his chest again. But now, for the first time, he sensed a mode of relief. And he couldn't help but take it, because he'd lived with this agony for too long, and he'd been feeling unstable ever since that night at Bella's apartment when she'd set something off in him, and the solution was standing right before his eyes and he no longer had the self-control required to resist his own doom.

Jamie rarely did anything without overthinking. But when he bent down and kissed Bella, his mind was empty. And when she returned his kiss, her sweet lips smoothing over his, the jagged, misshapen parts of him that didn't fit anywhere finally fell into place.

And then he made an ass of himself. Again.

CHAPTER TEN

There were some things Bella had never thought could happen to her. Finding a two-bed apartment within her budget was one. Being kissed by Jamie Star was another. Now both of those were happening at the same time.

His lips scorched a hot trail over hers. And just as she started to respond, started to get used to that perfect rhythm of his tongue moving over hers, he broke the kiss.

"Sorry."

Frustration welled up and exploded inside Bella. Was apologizing the only thing Jamie could do? She'd been so willing to let him off the hook for that almost kiss five nights ago, but she needed an explanation for his wishy-washiness this time. He'd been the one to initiate it, after all.

"What was that about?" Bella wiped her lips with the back of her hand, then stopped when she registered the hurt expression in Jamie's eyes. What right did the bastard have to be hurt after he'd rejected her first?

Jamie was staring at his palms like he was hoping to find answers between the lines etched on them. "I can't kiss women."

Whatever excuse she'd been expecting, she hadn't been expecting him to say *that*.

"You're gay?" Crap. Had she assumed too much about his sexuality without confirming? Had she made him uncomfortable by approaching him that time at her house? Wasn't that some type of harassment? Bella was paralyzed with guilt when Jamie suddenly spoke.

"No. I'm straight," he said. "I just can't kiss women. I can do everything else. Sex. Oral. Whatever."

"But you just kissed me," Bella said. "Unless your definition of 'kiss' is significantly different from the general population."

"That...I don't know what came over me." The pleading in Jamie's voice set alarm bells ringing in her head. He was taking this even harder than she was. "Please forget this happened. I will never try anything like this on you ever again. I promise."

"You're so freaked out over a kiss?" Bella asked.

"I didn't plan for this to happen." Jamie was talking to himself now. His eyes were unfocused, darting everywhere like he was not here in this apartment, but somewhere far away, surrounded by things that scared him.

"Jamie, you can tell me if there's something," Bella said. "I told you about my mother, too."

"My mother..." Jamie started. "She wasn't abusive like yours, but she was a user in her own way. Well, it's water under the bridge now."

His shoulder stopped trembling and he pulled himself straight. The haunted look was still stuck inside his eyes, but he didn't say more about his mother. Bella had a feeling she'd have to pry it out of him.

"What did your mother do?"

Jamie just shrugged. "She was a gold digger, obsessed with being beautiful and important. She married my father young, seduced by promises of being a top star's wife. But my father wasn't the faithful type. Neither did he suffer fools gladly. When he realized she was spending his money like water and that she'd only married him for his money, he divorced her."

"What happened to her after that?"

"My father got custody and she got a hefty settlement which she spent before the year was out."

"And then?"

Jamie paused. Bella knew this was the crucial piece. But he didn't continue, just shrugged, buried his hands in his pockets, and started to pick his to the apartment's entrance. "I don't know. I don't keep in touch with her anymore."

She followed him, but even in the elevator, he didn't disclose the rest of the story. When they got to the fitness center, he quickly changed the subject to the facilities that the building had and how much of a bargain the condo was.

Bella clenched her fists in frustration, the hormones from the kiss earlier still circulating in her blood.

She wanted nothing more than to know why Jamie Star couldn't kiss women.

Bella would've ended up thinking about Jamie and his mother and the kiss all day if not for the visit to Gracie Mansion that Kat had planned for her months ago. Since she had no excuse to bail, she went. After all, getting a personal tour from the mayor himself was a once-in-a-lifetime opportunity. Plus, she couldn't wait to share news about the apartment with her friends.

Although Alex, Kat's boyfriend, had been mayor for three years now, she'd never had a chance to see Gracie from the inside, because Kat didn't live with him. But today, out of the blue, she'd invited Ashley and Bella for a tour of the house.

"Had sex with Alex in the morning? You have that post-orgasmic glow on your face," Bella teased Kat as they gave each other a friendly hug.

"We were discussing the proposed gun control bill, actually." Kat blushed the exact shade of pink as her skirt suit.

Shaking her head, Bella sighed. "I swear; I'll never understand you guys."

"Nobody does. But someday, you'll understand the sexiness that is politics."

They negotiated a flight of stairs to what Kat called the 'yellow parlor.'

"So how's it going with Jamie? Anything happened yet?" Kicking her shoes off, Kat lounged on one of the uniformly beige wing chairs.

On a table in the corner, Alex had his nose bent over a stack of papers, and he was talking to one of his staffers. Since they were still waiting for Ashley and Andrew to arrive, they didn't disturb Alex.

Bella cleared her throat awkwardly, thinking of the best way to phrase her lie. But Kat had been her friend for too long to let this hesitation go unnoticed.

"Something happened," Kat surmised.

"We almost kissed."

"Almost?"

"He decided to be a jerk and pull away at the last minute." Kat gasped at that. "But I don't hate him too much for it. I think it was a good decision. I don't want to date a player. Jamie made it clear he doesn't believe in long-term and I'm not my mother. I won't put up with men who cannot invest in a relationship."

"Oh, right. I forgot about that." Kat shifted her gaze to Alex. There was a hint of concern in the way she looked at him. "He's so busy these days. He gets home from city hall and then he's having meetings here all through the night. I worry about his health."

"You worry about everybody's health."

Kat wasn't listening. Eyebrows furrowed, she continued to stare at Alex.

Bella shook her legs and decided to walk around. Sticking to the windows and the fireplace opposite Kat to not disturb Alex, she examined the furniture and paintings on the wall, as Ashley came in through the door.

A gasp hiccupped from her. "Ashley!"

Ashley had grown and expanded a lot since the last time she'd seen her. Giving Bella a cheery smile, she waddled towards Kat, one hand protectively on her belly.

"That's a big bump. Are you sure you're not having twins?" Kat inquired.

Creeping closer to Ashley, Bella beamed. "Hey. You look good. I haven't seen you in so long."

There was a distance in those words that shouldn't exist.

Ashley moved in for an embrace. "We've both been so busy. How's your acting career going?"

"Another two weeks and it'll be over. Honestly, I can't wait to go back to being a normal person." Recently, she missed being able to ponder deep philosophical issues.

"The show airs in six months, right? I'm on a break then so I'll definitely watch every episode. Maybe she will, too." Ashley poked her swollen belly, sniggering.

"I have good news to share," Bella said. Everybody's eyes darted to her instantly. "I have finally managed to buy my own house. It's a two-bed in Prospect Park. I'll move in next month and then you're all welcome to visit me."

Kat was the first to embrace her. "Congratulations, you made it happen. But how? Prospect Park's so pricey."

"I got a good deal from one of Jamie's friends. He wanted to get rid of his property quickly and was looking for a buyer who'd decide fast."

"I'm so proud of you," Ashley said. Her hug was a little more difficult to execute. "You've become a homeowner at last."

"Who's Jamie?" Andrew asked, all of a sudden.

"The producer of my show," Bella replied. Then Alex shepherded them all toward the library to continue the tour.

The library was all blue—blue walls, blue upholstery, blue carpets. Even the curtains were blue.

"Why're there so few books in the library?" Bella asked eyes on the lone bookshelf nestled between the door and a window.

"Yeah, it's confusing to visitors sometimes." Alex rolled up the sleeves of his shirt. "The thing is, it's called the library, but it's actually another parlor."

Sliding a provocative gaze to Kat, Alex cleared his throat. "I use this one for drinking coffee and reading," a muscle twitched in his jaw, "mostly."

And it was anybody's guess what else he used it for. They all shifted to the dining room. It wasn't big, but it was welcoming. Two large windows on the east brought sunlight inside the mostly blue and green-themed space. A long wooden table, polished like a mirror, with eight chairs, was the centerpiece.

"Is this where you eat?" Ashley asked, studying the wallpaper—a painting of trees, plains, and peasants.

"Not daily. But during formal dinners, yes. That wallpaper was manufactured in the 1830s by Zuber, a French company." Alex stepped back, bumping the fireplace. "It's more than a hundred years old."

"Looks new."

"Thanks to the dedicated cleaning team we have here." Setting one crooked candlestick at the center of the table straight, Alex launched into the history of Gracie Mansion and then led them through the hyphen—a hallway connecting the older wing to the newer wing.

En route, Andrew stopped at a corner to kiss Ashley's bump. Then, to make it worse, Kat took Alex's hand, and their lips met, too. She had to pretend to look at the framed sketches hanging on both sides of her until the PDAs died down.

The ballroom was the next stop. Huge and empty, with hardwood floors scrubbed to gleaming perfection, it was pretty much what one would imagine a ballroom to be.

"This is where most of the entertaining of guests take place." Stroking the black exterior of the Steinway grand piano standing diagonally opposite the entrance, Alex scanned the room. "Anyone musically talented here?"

"I can't even whistle." Kat ticked her heels on the glass-smooth floor.

"The last time my fingers touched piano keys was when I was ten." Nevertheless, Ashley at least tried to play a scale, which echoed richly.

From there, they exited the building so they could walk around the lawns. Circling the perimeter of the lawn, Bella oohed and aahed at the magnolia trees in bloom.

"Aren't they beautiful?" Kat extended her arms over her head. "Ah, I love this place. Every time I come here, I don't want to leave."

"Then why don't you move in here?" Ashley looked over her shoulder to Alex, who was trailing behind them with Andrew.

Kat rubbed the heel of her foot, which was getting red. "I can't. Only the mayor's family is allowed to live here."

"But you're—"

"I'm his girlfriend." Her brows drew down. "And it's okay. I like where I live."

They ended the tour back at the parlor where they were served coffee and snacks, and Alex took his leave. "I hope you can excuse me now. Former first lady Rosalynn Carter just touched down at JFK, and I need to meet her at Bryant Park."

"No worries. Thanks for the tour." Andrew drank some coffee.

"My pleasure." Alex passed around half-hugs to everyone before darting out of the parlor.

"That was a productive morning." Ashley munched a cookie and licked the crumbs off her lips. Then, she suddenly dropped the cookie, bending forward instinctively. Her eyes widened.

"The cookie's that bad?" Kat smiled.

Slanting her eyes to her bump, Ashley cased her belly with her hands. "Oh my goodness—she kicked."

"What? Let me feel it." Sitting right next to her, all Bella had to do was stretch her arm. "Wow. I can feel it. Something's moving."

"She's moved plenty of times before," Ashley said. "But every time it happens, I feel like it's something special."

"I can't wait to see her," Bella clasped her palms eagerly. "I'm sure she'll be the cutest baby since she has such good-looking parents."

"We'll love her even if she isn't cute," Andrew said, exchanging a visual yes with Ashley. "And hopefully we'll have her name sorted out by then."

"If not, you can always let me name her," Bella volunteered.

Andrew shrank back into his chair. "What would you name her?"

"Penelope."

It was the first name that had come to her mind, and she'd uttered it.

"That's a cute name. Penelope Smith." Face brightening, she jerked her head to Andrew.

Andrew nodded. "I agree."

"So Penelope it is."

CHAPTER ELEVEN

Jamie needed sex. His sex drive was raging since he'd returned from Gage's condo to the point that even a hand job hadn't brought him any relief. He needed the wet, hot heat of a woman's body to sate him.

His emotions were even more turbulent than his hormones, though.

The kiss had changed too much between Bella and him, set a horrible monster loose inside him and it wouldn't be satisfied until it etched new scars into his heart. His only option was a rebound hookup to erase Bella from his consciousness altogether. His feelings for Bella had, at that moment at the condo, tipped over into the territory of 'uncontrollable'. He'd wanted to do more than kiss her. He'd wanted to hold her and cling to her and take away all the sorrow that cast a shadow on her face. He hadn't felt so vulnerable in ages, not since he'd cut his mother off. The fact that a simple kiss could do that to him, could completely upend the order of his head and heart, was scary.

He couldn't lose control. He couldn't let Bella control him. He couldn't make that mistake again. If she was down for a one-night stand or even a string of one-night stands, he'd take her up on it, but his emotions were no longer something he freely shared with another person. That was a risk he couldn't take.

He shook off thoughts of Bella. He still had the number of the woman he'd slept with two weeks ago. The redhead from Tinder. She'd been great in bed and he wouldn't mind a repeat performance. She'd been pretty open to the possibility, even giving him her number. He hadn't managed to save it under her name to contacts yet, just as he hadn't managed to save the numbers of many of his production staff. He was terribly disorganized at organizing his phone. This resulted in him frequently calling Grant for hookups. Grant was cool, so he just laughed it off. And that gave Jamie even less of an incentive to store the numbers in his phone correctly.

It was late at night, but he crossed his fingers that the redhead would be awake. Booty calls weren't usually his thing, but this was an emergency. He whipped his ass down to the Duane Reade to buy condoms, but then, while he was browsing the aisle, he had a brilliant idea. He snapped a picture of all the condoms and pressed send to a number he'd registered approximately two weeks ago. He was certain this was the redhead's number. He remembered it ending with 08.

Jamie: At the store right now. Can't figure out which one to get, there are so many.

His phone vibrated with her reply.

08: Huh? Why r u asking me this?

Jamie: It's for you.

The next message came quickly.

08: I didn't ask you to buy me condoms.

Jamie: I'm in a generous mood today.

Jamie: What about the strawberry flavor? Would you like to suck that off my cock?

08: You're out of your mind.

Jamie: Come on baby, don't you remember me? We met on Tinder two weeks ago. We had mind-blowing sex in the afternoon. You said it yourself that you wouldn't mind a repeat.

08: I did not say any such thing.

Jamie: Oh, really? You begged me to tie you to the bed. Begged me to give it to your hard. Thrice. Jogging your memory yet?

08: Stop it. I don't need the details.

Jamie: Well, are you free now?

08: I am. But unless you explain what's going on, I'm definitely not letting you set one toe inside my house.

Jamie: You need to ask? I want to fuck you. Let's do it with handcuffs this time. You wanted to do that last time, didn't you? I'll eat you out as much as you want. So just say yes.

08: Okay, this is getting R-rated.

Jamie: Text me a pic of your hair. I haven't been able to forget about it.

08: Your requests keep getting more and more ridiculous.

Jamie: Come on, baby. I know you want to do it with me. You handed me your number yourself.

08: And I'm totally regretting that right now.

Jamie: Throw me a bone here, darling. I promise I'll be good to you tonight. I'll fulfill your every fantasy. Even the dangerous ones.

From 08'S belligerent tone, Jamie wasn't expecting a response, but he got a pic of the back of a woman's head. Her dark burgundy hair was the focus of the photo, so long it hid even her shoulders. Something about it made his stomach turn.

Jamie: Did you color your hair?

08: No, my hair was always this color.

Jamie: But it was red when we met.

Jamie: Fuck. You're not the redhead I fucked two Tuesdays ago, are you? Who are you?

08: I'll give you a hint. I'm part of your Netflix drama.

Jamie: Shit. You're Cathy, aren't u? I'm sorry, delete what I said. I know u love your husband. I would never think of doing anything inappropriate with u, ma'am.

08: Okay, that was hilarious.

Jamie: Ma'am, I may be a horribly disorganized dipshit but I have never, ever entertained sexual thoughts of you. Not saying you aren't sexy because you're totally hot for fifty. But you know what I mean.

08: Okay, stop digging your grave, Jamie. I'm Bella.

A terrible pain echoed through Jamie's head. This could not be. This was even worse than offending Catherine. He could not have possibly...out of all the people he could have sent a misplaced sext to... not her...

He typed the next string of letters with trepidation enveloping him like a blanket.

Jamie: Which Bella?

o8: The one you kissed this morning. I'm curious; how many Bellas do you know?

Jamie: Just wanted to make sure.

o8: Good night. And Jamie, you had better have an explanation ready for this when I see you tomorrow.

Jamie dropped his phone with a string of expletives. Was he never going to stop making a fool of himself when it came to Bella Hopkins? How had he managed to stir up the very woman he had been trying to forget? As he looked over their text messages, he realized he could no longer contemplate fucking the nameless redhead.

Because there was only one woman he wanted to fuck right now. The very woman with who he'd just shared the most embarrassing text exchange of his life.

Something acidic and repulsive spiraled in Bella's stomach. It wasn't jealousy, she told herself. Jealousy burned. This was just...emptiness. Had Jamie just been soliciting a woman for sex? Right after he'd kissed her this morning. What did she expect?

She didn't know which was worse—the fact that she wanted to actually be the redhead Jamie was planning to fuck or that she was jealous of this nameless redhead. While wanting to be her. Was this what they called madness?

Bella dug a hole in her couch with her head. She had vowed to never let men like Jamie Star, who moved on from one woman to the next like a bee tasting flowers in a meadow, ever put her mind in such a spin. But she hadn't been able to get him out of her mind. Since she'd returned from Gracie Mansion, she'd been thinking about him and their exchange non-stop. She'd felt a certain connection with Jamie when he'd talked about his mother. They were similar.

When his text had appeared, she had been Googling his mother. There wasn't much about Melanie Star except her recent arrest for possession of cocaine. So she was *that* type. Not so much different from her own mother. Only the substance of her addiction was different. Bella was trying to figure out how growing up with someone like that would've affected Jamie's views on women. He'd called her a user. How had she used him?

But now she couldn't think anymore. Because his sexts were stuck in her mind. And she wanted nothing more than to be tied up to a bed and be fucked by Jamie.

Jamie Star was going to be the death of her someday.

CHAPTER TWELVE

Grant looked over the top of his beer glass at Eve, who was serenely munching on mozzarella sticks. He'd seen her in power suits and evening dresses, but he'd never seen her look so sexy. In her faded jeans and Raglan T-shirt, sans makeup, her face glowed.

He'd managed to get her to this restaurant by telling her that the purpose of their meeting was to get to know each other better outside work. But all he wanted was to get into her pants and get her out of his mind once and for all. Given how she hadn't really bought his spiel about wanting to strengthen their teamwork through mutual understanding, he hoped his plan would go smoother.

Stifling a yawn when the amateur band took a five-minute break before starting to play the next set, he enquired, "Is this the point where I'm supposed to ask you about your hobbies?"

Eve scoffed. "I knew you couldn't do it."

Not one to admit defeat, Grant soldiered on. "Fine. Tell me about your hobbies."

The hoops a man had to jump through to get sex.

"I run marathons." Her features grew animated. "I ran the TCS New York City Marathon last year. And I like to read, cook, and do home improvement projects."

Grant closed his hands over his ears when a loud guitar riff wailed, and a swell of hoots followed. Usually, he avoided crowded, noisy places with live bands, but he'd been afraid that a silent dinner with Eve might end with him falling asleep on the table, so he'd picked this place.

"That's great..." He absently cheered her on, as she started telling him about the yoga class she attended.

How was he going to get through another hour of such inane conversation?

The music altered pitch and tune.

Eve picked up her head in the direction of the live band. "I love that song."

"You listen to Top 40?"

He wouldn't have thought she was the type to listen to anything but slow, boring ballads and country songs.

"I have two teens at home. I listen to everything."

"Even rap?"

He pulled his knee up to cross his leg. It hit the underside of the table. The contact with wood reverberated in his bones.

"I've been to every Kanye West concert in New York," she boasted.

Now that was shocking.

"And how did you fit in with all the kids in the audience?" Grant leaned forward.

"Didn't get too many stares," Eve said, her content face cupped by her hands, her elbows resting on the table. "A young man made eyes at me and said that I was the sexiest grandma he'd ever seen. It was quite flattering."

Beating his hand on the edge of the table, Grant released a throaty laugh. "If I'd done that, you'd have given me that look you usually give...yeah, that one."

She had that pissed-off face on right now, but it didn't bother him anymore. He was getting used to it. In fact, he was beginning to find it endearing.

"Enough about me, though." She ringed her glass of fruity cocktail with her hands. "Tell me about your hobbies. You have any?"

"Women," he threw, taking a long gulp of Budweiser. That was the best he could do.

She clicked her heels below the table, a frown etching into her lips. "That's not a hobby."

"It is to me." Angling for a bigger sip this time, Grant got that nervous feeling again.

"Of course it is." She gave her attention to the band. "Although, I'm assuming that when you said women, you didn't mean talking to them. Because you clearly don't excel at it."

"I don't have to. A simple gaze works most of the time."

Eve didn't look shocked, but she flinched. "I wonder why anyone would want to date you," she muttered, under her breath, reddening.

"You tell me." He pointed a sharp gaze at her. "Why don't we already do it? I mean, what's the point of this elaborate hoax? Sipping stupid cocktails and pretending to be interested in each other's lives. I don't give a fuck about your hobbies or your kids. I just want to fuck you. Why don't we cut the chase short and get between the sheets already?"

Eve hissed, collecting her purse. "You're the one who said you wanted to understand me better."

"I thought you were too smart to believe that. Didn't you honestly not see my intentions? Did you not understand?"

"Oh, I understand you well, Grant. You're a man who cannot take a 'no' from a woman. It hurts your ego, doesn't it? You wanted to take things further on the day I kissed you, and I said no and you just can't let it go."

"Damned right I can't let it go." His sanity was hanging in the balance here. He couldn't reconcile what he was becoming when he was around her. A desperate man. A confused man.

"Fine. If you're not interested in doing the team-building exercise, let's just go home."

Grant popped to his feet and lent her his arm. "I'm guessing it's my house we're heading to."

He flashed his teeth in a charming smile.

"You're incorrigible!" She threw her hands in exasperation and trotted away.

He waited. If she felt even half the attraction he felt towards her, she wouldn't be able to walk away. Not tonight. Predictably, she was back at the table a minute later. Nobody escaped Grant Star. Sometimes his sex appeal even surprised him.

"Changed your mind?" Grant coaxed, with a smug grin.

"No." Her eyes burned a hole through his skull. "I forgot to pay my share of the bill...a fiesta burger, a Cosmo, and mozzarella sticks...."

She studied the menu for the price and extracted the exact change from her purse. "Thirty-five dollars."

"We never agreed to split the bill." Knowing her, he didn't expect his words to make any difference.

She pulled up the neck of her top. "I never agreed to let you pay, either."

"It wouldn't hurt you to be gracious sometimes."

"There's nothing gracious about letting a man pay for me." Crossing him, she sat back down and waited for the server to bring them the check. Probably trying to make sure that he didn't pay for everything himself.

"I'll consider this a date." He tipped the waiter who cleared away the table. Honestly, he wondered sometimes whether sex with Eve was going to be worth all the time and effort he was investing into it. It had better be. "Which means we have only two more to go until the three date rule goes out of effect."

Aghast, she skated her palm over the smooth edge of the table.

"I don't have a three-date rule. I have an after-marriage rule." The words were firm.

Grant forgot to swallow. She didn't really mean that, did she?

"Come on, you wouldn't have a rule like that. I thought you believed in feminism and equality. Sex after marriage is..." He looked for a word that would hit her in the right spot. "...patriarchal. Outdated. Anti-feminist."

He tried to come up with more big-sounding words as panic hit him. It felt like something was slipping away from him. Something he didn't want to let go of.

"It's what I want." Eve held determination in her tone. "But to be clear, I don't want to marry you or anything. I just meant...we're not going to do it...well, it doesn't matter now. I think this is going to be the last time we meet. I hope for your sake you don't drag this into our work."

Zipping her Louis Vuitton tote hastily, she moved one foot away from the table when her phone went off, and its ringtone cut through the noise of rock music.

Glancing at the caller ID, she pressed her cellphone to her ear and murmured a concerned "Hello."

The chatter coming through was faint but hurried.

"Are you okay? You're not hurt anywhere?" Eve grasped her phone tight.

The crow's feet around her eyes intensified. Grant squashed the crazy urge to touch those lines on her face, feel their texture, watch her eyes widen when she reacted to his touch.

Time to cut your losses and move on, pal.

Because why in fucking hell was he wasting his time with a woman who never planned to sleep with him?

"Carla slipped on the stairs at home. She can't move. She says she probably fractured something." Dropping the call, Eve faced him, anxiety splayed across her features. "I need to go."

"Want me to come with you?" It was a polite question, perfunctory.

"Will you?"

He read the hidden plea in her eyes. She was scared. Her fear resonated with him. He'd almost lost his heartbeat when Jamie had had a clavicle fracture in high school. If she was going through anything like that, she'd need some emotional support.

"Since I'm not getting laid, I might as well be of service."

Her smile was withdrawn. "Thank you."

In the end, his presence had turned out to be useful. Carla had hurt her lower back so badly, she'd been unable to stand straight, so he'd had to help her to the ambulance. And now, against all reason, he found himself at the hospital where Carla was, cradling a bouquet of flowers and a box of Godiva chocolates.

Why did he care about this ugly, awkward girl again? There were thousands of employees at Star Studios whose children injured themselves. Yet, he didn't visit any of them in the hospital. Ignoring his racing thoughts, Grant knocked on the door to Carla's room, waited for a sound, then let himself in.

"Oh, it's you." Carla jerked her head up from the bed.

Scanning the room, he failed to spot Eve.

"Your mom—"

"She's talking to the nurse." Amber eyes identical to Eve's regarded the bouquet in his hand with interest. "Is that for me?"

Unenthusiastically, Grant brought himself over to her side. "Here. Get well soon."

"At least sound like you mean it." She sniffed the roses. "You used to be an actor."

"That was two decades ago." Grant took the flowers from her and set them on her bedside.

She crawled closer to the edge of the bed and tried to flip onto her other side. "Can I ask you something? Will you promise not to tell my mom?"

Grant whistled. "Sorry, kid. I don't know any abortion clinics or coke dealers."

Carla hurled the same scoffing eye roll that Eve hurled at him whenever he stepped on her toes. Like mother, like daughter.

"I read online that you've helped a lot of actresses land good roles." She drew a circle on the sheets. "Will you do me a favor?"

"No."

His icy expression didn't diminish her enthusiasm. "Actually, I want to kinda...become an actress...."

"No." Grant could already sense where this was heading.

She avoided eye contact but continued to talk. "I've taken a few classes...and done a few auditions...but there haven't been a lot of roles. Will you help me? Don't tell my mom. She doesn't understand. She wants me to get a college degree and waste my life slaving away in corporate America."

"Education's good for you. So is getting a job." He didn't feel those words, but it was the right thing to say. It was what Eve would want him to say.

"I don't want a job. I want to be an actress." She narrowed her eyes.

"Then keep auditioning. You're bound to find something."

"It doesn't seem to be going anywhere. If you help me…"

"No."

"Why not?"

Grant decided there was no point in trying to be nice.

Encouragement was one thing, but giving false hope was quite another. Even subtracting the natural lack of good looks, Carla didn't have the kind of face that could be cast easily. She wasn't photogenic enough to look good on screen, and her height and figure were caught somewhere between adolescence and childhood. Her face was unique in all the wrong ways. As a director, actor, and producer, he had an eye for stars. Within moments of looking at someone, he could tell if they were going to make it big or not. Ten times out of ten, he was spot on.

"It's gonna be tough for you to be an actress with a face like that. I mean, you could get supporting parts, but showbiz is a very beauty-centric industry."

"And I'm not beautiful?"

"She finally gets it." Grant cast his eyes heavenward.

"Are you allowed to tell a sick person that they look ugly?" She waved her hand when he tried to open his mouth. "Don't worry. I'm not hurt. I guess I get the weird face from my mom."

"Rubbish. Your mother's beautiful." Grant froze when he realized what he'd said. "It must be your father."

"Wow, thanks for that confidence booster." A belly laugh tumbled out of her.

At least the kid was easygoing. Worlds apart from her uptight, pain-in-the-ass mother.

Whistling low, Grant suggested, "Try YouTube. Lots of awkward kids become YouTube stars. You get more creative control, and the money's potentially better than what many actors make."

Her eyes sparkled with interest. "I've been thinking of that. But isn't it impossible to get noticed on YouTube these days? It's become so crowded. Everybody's starting their channel."

"Everything's competitive. You have to work hard if you want to get somewhere." The edge of her bed frame cut into his hands.

When she coughed, his natural reflex had him handing her a glass of water. The sudden wave of niceness surprised him. He didn't often do such things. His paternal instinct had gone into deep freeze the day Jamie had graduated high school.

"But I don't know if YouTube will be around ten years from now." She handed him back her empty glass since she couldn't reach over to the bedside table.

"As long as there are kids with more free time than brain cells in the world, YouTube isn't going anywhere."

Giggling, Carla halted abruptly when her gaze reached behind him. "You're funny. And my mom's here."

"Grant." Wariness colored Eve's tone as she entered the room and eased the door shut.

In one week, she'd acquired forty more fine lines on her face. He really needed to add in Botox with her bonus this year. And if she raised hell, let her.

Visually checking that her daughter was okay, she muttered, "What was he telling you?"

Eve didn't trust him around her daughter, and it was obvious. Taking a step back, Grant tried to align himself close to the walls.

"We were talking about YouTube," Carla said. "It's that website where you can watch videos."

"I know what YouTube is," Eve snapped.

Carla rolled her body away from Eve and, showing a very different side of her, sulked.

"I'm grateful that you granted me vacation on such short notice." Facing him, Eve clung to the box of chocolates way too tightly. "The doctors are going to keep Carla in the hospital for another day to make sure everything's okay. I should be back to work tomorrow."

"Take your time." He played the good boss, although he felt anxious at the thought of her prolonged absence. "This must be hard on you."

Eve chewed her fingertip. "It is."

Grant didn't delude himself. There was no way he could understand her situation. He might've been a single dad, but he'd had an army of nannies and maids to pick up his slack. She only had herself.

A knock resounded, and the door slid open again. This time it was a man.

"Dad." Carla's response was lukewarm.

Eve's was frigid. "You should've called ahead. I had no idea you were planning to drop by."

"I'm allowed to see my daughter whenever I want to." Prickly, her ex-husband barreled towards Carla. "Are you okay, lemon?"

Carla scrunched her nose at the nickname. "Don't call me that. You're embarrassing me in front of people."

"There's only your mom and...."

A big question mark dawned on his face when his eyes rested on Grant.

"I'm her boss." Grant identified himself.

Turning back, her ex cocked his head sharply at Eve, who tensed.

Crossing her arms in front of her stomach, she said, "I'll wait outside."

She left the room, and Grant assumed he was expected to follow, so he went with her.

He didn't know a lot, but he knew that her split with her husband hadn't been cordial. Immediately after the divorce, she'd switched from the company she was working at to Star Studios.

They settled into metal-backed chairs in the waiting area outside. There were a few other people— some asleep, others checking messages on their smartphones.

Silence blanketed them quickly since Eve wasn't in the mood to talk. Sifting through emails on her iPhone, she forgot about him. He should've done the same, but he didn't want to. He wanted to watch her. Catalog every detail of her fascinating face.

Her irises shifted around swiftly, reading.

Placing a hand on the back of the chair, Grant turned sideways and asked, "It's an intrusive question, but I'm curious. Why did you divorce him?"

Eve didn't lift her eyes from the iPhone screen. "Irreconcilable differences."

"That doesn't tell me anything."

"It's not supposed to."

"So you don't wanna talk about it?" Grant protracted his legs.

With a flourish, she buried the iPhone between her thighs. Her golden eyes bored menacingly into his. "No."

"Don't get so defensive. I wasn't forcing you to answer."

"Thanks for helping me with Carla on Friday. I didn't think you had it in you to be nice." Familiar contempt crackled in her voice.

"So will you let me take off your clothes now?"

Her sigh was deep and disturbed. "I don't have the energy to deal with your stupidity, Grant."

"It'll be good."

"Thank you for the offer, but no."

"Fine, then how does a relaxing weekend in Montana sound? I have a lodge up there. Been meaning to go there for a while now."

"I have a daughter in high school. I can't just leave her and go on a vacation." She pulled a face.

"Carla can come, too."

He was making all these ridiculous offers now. And for what? Why exactly did he want to take this surly, old woman to his lodge in Montana, let alone her annoying daughter?

"It won't work out, no matter how hard you try." Pessimism rung in her voice. "And why are you trying, anyway? Didn't I tell you clearly that I'm not having sex with you?"

He didn't know why he was trying. Lord knew that if he wanted a willing body to go to Montana with him, he could get one anytime. But no, he didn't want just anyone. He wanted *her*.

He was unhealthily obsessed with her. The three days that she'd been away from work had made him restless. Strangely, he enjoyed her sarcasm. Enjoyed the back and forth repartee they always shared.

"You need a break." Taking her cold hands, Grant warmed them up. "We'll be in separate rooms."

Shocked by his request, Eve forgot to free her hand. "If you think you can change my mind once we're in Montana, better think again."

"Don't change your mind, then," he challenged while battling the uneasy feeling of the ground shifting from under his feet.

He'd never had serious romantic relations with a woman outside the bedroom since his divorce. Had sworn not to.

"Give me some time to consider it. I'm not in the right mind to make decisions right now..." Touching her knees, she screwed her eye shut.

"Tell me what you decide tomorrow." Without a deadline, she might brush this under the rug.

Eve clamped her lips into a hard line when her ex-husband, exiting Carla's room, threw her a malevolent stare from across the waiting area. "You should go now."

"Remember, separate rooms. You have nothing to lose," he said, as she parted from his side.

In life, some actions had no explanation at all.

CHAPTER THIRTEEN

Monday morning on set was awkward, to say the least. Jamie tried to derive comfort from the fact that there was only one more episode to go, and then he and Bella would go their separate ways.

"You should totally come to the wrap-up party. It's at Lim's, a club uptown. That place's a hidden gem. It's not easy to gain access, so don't miss out." This was Cathy, sharing sage advice with Bella. They were rehearsing their lines together, even though Cathy had three times as many dialogues as Bella.

Jamie wanted to tell the veteran actress to shut up. He didn't want to see Bella at the club. The less he saw her from now on, the better it'd be for his mental peace. Those texts from last night were burning a hole in his pocket. He should've deleted them, but clearly, he loved torturing himself with reminders of her way too much. Maybe he should let her tie him up and flog him. He was clearly the masochist in this relationship.

"It was a mistake. I'm sorry. Here, I wrote a detailed explanation." He handed her the three-page document he'd spent all night typing up because he was certain he'd melt with embarrassment the moment he was in her presence again.

Bella scanned it quickly. "So it wasn't a prank?"

"Of course not. I'm not a jerk, despite what you think. It was an honest mistake."

"You seem to make a lot of mistakes when it comes to me," she said.

Jamie felt heat circle his neck, creep up to his cheeks, and fuck with his head again. She'd got him with that one.

"I'll try to be careful in the future."

When he said that, he couldn't possibly have known that he was going to break his promise a week later.

Club music tickled Jamie's ears. The bass, deep and groovy throbbed in his body, intensifying the throbbing of his heart.

"I didn't expect her to come," Daniel, the accountant, remarked, his curious gaze pinned on Bella, who was slamming back shots with Catherine, her hair tumbling down her shoulders wildly. "But Cathy somehow convinced her. They've grown close."

The original plan had been for the club night to be after the sixth episode, but things had gotten so busy that it had been delayed. Now that they were officially finished filming *Troubled Domesticity*, and all that remained was editing, they'd all decided to go to The Revolver, a new nightclub that had opened on 91st street.

On the floor, Rosie was grinding herself against Liam Hemsworth. At least she'd found someone else to bother, so he was free.

Jamie tipped whiskey sour into his mouth, but it was no match for the heat circulating around his body. He hadn't been able to stop thinking about Bella since their kiss. Then there had been that screwed-up sexting with her on the phone, and he'd been imagining Bella's body all the way through. Her large breasts were displayed prominently by the low cut of her bandage dress. She must be a 36D, at least.

Oh, hell. Jamie pulled at his hair. Now he was speculating on her cup size. Could this possibly get worse? He'd shoot himself before he succumbed to her. He should've feigned a fever and stayed home instead of voluntarily putting himself in the path of a disaster.

With a woman like her, there could be no one-night stand. There could be no short-term fling. No goodbye. She haunted his mind all the damn time. And when they'd met on Tinder, she'd said that she was looking for long-term.

But with the aid of testosterone, even bombs looked like good ideas.

"Any particular reason you've been staring at her for the past half hour?" There was a clear accusation in the way Daniel said that.

"She just happens to be in my line of vision," Jamie said. "And even you've gotta admit that she looks stunning tonight."

More than stunning, actually. She looked like an angel descended to earth.

Daniel played with the glass between his fingers. "She does."

Jamie wondered whether he should go over and talk to her. He'd been ignoring her all night. In fact, he'd been ignoring her since the kiss. His own feelings were bubbling under the surface, threatening to burst like a volcano. He should try to remain sober because otherwise, this night was going to end in a regrettable mistake. "I hope she'll return for season two."

"If there's a season two." Daniel's eyes acquired a dark look.

"There will be."

There had to be. He'd taken a huge chance on this show, foregoing a year of work in Hollywood so he could concentrate on Netflix. It had to pay off.

"The show business is fickle." Daniel rested his elbow on the table.

While Jamie knew where that cynicism was coming from—Daniel had written a show that had been canceled before—he didn't share it. He'd never tasted failure before—even *Love Me Like You Do* had made back most of its production costs—so he believed his luck was invincible.

"Not as fickle as Hollywood." He touched the rim of his glass to Daniel's. "Cheers. I hope *Troubled Domesticity* becomes an enduring cultural icon like *Friends*."

Daniel snickered, swinging his glass to his mouth. "Aren't you ambitious."

"We weren't born to dream small dreams," he imitated Grant Star.

"So stop dreaming about her and act." Daniel gave him a shove in Bella's direction. "She's not that out of your league."

As if on cue, Bella tipped her head up and blinked, like she knew they were talking about her.

"Come on. I don't want to destroy my relationship with an actress. Did you forget we need her back for season two?"

Still, Jamie bounded to his feet.

It was worth a chance, at least. Not a relationship, but just talking to her. He could do with some of her humor in his life tonight. And since they wouldn't be seeing each other until next year, he should thank her. After all, she'd done a pretty good job for someone who'd never taken an acting class in her life.

Before he could make a move though, someone else did. Jamie couldn't see anything more than the shadow of a brown beard and a black leather jacket, but the man was tall. Cathy had drifted over to someone else by now and when the man opened his mouth to talk to Bella, she started looking around like a deer in headlights. The distress on her face was as clear as if she'd screamed it out through a loudspeaker. That's why it surprised Jamie when Bella let the man sweep her shoulders into his embrace, let him whisk her away from the club's main floor. The pair of them fled the stifling heat and pounding music.

Jamie wondered whether he should follow them, but his feet were already moving without waiting for his mind to get its logical bearings together. When it came to her, he tended to make decisions without thinking. But this time, she might be in danger. Jamie weaved through the crowd, eager to get to her.

CHAPTER FOURTEEN

Bella attributed the fact that she hadn't slapped Bryan yet to her state of shock. She should be getting herself away from him, kicking him, shouting at him, making a scene. That was what she'd sworn to do if she ever met him again. But instead, she was letting him force her out of the bar, carry her towards some unknown destination.

His fingers bit into her wrist as the music died behind them.

"B-Bryan, what're you doing?" Tight and strained, her voice barely functioned.

Their conversation from before was a choppy memory inside her head. He hadn't said all that much, just that he wanted to talk. In private. And her legs had trembled as they always did when he was near. She'd been too scared to refuse, even though she wasn't alone this time.

That had caught her off guard. After eight long years, why was she still the same? Still so terrified of displeasing him. It was disgusting how much her mother's influence pervaded her life.

Bryan's fingers left indents on her skin when he turned into a dark corridor, still linked to her. He twisted her wrist and turned her body so she faced him. A weight dropped into Bella's stomach. This was her nightmare playing in slow motion. She shouldn't have agreed to act in the show. Then she could've avoided seeing Bryan Singer again.

"Let me go!" It felt like she was shouting, but whether anything actually came out was anybody's guess. They were zooming beyond the doors of the club now. Summer breeze spiraled around her, blowing strands of hair into her eyes. The scraping of her heels against the rough asphalt sounded like the last, dying roar of a lion.

"No." Bryan's eyes glittered darkly. "I'm never letting you go again."

An ominous statement like that should've kicked adrenaline production into high gear. But her heartbeat didn't move a blip.

"W-what do you mean?" That question found its way out of her lips.

There was no reply, however.

Her world was swallowed up by darkness as he pulled her into his car. Though Bella realized what was happening, she was too stunned to speak until the engines roared.

Then, Bryan didn't give her a chance to talk.

"What were you doing at the club looking like this?" He palmed her breasts through the spandex material of her dress. The pressure of his fingers against her body made her want to throw up.

"What were you doing in that club? You don't even live in New York." Bella ripped his hand away from her body, exerting every ounce of her strength. But that didn't do anything to return a sense of control to her. She had no idea where he was taking her. "And stop the car. This is kidnapping." She tapped Bryan's chauffer who was driving without bothering about the commotion in the backseat.

"I want you back." Bryan's hands, now away from her wrists, bracketed the sides of her face.

Their breaths mingled, spreading heat in the air, condensing into sweaty little drops that trickled down uncomfortably between her breasts.

Without another word, he tore away the fabric covering her boobs and ran his thumb over the underside of her breasts, caressing her, feeding her starved body with a human touch. She didn't deny how good it felt. He knew her, and he knew what she liked. But no matter how good it felt, it wasn't right to do this. Even if her entire body was betraying her and her hormones were leading her down a destructive path, she had enough common sense to recognize it for what it was.

"Stop. You're getting married next month. You can't…"

"I can. I'm not married yet." Angry, he tried to take her mouth in a kiss.

With great resolve, she forced her head away. "What do you think I am? Some toy you can pick up anytime? You dumped me without a word eight years ago, and now you want to kiss and makeup like nothing happened? That is not fucking happening."

"Don't do this to me now, sunshine." Those magnificent silvery-gray eyes that had been her entire world for three years met her again. Trying to seduce her again.

And failing miserably.

"If you expected me to fall into your arms after the way you cheated on me, you're way too drunk." She shifted away from his reach, covering herself up. She needed to call someone. She needed to get help. Bella patted herself down. Where was her phone? Had she left it in the club?

Bryan gave a half-hearted sigh. "I know you're angry. I messed up, okay? I'll make everything right. But tonight I need you, Bella." His finger traveled down the exposed skin of her throat, all the way to the thin crease formed by the squishing of her breasts. "I want to fuck you like we used to. I want my head to be filled with your face, my nose with the smell of your pussy when I wake up tomorrow."

Shuddering at the thought of Bryan's anything anywhere close to her pussy, Bella brought her arms up over her chest. "If you want sex, fuck Nicole. As for me, I'm not available."

She refused to give him the power to push her around any longer.

"Nicole's not you. She's too perfect, too bony. There's no art in her body, no curves. She doesn't feel the way you do. You feel like heaven, babe. You're special. You were always special. I was just too stupid to realize it."

Whatever he'd drunk at the bar was capable of producing mind-altering effects. Just a few years ago, she'd been too fat, too ordinary, too ugly for him. Now she was curvy and special, huh? Went to show what desperation could do to one standard. But she wasn't desperate like him or her mother. She had vowed to never let bastards like Bryan Singer into her life again. She had her hands full with that jerk, Jamie, already, and she did not need another case to drain her emotional energy.

"Too late to pull that shit on me now." Bella kicked Bryan in the shin and felt a small spark of satisfaction at her retaliation.

He raked his finger across her forehead. "I'm sorry, sunshine. I know I didn't handle our break-up as I should have. I was an ass. I'll apologize all you like, but let me do it my way..." Finding the curve of her butt, he stuck his fingers under her and tried to lift her up.

He couldn't.

Being big-boned had its advantages, too. Fighting away his intrusion, she slammed his hand to the back of the seat.

"For fuck's sake, Bryan. Get your act together already. You're getting married in a month." Acid sputtered in her voice.

"I don't want to get married." He gave her another one of those smoldering looks. "I don't want to marry Nicole."

"Well, then you need to tell her that. I'm not the cure to your pre-wedding jitters."

"But you're the cure for my broken heart," he said. 'Since you went away, I've been only half-alive. I know I was too foolish to understand that when I was young, but I want you now. And I'll give up everything I have to keep you this time."

Her heart skipped one beat. Only one. Then she was back to reality. This was like all the times her mother's lovers said they'd marry her. Smoke and mirrors.

Rearranging the strands of hair that he'd displaced, Bella tried to latch onto a steady rhythm with her breaths. "There are dozens of beautiful women in Beverly Hills."

His hands enclosed hers. "Nobody comes close to you. You're the sun, baby, and all they are is just space dust. Pale imitations of your brilliance."

Oh, please. What was he trying to pull there? A Wordsworth?

Bella refrained from rolling her eyes. "You don't need me."

If he couldn't stay faithful to the most beautiful and talented singer on the planet, what chance did she have?

"I do. You and I had something great. I've never been with anyone as long as I've been with you."

True fact. But that was not because they'd had something special, it was because she'd been way too tolerant of him. She wasn't proud of the weak, insecure woman she'd once been, but she wasn't that woman anymore. She wouldn't be won over by declarations of love unless they were backed up by commitment and respect.

"Stop the car. I want to get off." Bella sharpened those words so he wouldn't ignore her.

"If that's what you want." He barked out an order to his chauffeur. The wheels screeched to a halt. "But trust me, you'll regret this. You'll regret having wasted this opportunity."

"Not as much as I'd regret sleeping with you."

She clambered out of the car faster than he could blink.

"It's not over between us yet." Bryan's warning dissipated in the cloying humidity of August.

Without sparing a backward glance, she picked out the clearest route back. Traffic on the Upper West Side being what it was, Bryan hadn't gotten her far. At the entrance of the club, she spotted Jamie. His face defused some of the explosive anger in her. And triggered something else.

That sexually charged encounter with Bryan had left her with a lot of hormones circulating around her body. And Jamie, with his easy smile, chocolate hair, and tight, sexy butt was the last thing she needed when she was so hormonal.

"Where did you go?" He scanned her face, worried. "Everything okay? Who was that man? Did he do anything to you? Why is your hair so disheveled?"

Jamie was visually checking her like a cop checking a drug dealer for any signs of abnormality. Jamie Star had no right to be concerned for her after what he'd done, but she was thankful for his concern nonetheless.

"He was my ex," Bella said.

Jamie's eyes narrowed. "The one I should've sent to sleep with the fishes? You said there were people in showbiz you didn't want to see again."

"Yeah. That was him."

"What's his name? I'll do something—"

"I'm fine."

"Bella." Jamie stepped into her space, but he didn't touch her. "I know we're not on the best of terms these days, but I'm begging you to tell me if he did something to you. You shouldn't go through this alone."

"If I tell you what happened, will you tell me why you can't kiss women?" What had induced her to say that? She was an idiot, making it so obvious that she cared for him. Making it so obvious how his two rejections had stung her.

"I told you already," Jamie muttered.

"I don't accept that bullshit. Your mother? Really? I get she was horrible, but how could that have anything to do with you rejecting me?"

Jamie exhaled. He expanded the distance between them.

"Forget it," she said, fighting the desire blooming inside her. After that failed kiss, it was stupid to expect anything from him. "I think I'll head back home."

She'd eat and engage in some form of escapism to get her mind off Bryan. And Jamie's cute butt.

Jamie fell into step beside her. "I'll have my chauffeur drop you home. It's not safe for you to walk alone at this hour."

Shooting him an angry look, Bella brought her arm between them, like a shield. "Go away."

He stayed. "Something's bothering you."

"A lot of things are bothering me."

"Does any of it have to do with that guy?" A step later. "Does any of it have to do with me?"

"If I say it does?"

"I'm sorry. I know I've been a flake with you recently. I swear, there's a reason for everything I've done and...I didn't want to share this with you, but I guess I have to." They trudged on a few more minutes in companionable silence without any destination in mind, just two lost people wandering the streets of uptown Manhattan past midnight. When she thought he wouldn't say more, he started, "I had a girlfriend before, when I was younger. She was an aspiring model and I was attracted to her ambition. I was serious about her. I wanted to support her dreams so I did my best to earn money to help her out. Every time she asked for something and I agreed, she'd kiss me so passionately. A thank-you kiss. And I was addicted to that. Even when some of the stuff she asked for made me uncomfortable, or was more than I could afford, I couldn't refuse her. I was her puppet."

"She took advantage of you, then? Using intimacy as her bargaining chip." Bella could fill in the blanks from here. She'd seen those types of women, too. Not just women. She'd seen those types of men, too. Bryan was one. He wielded sex and romance like a whip, using it to beat anybody he desired into submission.

"I know this sounds pathetic, but kissing women makes me uncomfortable. I'm okay with sex, but not with kissing."

"Then why did you kiss me?"

Mild shock passed through Jamie's blue eyes. His voice dropped an octave, grew husky. "It felt right. Not like a kiss exchanged for a favor."

"But it *was* a kiss exchanged for a favor. You got me a deal on that house. Did you feel entitled to kiss me because of that? Because you think I'm like your ex-girlfriend and I'll fall at your feet because you did something for me?"

Jamie paled at her accusation, and she didn't need to hear the words to know that hadn't been the case at all. So he wasn't an unsalvageable jerk, then. He had some decency left in him. "I didn't think of it like that. But maybe you're right. Oh god, I'm so fucked up. I'm so sorry. I just don't know what to say. How can I fix it?"

Bella's gaze accidentally drifted to Jamie's lips. And her heart zoomed off. The urge to kiss him bit her. Hard. The shooting for *Troubled Domesticity* was over. They'd have no opportunity to see each other anymore. Today could be the last time she ever talked to him. This was her last chance to act on her feelings for him. She couldn't let this moment slip away.

Gathering courage, she asked, "Kiss me now."

"What?" Jamie recoiled.

"I'll give up on that house in Brooklyn. That way, if we kiss now, it'll be just a kiss. Nothing more, nothing less. I expect nothing from you after this. I'm making that clear."

Trailing his eyes down to her lips, Jamie twitched. "Why're you doing this?"

"Because I want you to know that not I'm not a user or a manipulator. You helped me out with the house, so why shouldn't I help you out with your intimacy issues?"

He paused for a moment. Turned the full force of his aquamarine gaze at her. Then murmured softly, "You can't mean that."

Crumpling his collar under her fingers, she yanked his face close to hers. "I do."

It was official. She was a nutcase. The encounter with Bryan had messed up her brain waves and now she was going to kiss and, if it all went well, sleep with Jamie Star. She waited for guilt to snap her awake, to make her abandon this game, but she wanted it too much. Wanted him too much.

Jamie stalled, although from the ticking of his pulse in his throat, she knew he couldn't hold it any more than she could. "I'll be honest; I find you incredibly sexy and always have. But I don't want to give you the wrong idea again. I'm not a forever kind of guy and can't commit to anything with you."

She shook her head. "I'm not looking for forever with you."

For her sake, she hoped she wasn't lying about that to herself.

Without another protest, he took her lips. She gasped under him. Her hands came out and enveloped his body. His lips moved like wet satin under hers. Magnificently welcoming. Headily intoxicating. Swiping his tongue against her bottom lip, Jamie swept away any crumbs of Bryan that she was still holding onto. With every contact, more of the explosive chemistry between them exploded. They panted, taking short sips of air before launching back in. Closing his teeth over her bottom lip, he tugged it and she moaned.

They were smack dab in the middle of a street, with cars and pedestrians whooshing past them, but in his arms, the world outside disappeared. All that mattered was wet, impatient tangling of their tongues.

Nudging his hand up her tummy to her breast, Jamie rubbed a nipple until it was pebbled.

Bella peeled herself away from him.

"No?" he asked, anxious.

"Yes, but not here."

CHAPTER FIFTEEN

By the time the door to his apartment clicked shut, Bella had managed to get his shirt off and he'd managed to get his belt. Her dress left her body next, trailed by her pumps. He flipped her, backing her up against the wall.

The curtains were drawn and the lights out, so it was pitch dark, except for specks of light coming from under the door. Bella hoped it would remain dark because she was not having sex with lights on. She didn't want to see the mistake she was making in bright light. It'd just make her hate herself more. All these years, all those vows, but underneath it all, she was just like her mother. A bitch in heat who fell into the arms of the first man who made her feel desired.

She tried to put her arms around Jamie, but he bound her wrists and raised her hands over her head. Letting his tongue dive into her mouth, he pressed her harder into the wall. His tongue plundered her mouth ruthlessly, milking every sensation from her. To accommodate him, she circled his waist with her legs. Heat buzzed between her thighs and streaked up.

Jamie cupped her ass and gave it a squeeze. Sliding his fingers up and down the crack of her butt, he infused her with anticipation. His lips carved a trail down her stomach as he kissed each and every fold on her stomach lovingly. She'd been afraid he would be critical like Bryan and she had seen enough of Bryan for one night. But Jamie was different.

She loved the way his lips skated under the two folds on her belly, and when he clamped his lips around the loose flesh, she almost choked on tears. He didn't treat these folds like ugly flab or extra weight. He treated it like it was a part of her.

"Ah—" Her words snuffed out when his lips met her pubic bone.

She slanted herself back, closer to the hard wall, and closed her legs, though she didn't have to try because her thighs naturally stuck together.

"Open." He tried to get her thighs to unglue.

"No. Not yet."

Attempting to get her bra off, she was stopped by him.

"Keep your hands up." The heel of his hand slid over her wrists and pinned her hands over her again.

Jamie's tongue tickled her nipples through the sheer lace of her bra before he got her hard, aroused bud with his teeth. Bella groaned. Gooseflesh pimpled the nape of her neck.

"Take me against the wall," she begged.

The unzipping of his jeans tore through the silence in the dark, empty living room. He snaked one arm over her and pulled her closer to him, while his other arm worked to get rid of his jeans. Lowering her against him, his hard arousal pressed into her hungry wetness, feeding it with delicious friction. She almost ripped his boxers because she couldn't bear not being able to touch his hard length with her hands. Closing her fingers around his shaft, Bella brought her hand down to the tip.

Jamie's cock turned harder. Strangled, animalistic breaths ricocheted off her skin. Pressure grew against her closed fist. Powerful. She felt powerful controlling him this way.

Rubbing his tip against her opening, Bella pleasured herself. The way he went breathless, Jamie must be enjoying the tease, too. Bringing his cock up to her clit, she circled her sweet spot, until she was dripping and ready to be entered.

Then, she asked him for it. "Fuck me hard."

"I was planning to."

Squatting, he held onto her and dipped to the ground to fish out a wrapper from the jeans he'd discarded. Had he been planning for this even before it had happened? If she was feeling up to it, she'd question why he'd had a condom on him. But at this particular moment, she didn't really care.

Slipping on the condom, Jamie walked his fingers over her pussy in a sensual rhythm.

"You're so wet." He spread her damp folds apart. "So hot for me."

"Yes, give it to me," she begged.

Nobody had gotten her this wet and excited since...since...Bryan.

For one second, her blurry mind confused Jamie for Bryan. But that illusion snapped when his eyes—deep, dark, and desire-laden—swept over hers. Bryan's eyes had always been cool, cynical, judgmental. Jamie's held nothing but blatant yearning. They screamed for her. Only her. Not any glamorous thing with a pair of tits, but her. When he drove two fingers into her and curled them inside her, she dug her claws into his back. Coiling through her chest, the delight was fluid.

Pulling his fingers out, he smeared the wet moisture across her nipples, then licked it off. "Mmmm. Delicious."

A flurry of shivers went down her spine. God, this was so erotic.

She tilted her pelvis up and brought her pussy closer to his touch. "Come into me."

"Hang on a sec...." His fingers darted past her...what was he doing? Her eyes followed him. He was reaching towards a switch. No, no, no...

A snap later, illumination fell over her.

Automatically, Bryan's snicker echoed inside her brain. She remembered how degraded, inadequate she'd felt when he scrunched his nose at the sight of her stomach. Clicked his tongue at her sagging breasts. Flicked his fingers disapprovingly at her thighs, telling her to stop being lazy and get on the treadmill.

Fear overcame her in a rush. She knew he wasn't here anymore, but his barbs were still stuck in her head. They were all false, all stupid, but nevertheless, they made the experience of sex with Jamie bitter. Polluted it.

"What's the matter?" Jamie was confused by her sudden panic.

"I don't—" She stopped herself right there.

No way was she letting Bryan ruin her sex life. She had to forget about him. She had confidence in her body now and Jamie's experience was inflating her ego at an exponential rate.

Jamie sucked in a breath. "You're gorgeous. It makes me regret not having made love to you with the lights on."

She wrapped her arms tighter around her breasts. "You don't have to compliment me."

But it did feel great to be complimented for her body. She wasn't usually insecure about her figure, but sex had a way of dredging up old hurts. But with this sex session with Jamie, maybe she could finally put the past behind her. Erase those bad memories and replace them with the ecstasy of tonight. Yes, she'd made a bad decision by sleeping with him, but she'd gained something out of it at least.

"Is there something you want to tell me?" Jamie asked.

"You're pretty hot yourself."

He'd never understand how much it meant to her to overcome years of insecurity and let someone see her close. This was her body. And it was perfect.

Sweat beaded on Jamie's neck. He was completely absorbed in looking at her. "Not so sure I can go slow anymore."

"Who asked you to?"

He pressed a tight kiss onto her forehead, then trailed further down to her breasts. Ecstasy folded into her in slow, lazy flicks, rapidly evolving to bursts of euphoria that throbbed and swelled when his cock thrust into her. Clenching her pussy, she wound all her eager wetness around him, forcing him to drive deeper, to her core, absorbing every shock of delight he sent her way. They were so perfect inside each other. So flawless.

She rode him until they were both enveloped by a heady, sweaty orgasm. Intense contractions poured through her body. Inhaling and exhaling alternately, she relaxed into the moment.

"I've never come so fast." She let out a satisfied sigh.

Jamie didn't answer. And when he came on her stomach a moment later, she knew why.

CHAPTER SIXTEEN

Good things never lasted long. So Jamie knew that having Bella curled under his arm, her skin resting against his was going to have to end.

"We need to talk." He cringed as he said those words.

They sounded so wrong in his voice. He'd never been the let's-talk-about-where-we-stand type. Mostly because it was clear from the start where he stood with most women.

"Right now?" Sitting on his bed with her armor of clothes back on her body, Bella hugged his pillow. Expectation and hope sat behind her baby blue eyes.

Fuck. If she felt half as romantic as she looked, she was in trouble. So was he.

"Since you're staying at my place tonight, and we just had sex, I want to make sure we're both are on the same page." Clearing his throat that had suddenly become scratchy, Jamie walked around to buy time.

"Who said I'll be sleeping over?"

He squared his gaze with hers. "I did."

She didn't argue.

"Look. I respect you, Bella. You're intelligent. You're hot. You're funny. But..." For hell's sake, did she have to give him that disappointed look right now? His throat already felt like it was stuffed with nails. Counting to five, Jamie soldiered on. "I'm never gonna marry you."

"Don't be so conceited. I didn't ask you to marry me." Clinging to her pride, she tossed her chin up.

"Not yet. But you're looking for someone who's eventually going to settle down with you. I can't be that man. Ever. I don't commit." Since she was looking almost sick, he gave her time to process it. He had no space for commitment in his life right now. "But that said, I'd very much like to keep seeing you. I think it'll be fun. We can have a good time. We're very sexually compatible."

She sucked in her nostrils sharply, making a grunting sound. Jamie hoped it wasn't tears that had blocked her nose. "I'll consider it."

"What's there to consider? Your mind wasn't blown by that orgasm just now?"

She blushed. He was relieved she'd enjoyed this just as much as him. And that she was struggling with the strong feelings that their sex had lain bare. Both of them probably had a lot to reconcile. But Jamie was done with trying to avoid Bella or the lust he felt for her. The best way to forget about a woman, as Grant said, was to fuck her out of your system.

She pushed her body further into the bed, jumpy. "When I saw Bryan again today, he treated me like a slut, like I wouldn't protest even if he put his hands all over me. Made me wonder if I used to be like that in the past if I was the kind of woman who was easy. Like my mother."

Jamie didn't know what to say. "Bella, I did not intend to disrespect you. I just am very attracted to you."

"But I'm tired of flings and fucking. I want something deep and intimate. Emotional and lasting. Real. Fun's not fun anymore. It feels pointless afterward like there wasn't a connection in the first place, nor any purpose to the relationship."

He felt her dress sliding up against his side. She threw it on. "I think I'll be going."

"Weren't you going to stay here?" Jamie tried the classic cop-out excuse.

"I can't. It'd be too awkward to do the walk of shame in the morning."

Her uncomfortable expression said it all.

"So this is the last time?"

"Yep." She bit her nail, shuttering her eyes. "You've made yourself clear, and I've made myself clear. I'm not looking for forever with you, but I'm looking for a deep connection with *someone*. Unless I end this now, my chance with that person might slip away."

Jamie dropped his hands to his sides. Even the knowledge that she was nothing like his ex-girlfriend didn't comfort him. Because even if she was the perfect woman for him and she'd never take advantage of his feelings, he'd never see her again unless he got over his heartbreak and agreed to open himself up to her emotionally. And it infuriated him because he couldn't—didn't want to—give her that.

"You're young. You want to enjoy life. You want to play around. And I don't blame you." She stretched her neck. "But having someone to love me and understand me deeply is all I've ever wanted. It's all I want."

He bowed his head. "Fine. It's your decision. What can I say?"

"Thanks for tonight. I had a great time." There was hardly any warmth in her tone when she said that.

She limped to the living room. Then without saying good night, she slammed the door behind her.

CHAPTER SEVENTEEN

The fall semester started with the promise of great things.

The *Journal of the American Philosophy Association* accepted her paper on 'The Political Theory of Possessive Individualism' for publication. Her landlord agreed to not increase rent for another year. The matchmaking agency she'd recently joined managed to hook her up on a date with a hotshot banker. Best of all, though, *Troubled Domesticity* aired to severely disappointing ratings, which meant Netflix wouldn't be renewing the show for a second season. Which in turn meant she wouldn't have any reason to see Jamie again.

All in all, life was good. Except for the moments when it wasn't—the moments when she thought of her one night of wild passion. And wanted it again. And again. And didn't understand why. She was old enough to know that physical attraction like that was hollow, meaningless. It'd leave her empty and more desperate for real love. If she went down that path, she would turn into her mother, who'd ruined her life over fleeting pleasures.

Jamie thought all she wanted was a commitment, but that wasn't true. She wanted love and security and deep intimacy with someone. She wanted someone to emotionally invest in her, unlike her mother who couldn't invest in anything but alcohol. She wasn't going to turn into her mother. She had to do better than that. She had to search for the real thing instead of drowning in empty pleasure.

After their one-night stand, she'd ghosted. Deleted Jamie's number.

Jamie didn't want long-term. It wasn't clear what he wanted except for more sex. And she definitely didn't want heartache from another confused male. As she stared at the photo of Mr. Banker Extraordinaire on her screen and her heart sagged lower than her droopy butt cheeks. Three months of not dating had been wonderful. No bikini waxing appointments to worry about. No crash dieting before a date. No Spanx. No agonizing over what to wear. No stress.

But she needed to find love as well as a new apartment since she'd given up the chance for that Brooklyn dream house in exchange for one kiss from Jamie. If she went back on her word, she wouldn't be any different from his ex-girlfriend who had kissed him in exchange for favors. And just like that, she'd ruined her shot at her dream for an instant of temporary thrill.

"Hey," a familiar voice called to her, while she was spacing out in front of her computer screen and wondering how she could get Mr. Hotshot Banker to shave off all that facial hair.

Her heart jumped out of her chest.

Jamie. Pushing the door to her office open, he materialized, along with Rosie.

Inwardly, Bella broke into a happy dance. Wait. She had no reason to be happy. Hadn't she, after thinking over things, decided that Jamie was not right for her? She wanted more than the no-strings-attached sex he was willing to offer. He may have been a nice guy in the past and been betrayed by the woman he loved, but he was just as emotionally unavailable as all of her mother's boyfriends had been. The reasons didn't matter. She wasn't going to make a fool out of herself over him.

"What're you doing here?" Bella felt awkward with her nerdy glasses on but didn't dare remove them for fear of seeming desperate.

Jamie dug his hands into the pockets of his faded, distressed jeans. "Rosie wanted to see you."

Emerging from behind Jamie's back, Rosie waved a plastic bag with

Target's logo. For a change, she was wearing jeans and a sweater, instead of her usual over-the-top outfits.

Traipsing across the small, messy office, she dropped the package in the middle of Bella's desk. "Gift for you."

"What's..." Deciding it would be quicker to see what was inside rather than asking, Bella pulled out the pink T-shirt inside the cover. It had the words *Miss Gorgeous* sewn across with sequins. The caption on her old T-shirt had been different, but Bella liked this one more. Seemed to be about the right size, too.

"It's a replacement for the one I ruined that day," Rosie offered, looking embarrassed rather than apologetic.

"Did you ask her to do this?" Bella jerked her head in Jamie's direction, pointing him an accusatory look.

She knew he felt guilty about her first bad day at the set, and he might be trying to get her in bed again with this move, but she didn't need a new T-shirt. Nor did she need an apology that wasn't sincere.

"Nope. I'm only here because Rosie pestered me to come with her." He raised his hands in a gesture.

That surprised Bella. Rosie apologizing to her on her own accord? What was happening in the world these days?

Trailing her gaze to a very queasy Rosie, she said, "Thanks. I'm touched."

Rosie scooted over to the chairs in front of her table and parked her slim, shapely rear on one of them.

"I'm sorry. I was mean that day." Rosie's shoulders flumped. "You know, I thought about it...and it doesn't matter that you got the role easily. I mean, I'm so gorgeous and talented. You could never hope to compete with me. I'll consider it God's way of compensating."

She and Jamie both sucked in their lips, trying to suppress an untimely snigger. This girl had unflappable self-confidence.

"That's generous of you." Bella accepted the gift.

"Wow, these old books are cool."

Mercurial, Rosie forgot about the apology and her attention flitted to the next shiniest thing—which happened to be Bella's bookcase, where volumes of golden bound books were stacked next to each other.

"Let's take a selfie together for my Instagram." The phone in her hand was quickly brought to the correct angle.

Puckering her mouth and making a duck face, she snapped before Bella was ready. When Bella opened her mouth to suggest that they try again, Rosie waved her concern away.

"Don't worry. I'll make you look thin."

"I'm okay looking the way I am."

Rosie squinted as if Bella had just admitted to being an alien.

"I can't have my followers thinking that I associate with..." Her irises swam all around the whites of her eyes, struggling for something non-offensive. "Unhealthy people."

Bella let it slide. She could have argued, but Rosie wouldn't change her mind. Whose mind had she changed by arguing, anyway? Bryan had treated her like something pitiful until the end, despite the million arguments they'd had about how degraded she felt when he made unkind comments about her body.

"He's hot.' Rosie's attention was drawn to a hot grad student drifting outside her room, and she pursued him immediately, leaving Bella alone with Jamie.

The heat from the radiator instantly became fifty times more stifling. X-rated images flickered before her eyes. His tongue whispering dirty words over her pussy...his cock driving into her. Heat burned her face and spread down to her stomach, between her legs. Why was she making herself miserable? Why?

"What're you gonna do now the show's over?" Bella asked, dispassionate. "Back to LA?"

"Not until next year." Jamie slid into one of the chairs meant for her students. "I sub-let my place until the end of the year, so I'm going to stay and experience the miserable New York winter."

Bella opened the window, to ward away the oppressive heat...most of it coming from her body. "You could write something in the meantime." With a loud clap, she gave herself an ultimatum.

Snap out of it, you fool. Jamie and you cannot be. "*Love Me Like You Do Part 2*. You could write a sequel."

"You really love that movie, don't you?"

"The ending was incomplete. How about giving Damien and Maddie another chance? Maybe a happier ending."

"Yeah, that'd be nice." The disinterest on his face started to change...but then it was back to apathy. "But I can't."

Clearly, he didn't mean Maddie and Damien when he said that. The way he squared his jaw at her told him he meant them.

"Too bad." Bella scribbled intelligible letters with her pen. It kept her distracted from his face.

"By the way...Kelly McKenna, who played Maddie, is in town today. She'll be at a party at Grant's...my dad's place. Wanna go?"

"Kelly McKenna? Grant Star?" Her eyes widened and sparkled, full of excitement. She'd never met Grant Star before, but she wanted to. He was a legend. And Kelly McKenna....could she squeal in fangirl excitement?

Jamie wiped the screen of his phone with his thumb pad. "I'll call you when she's there."

"Oka—" Bella sliced off her approval midway. What was she thinking? What was she doing?

She had a date with the boring investment banker tonight. She couldn't go to Grant Star's townhome. Besides, hadn't she'd decided to stay away from Jamie?

Battling the lump in her throat, Bella breathed. "I don't think I can make it. And lose my number. We have no reason to remain in contact any longer."

"Sure we do. What if you change your mind and decide that you want to sleep with me again?" He seemed way too confident for that to happen.

Bella crushed the pen in her grip. "That'll never happen."

Unless he got clearer with what he wanted, she wouldn't waste any more time on him. She needed to be hunting for good men to date.

"Okay. But can't we remain friends? We used to be friends."

"No, we were not friends. We just hung out on the sets sometimes..."

"And had sex—"

"Once," she asserted, uncomfortable that he was bringing that up now.

"But it was good. Very good."

"An irrelevant detail."

"You didn't think it was irrelevant when you were coming."

Someone must've dunked her face in hot water because she felt scalded. Why the hell did he have to remind her of that mind-blowing orgasm? This was already hard enough without having to fight her hormones.

Bella coughed. "What matters is that we have different life goals. You're leaving for LA in January. End of discussion."

Yes, she liked him. He was funny, hot, ticked off most of the boxes on her list. But sacrifices had to be made if she hoped to break her pattern of toxic relationships and find true, lasting love.

Jamie made puppy-dog eyes at her. "But can't we have fun until then? In three months, I'll be gone, and you can go back to finding true love."

Impatiently, she clicked her fingers. "Do you think any good will come out of us being friends?"

It'd be like dangling temptation in front of her eyes. She could maintain her cool if they met a few times...but she didn't know for how long. In a perverse sense, she now understood her mother's relationship with alcohol. It was like an unhealthy dependence, a yearning so deep for the thing that can destroy you. Yet all you saw was the glittery exterior, the pretty reflection made of smoke and mirrors.

Jamie leaned forward. Yep, that was definitely an eye roll from him. "I'm just asking for you to be a friend. Is that too much?"

"I have friends." She had to resist his charm. She had to resist those eyes. She had to. Otherwise, she'd spend her life chasing illusions like her mother.

Jamie climbed to his feet lethargically. He must've realized that he couldn't dent her determination. "If you change your mind about meeting Kelly, text me. Just make sure you don't wait too long."

There was a warning seething under his final words. He made one final attempt to tempt her with a seductive swipe of his eyelids, but she'd swum around in the dating pool long enough to know the difference between guppies and sharks.

"All the best with your move to LA," she finished. "I'm sure you'll find plenty of fishes on the beaches there."

A double reference, which he pulled his mouth at.

"But the species I like is native to New York." He winked, grasping her insinuation.

"There are no fish species native to NYC."

"Oh, there's one. Its name starts with B." He parked his fingers under his chin, pretending to be thinking.

Bella hammered her fist on the table. "Get out."

"Someday, you're going to regret saying that."

He was right.

Someday, she might. But that day wasn't today.

CHAPTER EIGHTEEN

Before today, the greatest achievement in Grant's life had been winning the Academy Award for best actor in 1988.

But here he was, twenty-eight years later, surveying his second major accomplishment—an aging woman in khaki shorts and a gray T-shirt. Persuading Eve to spend the Labor Day weekend with him at his lodge at Whitefish Lake was surely worthy of an Oscar. Even two.

He'd pulled out all his acting chops to cajole her into taking this weekend getaway with him. And he'd charmed lady luck, too—Carla was in France on a cultural exchange for three weeks, and Alana's fall semester had begun. So no annoying kids to disrupt the adults.

As much as he had grown to find Carla tolerable—he'd met her five times after she'd been out of the hospital—he really needed some alone time with Eve.

She already despised him and distrusted him. Then she hadn't gotten the promotion she'd been coveting. And boy, had she taken that out on him. Last week had been a cold war. He'd been afraid that she'd resign and refuse to come with him to Montana this weekend, but she had shown up. Kudos to her commitment.

Still, he'd be surprised if this weekend didn't turn out to be an unqualified disaster.

"It's hot." Eve's breaths were labored as she navigated the dusty, dirty trail they were walking on. "I didn't expect it to be so hot in September."

"It's only the beginning of September. The weather will start changing soon."

Flattening pebbles, dirt, and leaves under the soles of his shoes, Grant gazed at the blue sky. No tall buildings were cutting the sky into a jigsaw puzzle piece, the way there did in the city. Only miles and miles of nature and nothing else.

Having grown up on a ranch in Ellis county, nature spoke to his heart. It was the reason he took two trips a year to his property in Montana. He enjoyed living in the quiet. Although, since adding a spa and restaurant to his lodge and opening it to tourists, it was getting noisy here, too. It was time he bought that vacation home in Miami he'd had his eye on for a year. Rumor was, it was back on the market and selling for a steal.

"Carla wanted me to let you know that her YouTube channel has three thousand subscribers," Eve's eyebrows arched. "I still don't know what she's doing in her room behind the camera. She doesn't tell me anything. It isn't something...weird...right?"

"If you want to see what she's doing, just check out her YouTube channel. CarrieComedy."

"Comedy?" Eve's eyes widened. "I didn't know she was interested in comedy. She's always liked science..."

Inner conflict showed up as a darkening of her irises. Sticking to his oath of never dishing out parenting advice, Grant slipped his fingers between hers, holding her hand as they continued walking down the lakeside.

The corners of her lips curved up slightly. It was a small thing, but it was significant to him.

"Sally told me you asked the board to promote me." Eve looked more relaxed than she had all week. "Thanks."

"If you knew that, why were you angry at me all week?"

She looked at the grass springing under her feet. "I wasn't angry at you. I was just...angry."

Yellowing trees and the whispering of water followed them. A canoeing boat shot past them, and the two young girls rowing waved at them. He waved back at them with a hoot, which made Eve roll her eyes.

"Hey, I was just bein' friendly." Grant brought his hand back to his side. "They looked like they needed a little encouragement."

"I know, I know. You're not going to sleep with one of them later or anything." Her vexed tone bothered him.

"You're right. I'm not."

He didn't like Eve doubting him. She might have every reason to, based on his past behavior, but recently, he felt like a different man.

He no longer got any thrill or comfort from sex. If he was honest, he hadn't been enjoying sex for a long time. He'd just been doing it because he couldn't justify to himself why he wouldn't want it.

Lack of desire meant that he was growing old, weak, frail. It meant he was losing himself. After having been a sex symbol for the greater part of his life, his ego was firmly tied to his sexuality. He couldn't lose the only identity he had.

"Do you know how to get back?" Eve whipped her face around. They'd walked quite a way around the lake. "I can't see the lodge anymore."

"Honey, I know my way around this area better than I know my way around the female anatomy. You have nothing to worry about."

Eve choked in shock. "I...can't believe you made that comparison. That's...so...uh. That's so like you."

Turning up his chin, he gave her a cocky smirk. "If you want proof, I'll be happy to show you later."

Her foot beat on the ground. "I'll take your word for it."

"C'mon. Be adventurous. You won't die if you sleep with your boss." Grant clicked his tongue.

"You can't know that for sure."

"Really, woman." He wanted to hurl his frustration at her, but he gave up.

She'd have to be led into it gently because she had so much resistance. And once that resistance crumbled, he wondered what sort of woman she'd be. Not adventurous, definitely. But sensual. And very pleasant.

A sound passed into his ear. A twig snapping.

"What was that?" Eve asked, unknowingly handing him her palm. "I heard something."

"Could be a bear. There're a few around here." Grant kept her palm snuggled in his. "You'll be alright as long as you're with me."

"I'm not...scared."

She sucked at lying.

A huge overgrowth curved along the path they were treading on and pushed them closer to the edge of the lake. Since their legs were already squishing into each other, Grant took the opportunity to put his arm around her nice, round hips.

Her reproachful gaze pierced through him. "Hands off."

"It's good to stay close, in case something attacks you."

She let her guard down. Probably the mention of bears did the trick. "I guess."

Rustling leaves marched along with them. None of them dared speak.

"What was that?" Eve's voice shivered when she spoke.

Grant glanced to the right when the sound of the leaves broke, and an animal grunt took its place. A shadow lunged towards them from between the foliage. Eve's muscles tightened under him. The hair on the back of her neck stood up like a porcupine's spikes.

Her arms swiped the air, and before he could make sense of things, she was tripping over him, dragging him with her, until they tumbled into the lake with a splash.

"AAAAAAAH!" Her scream was ear-splitting.

Cold, wet water got into his clothes, his hair, his ears, his mouth, his tongue. It had a disgusting taste—mud mixed with dead fish.

Flailing, Grant popped his head over the surface of the water. Ejecting the water that had infiltrated his mouth, he swam around for Eve, looking for a trace of her blonde head on the smooth, glassy surface. He couldn't spot her.

Panicked, he scanned behind him. A manicured arm shot out amidst a bed of ripples. Paddling with his legs, he propelled himself to her. But by the time he got there, she'd gotten her head up and was floating.

"I was a girl scout," she announced, triumphantly.

Soaked to the bone, her hair was brown and damp. She was blinking vigorously trying to see through all the water that had gotten into her eyes.

"Looks like we escaped the bear." She spat out water, her gaze held to the spot where the shadow had been.

The branches of the shrubs shook.

The dark figure hopped out into the light. With its red eyes, it blinked at them and flopped its fluffy ears.

A rabbit.

Its nose sniffed the ground. Found nothing. Twitching, it hopped away to scare the next couple.

"It was a rabbit." Red climbed over Eve's cheeks. She ducked her head under the water, too humiliated to face him.

Grant couldn't resist laughing. A grown woman scared of a rabbit? Hilarious.

He continued to laugh until Eve couldn't hold her breath anymore and had to come up for air.

"It could've been a bear." Annoyed, she struck the surface of the lake and made water splash on his face. "We were just lucky."

Feeling like a completely different person, Grant ruffled her hair. "Who knew you could be cute?"

Out of the blue, she smiled too, and then they were laughing like kids, with seaweed and dirt caught in their hair. Age just faded away, leaving only two people having fun in the unlikeliest of situations.

His iconic line from *Unfinished Business* came to mind.

Two people who can laugh together have a special kind of bond.

When they finally managed to get themselves out of the lake and trail back to the lodge some two hours later, they were smelly and dripping with sludge. Grant could've sworn that the staff at the reception wouldn't have let him in if he hadn't been a world-famous superstar.

After a lengthy shower, Grant slid into a new pair of dry jeans. Facing the mirror, he spotted subtle differences in himself. There was a light in his eyes, a radiance in his skin, and his lips were still in a U. He straightened them out. He didn't want to look loony when he met Eve to embark on their afternoon sightseeing program.

They ended up leaving their rooms at the same time, and she was dolled up this time around, in a pink dress.

"That's some dress you're wearing," he complimented, with a kiss on her forehead, lingering. She let him linger. Eve seemed to enjoy his attention.

Wrapping her arm around him, she asked, "Like it?"

"Not as much as the ass it's hugging." His appreciative gaze rolled over the curve of her butt. If he was delusional, he'd believe she was flirting.

"I should've known you'd say something like that." Her hand perched on the curve of his neck. "You look good, too."

"As always," Grant added, with a touch of pride. Receiving compliments on his appearance was nothing new for him. He got them all the time.

But this was the first time Eve had given him one.

"You weren't looking very handsome with pondweed in your hair a few minutes ago."

She had to bring that up, didn't she?

A waiter bringing someone a late room service lunch passed Eve, the wheels of his cart creaking behind them.

"We're going to the Glacier National Park next," Grant informed.

Without any more bodily contact, they glided across the corridor.

"Tell me there are no bears there," she pleaded, with a note of humor. Her blush-dusted cheeks stretched against her high cheekbones, shimmering.

"We're taking a helicopter tour, so you don't have to worry about bears."

She breathed a comic sigh of relief. "Thank goodness."

The day only got shorter and sweeter after that.

The helicopter tour was exciting. Floating over the glaciers, the lakes, forests, they covered the whole expanse of the park in an hour. Sitting in the small space for so long cramped his legs, so Grant forced her to get a deep tissue massage with him at the spa, which left them both relaxed and hungry. So, deciding on an early dinner, they went to the boat club restaurant at the lodge.

Owing to the early hour, there was nobody except Eve and him, so they had the place all to themselves.

"The glaciers were unbelievable. I never thought we'd see the snow up close like that," Eve remarked, tearing a piece of bread from the breadbasket.

Sunlight hadn't faded yet and hit her face at all the right angles, since she was seated right opposite a window. Objectively speaking, she had a very pretty face, one that must've been truly stunning in her twenties and thirties. Age had pressed wrinkles and spots into it, but with makeup, one could hardly spot them. He'd been condescending about her figure for years, forcing himself to hate her because dating old women would mean the end of his life, but he found that he was rather strongly attracted to her body.

They ordered food. Surprisingly, she let him pick for both of them. Grant took that as an indication that he was winning her trust.

Folding the cloth napkin over her lap, she regarded him mockingly. "You haven't mentioned sex in the last hour. Are you sure you're not sick or something?"

"My health's better than it's ever been, thanks for asking." Grant pointed the sommelier to Eve's glass to pour wine. "And I haven't forgotten about sex. My plan is to ply you with wine and then ask."

She sneezed. "I hold my alcohol well, so better come up with another idea."

Touching the stem of his glass, he moved it to hers as a gesture. "You might feel differently after a few sips."

The first bit of liquid went down her throat. "We'll see. What're we doing tomorrow?"

She wasn't closing off the possibility that there might be something later. A good sign.

"Nothing. Staying in and eating room service. If you feel up to it, we'll go to Main street and have a look. You might want to get something for the girls."

"That sounds like a plan." By now, the charcuterie board was on their table, and Eve was nibbling on blue cheese. "See, it's not that difficult."

"What's not difficult?"

"Dating. Caring about someone else's life and interests."

Grant blinked. Were they dating? Did he *care* for this impossible, uptight woman?

"It isn't," he admitted, albeit grudgingly. "So now do the honors. Tell me what's gonna convince you to sleep with me tonight."

Lines gathered at Eve's eyes. "Can I ask you something? Why are you so interested in me? I mean, by Hollywood standards, I don't look anything special."

"You're real." Not exactly the reason Grant had hoped to give, but it poured out of him. "Sometimes, a man gets tired of the illusions."

He rolled his finger over the polished silver of the fork. "Women feigning attraction, feigning love, feigning agreeability, so they can get a piece of me. Pretending to love me. Faking orgasms. Faking smiles. Faking entire personalities."

Now, he had nothing against the fake and shallow, but that stuff got old. Fucking beautiful bodies without souls might be pleasurable, but it made him feel hollow. He hadn't realized how much until he'd met Eve. Maybe that was why he liked Eve. She had something more to give. Something more than an orgasm.

Eve needed nothing from him. Wanted nothing to do with him. She didn't back down from chastising him when he needed to be chastised. She'd never fake orgasms. Or laugh at something she didn't find amusing. In a way, she was refreshing.

"Women only see Grant Star, the seventies heartthrob, not the man under the mask."

She boxed his face between her palms. "Why do you think I see the man under the celebrity?"

Smothering a yawn, he said, "Because you'd never have called me a jerk to my face if you didn't."

She managed a smile. Now that he'd nailed the reason for why he liked her so much, he could see it wasn't going to go away. They talked about the places they'd traveled for the rest of the meal. She'd been to a lot of countries and by the end of it, they decided to take a trip to

Korea together someday. Time rolled by without him noticing. Soon it was time for the evening to end. For him to go back to his room and for her to go back to hers.

He tried to prolong it, creeping at a snail's pace as they neared their rooms.

"I loved the ribs. I'm glad I left the choice up to you," Eve praised, rubbing her tired eyes. The day's exhaustion was obvious to her.

He glowed. "Since I personally supervised the menu when it was created, I know what's worth having."

Her hair was sticking to the sides of her neck. She pushed them aside. "You hired a talented chef."

"Came recommended."

His room was ahead of hers, but instead of stopping at his door and turning in for the night, he followed her.

When she turned to say goodnight, he found her hand and tugged it towards him. "No goodnight kiss?"

"How could I forget that?"

Eve met him halfway for a kiss. It tasted of wine, cheese, and forbidden desire. He licked the inner rim of her lips, but when he tried to venture deeper, the tip of his tongue hit her teeth.

"Open your mouth," he demanded, savagely.

"We just ate," came her squeak.

"I don't care."

In the heat of the moment, everything vanished. He buried his tongue into her mouth, and this time, she let him in. Her whispers and moans vibrated against his lips as their tongues became lost in a passionate dance. When the kiss came to its natural end, he knew he had to have more.

Tracing the nubs of her nipples, he trailed his fingertips up her neck and ears. "So, wanna do the deed now?"

He could've been subtle. But he wasn't a subtle man.

The colour on Eve's cheeks intensified. "Sorry, the wine didn't do its job. I'm still clearheaded."

Grant tried hard to make his impatience invisible, but his voice betrayed him. "Once won't kill you."

"At my age, a woman can't afford to be burned." Sadness shifted in her eyes, and her legs moved away from his. "I know you're charming, but I have the wisdom of experience."

And didn't she look sagacious? But when she tried to open the door, she couldn't. She turned the key again and again, but the door didn't budge.

Confused, she stumbled back. "It's not working."

"Let me try." Grant pulled it out of the keyhole. "You inserted it upside down."

Touching her head, she groaned. If she was so muddled, didn't that mean the wine had taken effect?

"Thanks." She pushed the door wide. But she didn't go in. Her eyes pinned him. With her tongue skimmed over her lips, she asked, "Grant, do you read?"

A random question at a random hour, but anything to lengthen her presence in his life. He couldn't imagine going to sleep with so much unresolved tension. "Sometimes."

"Can I ask you to read to me?" The door was now invitingly open and so were her eyes.

"Come again?"

"I forgot to pack my reading glasses." Sailing to the edge of her bed, she caught hold of a book with John Grisham's name printed in bold typeface. "I've been reading this book, and I want to find out how it ends, but I can't see the words clearly. There are only five chapters left. Can you read them to me?"

She was asking a semi-drunk and horny man to read her a bedtime story? Was she out of her mind?

Ordinarily, he wouldn't have batted an eyelid before turning her down, but his emotions that had lain cold as a stone for years were thawing out all of a sudden. It was just a simple request. Why couldn't he do it? And if he stayed long enough, she might even change her mind.

"Sure. I'll get my glasses from my room." The words didn't feel as if they'd come from him.

Even when he got back with his glasses and found her on her bed, gripping her forehead, he didn't think of doing anything inappropriate.

He only handed her Tylenol from her luggage. Then he rubbed her head, even though she didn't ask him to.

Odd.

Maybe there had always been this part of him that could be caring and loving, but he'd never had a reason to utilize it. Moreover, he'd decided to not use it, after Melanie had sapped away all his emotions with her antics.

"Chapter Thirty-Six," he enunciated, adding a dramatic flair to his voice like he was reading it from a script instead of a novel.

Eve's eyes were half-closed, but she listened. The five chapters took him an hour to finish.

At the end of it, all she mumbled was, "I should've bought the audiobook."

"Remind me never to read you anything again."

A soft laugh gurgled in her throat. "I'm sorry. I should've said thank you." Her eyelids were struggling to stay open. "Thank you for everything. I really enjoyed today. I think this is the best vacation I've had since I became a mother."

"My pleasure." He put the book down.

Seeing Eve so vulnerable, so defenseless, lying on the bed where he could easily seduce her did things to him.

She reached for the book he'd put down and held it to her chest. "You're a good man, Grant. If only you had a better grasp on feminism..."

Grant couldn't hold it in any longer.

"I can be respectful." He spat the words like they were a curse. "I can be faithful to you as long as we're together."

He could be that, couldn't he? He'd been faithful to his first wife. Mostly. She had cheated first, and then he had just done it for revenge. He could be trustworthy. He could be a good father. He could be all that. The question was, for how long? And the more important question was, why did he want to be all that for a woman who hadn't even slept with him?

"I'm sure you can." She wasn't paying much attention now, very drowsy. Grabbing his hand, she slurred, "Do you want to sleep with me?"

A swift rush hit his gut. Denying how tempted he was would be foolish. She was giving him everything he'd ever wanted. But now that it was dancing in front of him, he was afraid to take it, because he feared it would change him. Change him in a way he didn't want to change.

It was no longer plain lust that he felt when he looked at her. It was something warmer, deeper. He didn't want something like that with her.

"The wine's messing with your head." He craned his neck.

"No, it isn't. I know what I'm saying."

"What day is it?"

"Saturday. The tenth."

She'd gotten that right. Still, that didn't convince him of her readiness. That he was ready. "You have a headache."

"I feel better now." Her syllables fell out lazy and uncoordinated. "If you miss this chance, you might never get it again."

"Sleep." Grant extricated himself from her grasp and laid a kiss on her head. "Good night, baby."

Then he did the unthinkable—he turned off the lights and left her alone.

CHAPTER NINETEEN

Bella's date with Mr. Hotshot Banker crashed and burned sooner than she'd anticipated.

The guy was seriously an egomaniac. All he could talk about was himself. He yapped on about his brilliant career, his bonus last year, his Harvard MBA, and the daily grind of his job. Repeatedly, she yawned, hoping it would shut him up, but he threw in more complicated words until she was snoozing with her eyes open.

"This year's not been the strongest for the Stock Exchange." He tapped on his receding hairline.

She shook her head on autopilot. "Uh-huh."

And he was boring. Not hot, either. If she married him, she would be trapping herself with a self-absorbed bonehead whose entire vocabulary consisted of jargon and numbers.

Plus, he was over forty and divorced. Now, she had nothing against divorcees, but he'd told her that he had a heavy child support burden and his old house now belonged to his wife. In her language, that translated to *'I'm borderline broke and will remain so until my son gets through college.'*

Still, she sat through the date and heard him drone on about equity portfolios, market risk, and the like.

"Isn't the soup too salty?" she butted in politely when she couldn't take it anymore.

He tasted the soup, then carried on as if she'd never spoken. "If you were to invest in the fund, you could double your money in five years...."

At some point, around the time she forked vinegary kale into her mouth, Bella forgot whether she was here to buy stocks or to find a husband. Through it all, she cursed herself for not having agreed to meet Kelly. An evening with Jamie would never have ended up like this.

Jamie listened to her. He made her laugh. Even when he was sending her sexts that were intended for someone else. Especially when he was sending her sexts intended for someone else.

"That's great." Doing her best not to fall asleep, Bella sprinkled pepper into her soup. "Do you go out on weekends?"

"I don't have the time." He locked his arms over his chest, a gesture that her questions weren't welcome.

"I usually go out with my friends on weekends—"

"Isn't the beef overcooked?" He held up a chunk of beef that was stuck to his fork, cutting her sentence short. "This is not how it should be. My mother makes the perfect beef and broccoli stir fry. The trick is to *stir-fry* it."

"Oh."

Ugh. A mama's boy.

"Do you want to ask the manager—"

"No need to make a scene." He didn't let her finish.

Every time she interrupted, he became more impatient. By the end of the second course, she'd made up her mind to not stay for dessert. If she did, she might end up smearing cake on his face and becoming a living cliché.

But the thought of the rest of the night alone at her apartment wasn't appealing, either. Spending Friday nights by herself made her feel twice as lonely.

You could go to Grant Star's house, her inner voice suggested.

Too late for that now. She wasn't dressed in the right clothes, and she didn't own any party-appropriate clothes. Anyway, she wasn't going to go, because that'd be like telling Jamie she was willing to hook up with him just for fun, which she wasn't. Even if Mr. Financial-jargon had failed her, there were other men in the world.

By the time the check came around, her ears were bleeding, and she wanted to disappear to a place where words like 'financial' and 'return' wouldn't bother her.

Tossing him the well-worn, "I don't feel any chemistry between us," dialogue, she waved him goodbye.

Honestly, he seemed quite relieved, too. The jargon he'd smothered her with all night was ringing in her ears when she a text appeared in her inbox.

Not coming today? I'm waiting for you, you know.

Bella knew who that was from. Her thumb dragged over the number. Called Jamie. It was pure reflex. She didn't consciously tap on his name. It just happened. And then she didn't feel like hanging up. She could give him a chance.

Of late, a thought had begun to take root in her mind. What if she just had mindless sex with him for three months? What if she gave herself a hard deadline of three months and cut him off after that? Even an addiction, if it lasted only three months, couldn't ruin your life. And Jamie was a good lover, better than most she'd had. He could satisfy her desires.

You're sounding more and more like your mother. Unsettling visions of her becoming an alcoholic floated past her eyes. Kat might call her fears unjustified, but she'd grown up with her mother. She'd seen her mother chase an illusory vision of love, contented even though she never had a deep bond with anyone. No man stayed with her. No man invested in his relationship with her. And she was satisfied with the crumbs of affection they granted her between their other commitments. But Bella wasn't stupid. She had seen the hope in her mother's eyes. The hope for more. More than just being someone's convenient sex toy or current interest.

Alcohol, dreams, and heartbreak were bedfellows. The reason her mother had started drinking was because of the emptiness. She needed to fill the hours between her lovers, needed to fill the void left by a string of unhealthy and ultimately, pointless relationships. Some women were so addicted to the affection that they took any piece of it without bothering to consider what they wanted and deserved. She wanted someone to invest their emotions in her, to at least *try*.

She shook her head vehemently.

"Hey." Jamie's cocky tone rippled through her, sending every other thought flying. She was so deep in her thoughts, she didn't hear him answer. "Changed your mind?"

"Maybe. You still at the party?" she hollered because she wasn't sure he could hear her over the deafening beat behind him otherwise.

She'd taken three months off dating already. Might as well take the rest of the year off.

"Yeah. But don't come. Kelly already left." The music in the background gradually grew softer as Jamie moved away.

"That's okay. It's you I wanna meet. Can I come to your apartment right now?"

"My apartment." There was no missing the underlying question.

Defensive, Bella said, "What's the big deal? You've watched a movie at my place before."

"So we're going to watch a movie?" There was clear derision in the way he asked it. Like he didn't believe for a second that she'd want to watch a movie with him.

And he was mostly right. There were a million possibilities racing in her mind, but all of them were more physically intensive than watching a movie. After weeks and weeks of longing for more sex with him, dreaming up scenarios, fingering herself while thinking of him, she couldn't let her desperation wear down her willpower.

"Why not? We'll eat some snacks and watch a movie."

"Okay." He drew out the 'ay.' "I'll pick up something to eat on the way. Any preferences?"

"Condoms. Banana flavored."

Oh fuck.

I didn't actually say that, did I?

Wait...had she actually said that? She'd been thinking about it, but...

"Can you repeat that? I thought I heard condoms," he emptily echoed.

She couldn't see him, but she imagined the smirk on his face died then. She kept going, mostly because there was no way to backpedal out of this. She'd trapped herself.

At least my bikini wax won't go to waste.

"Yeah. I said condoms. And if they don't have banana flavored, get orange. But not chocolate."

Jamie's silky laugh ran up her ears. "I swear; this is the most interesting conversation I've had with anyone over the phone. So tell me, what are you planning to do with all these condoms?"

"Put them on your cock and suck you, what else?" Yeah, she was totally in over her head.

She'd never been so crazy with a man before. She'd never told anyone her unfiltered, weird thoughts. But with Jamie, she could just do all these strange things. Because what did it matter? At the end of three months, he'd be gone.

"Crap." He coughed. "Have you hit yourself over the head?"

"No, I've organized my thoughts. I'm willing to have a sexual relationship with you until you go to LA. But after that, promise you'll cut me off. Even if I call, don't pick up." She wouldn't get her hopes up too much.

"That's extreme."

"Those are my terms. Three months, then we disappear from each other's lives."

"Fine." He dropped a heavy exhale. "So I'm seeing you in a bit?"

"Count on it."

This time, they at least made it to the bedroom.

I'm so, so gonna regret this, she thought, sandwiched between his body and the mattress as Jamie fitted his mouth against hers.

In a matter of moments, they were ripping hot, hungry kisses from each other's lips. Throwing one thigh over his legs, she straddled him, unbuttoning his shirt and running her hands down his tight muscles.

"Bella..." he grunted her name as a buzz overtook his groin and testosterone blocked all rational thought.

Moaning, she sunk her hands lower, rubbing over the bulge in his pants until his arousal was digging into her, hard and powerful. Jamie had her stop to get his clothes off because the scrape of his cock against his briefs was way too painful. Then, she got onto her fours, lifted up her dress over her waist, dropped her panties, and stuck her ass in the air, grinding her butt against his erect penis.

Leading him downwards, she closed her thighs around him and smeared the moist heat between her legs all over his cock. "This is how damp my panties feel when you're around. You make me so wet, Jamie."

She squeezed her inner thighs around his length, and he lost his breath. "Fuck…"

Being embedded between her hot vagina and her cool flesh was heavenly. He'd never experienced something like it before.

"I'm never again sleeping with a woman who doesn't have big thighs." His husky whisper rode over her neck. "This is the best damn feeling in the world."

"Oh yeah?" she challenged, bringing her hands into the mix.

She teased circles around the tip of his cock that was already dripping with her wetness. Ecstasy hummed in his blood and with every clench of her thighs, every little swipe of her finger. The muscles around his groin tightened in anticipation of his inevitable climax.

But he didn't want to come yet. It was too soon. There was so much more to see and do.

Jerking himself away from her, he spread her dripping folds and rubbed her swollen clit. Crying, she lifted her butt up. "Lighter."

"Sorry, baby."

Switching his touch to a tease, Jamie played over her clit with gentle, playful movements.

Warm honey poured from between her legs and drenched his fingers. Bending down, he licked her sweet wetness. A ragged gasp drifted out of her.

"Take me now." It was a desperate command.

"What about the blowjob you promised?" Mocking her with a twist of his lips, he continued playing her with his fingers.

"Later," Bella said, voice quivering. Her impending climax must already be getting to her. "I'll return the favor with interest."

"I'll hold you to that promise."

He was glad to finish what he'd started. Going down on her again, Jamie kept to a steady rhythm with his tongue until she was screaming as her body spasmed with delight. And then he tasted the last drop of her and wiped his mouth.

Mission accomplished.

"Uh..." Her chest rose and fell with fast exhales as she sunk into the full beauty of her orgasm. He put his hand over hers and enjoyed the moments of stillness with her. Having some peace in the midst of sex was great.

"Okay. Now it's my turn." Tossing, Bella forced herself up from bed.

Sometimes he envied how quickly women could recover.

"Did you get what I asked you to get?"

"Right here." He had a condom ready for her.

Tearing the packet, she wiped away the pre-cum on his penis with a tissue before rolling it on. Then she knelt on the floor so the height difference was ideal and steered the aroused flesh in her hand to her mouth. Swiping her tongue over his aroused length, she lightly brushed over his balls, too, before taking all of him into her mouth. Deep.

And then she sucked it hard enough that he came.

"Jesus." Jamie's voice was cut up by heavy breaths, as strong currents shook his body.

The wet, slurping sounds she made became erotic background music as he succumbed to the heady high of orgasm and spilled—thankfully not in her throat. He wasn't sure Bella would have liked that. She freed him from her mouth. Laying back, he enjoyed his orgasm to the fullest, screwing his eyes shut and letting every muscle bathe in the glorious release.

"You're something," he said, when he was normal again, dangling his fingers between strands of her hair. "Do you think you could do that again someday?"

"I could do it again right now." She slapped her lips together.

"Could you?" With a giant grin, he slid his arm under her waist and scooped up her body. "Then do it."

"Mmmm," Bella moaned, resting her cheek against cotton sheets as the last traces of her climax evaporated from her sated body.

Jamie's low, even breaths alternated with hers.

He stroked her hair gently, murmuring, "That was something."

"I know," she whispered, crawling closer to him under the sheets. "I can't believe what we just did."

"Yeah." His eyelids rolled up, and he shook off some of his post-orgasmic inertia.

Shooting his hand to the bedside, he passed her a bottle of water, along with a box of Ferrero Rocher he must have gotten at Duane Reade with the condoms. "Listen. I know you said you hate chocolate, but I just had to get some."

Unwrapping the golden foil, she dunked one round, caloric ball into her mouth. Sugar-coated her tongue, delicious and heady, almost as heady as the orgasms she'd had.

"You could change my mind about chocolate," she said.

"Oh, I just remembered...how was your date with the banker? Did he propose to you? Have you booked a wedding planner yet? I hear they book out quickly." He poked her nose.

"Shut up," Bella sneered, slapping away his teasing grin. "I'm not that desperate."

This was not the ideal conversation to be having after an orgasm, but it was better than murmuring 'I love you' or 'This was the best orgasm of my life,' neither of which meant anything.

"Really, was he so bad that you had to call me and beg me for sex?" His chest pressed against hers.

"I did not beg you. I negotiated with you." Wriggling, she stole another delicious little Fererro Rocher. The rustling of the wrapper tearing echoed loudly. "I'm sorry. You don't mind, do you?"

Expecting him to judge her, click his tongue, make fun of her binging, she almost put the chocolate back, but instead, he handed her the box. "Not at all. It's all for you. I bought another box, too, just in case."

"I'm going to get fat if I eat all that," she chided, swallowing.

"Don't worry. You've already burned your calories during sex." He trailed his hand over her thighs. "And since I love your curves, it's in my interest to ensure you don't lose them."

She shivered when he fed her another piece. Tears almost wet her eyelashes. For crying out loud, why was she getting so emotional over him feeding her chocolates? It was a perfectly normal and legitimate thing for a man to do. Even sweet.

And that was the problem. She didn't want him to be sweet. Because they didn't have that kind of relationship. And she didn't plan on becoming clingy.

Dragging the edge of the bedsheet over her cheeks, she dried her face and succumbed to temptation again when he fed her another chocolate. But when the flavors melted on her tongue, she tasted longing rather than hazelnut.

Pushing the box towards him, she said, "Your turn now."

He put the box next to the lampshade. "Not in the mood."

To make herself feel better, Bella scooched over to his side and cuddled. "My classes end early on Thursday. Do you think we could do this again?" she whispered against his ear, nibbling his earlobe.

She had no idea where they were going or what they were doing. All she knew was she was in love with this heady feeling. And she was ready to barter some of her secure future for more of it. Everything in moderation was good, as long as one had control over it. Like the chocolate she'd just eaten.

"Ha. Giving up on your search for your commitment already?" he taunted.

"Temporarily suspending it," she replied. "I'll go back to it in the new year."

"If that's what you want."

"It's what you've made me want," Bella shot, mildly bothered that he behaved like this was a foregone conclusion.

Freeing himself from the tangle of sheets they were lying under, Jamie got to his feet. "I need to take a piss."

Jamie's body moved in the shadows and then light covered his skin. She'd never seen him naked before. While she'd felt some muscles under her skin, she could not have been prepared for the gorgeous male body that she was now witnessing. Jamie was mind-blowingly handsome. He had no six-pack, but his stomach was flat, taut and she wanted to place her hand on it and feel his heartbeat.

"If you want to go, the other bathroom's down the hall." Pointing his finger, he shut the door to the bathroom that was attached to his master bedroom.

Bella didn't have to pee, but she didn't want to be here alone where sin, in the form of more chocolates, was close at hand, so she made her way to the other bathroom. Her reflection crept up on the mirror as she locked the door behind her. He must be having someone in to clean his place because, in her experience, most men did not clean their own toilets so well.

Washing her face, she realized there was some semen stuck to her hair (all the disgusting things that could happen during sex) so she found his shampoo and rinsed that out. Then she wandered back into the bedroom.

By now, Jamie had thrown on his boxers.

"I'll be going, then." Because she was hungry, she had to stop and get that last Ferrero Rocher from the bedside table.

"No. Stay and cuddle with me." Circling her wrist, he pulled her back to the bed.

Bella raised an eyebrow. "But isn't staying and cuddling like a...relationship? We're going to keep this purely physical."

"Cuddling is physical," Jamie argued.

And since she had nothing to retort with, he won that argument.

His fingers climbed up her arm, and she dropped onto the bed. "You're not just a sexual plaything to me. You're too good for just sex. I want us to at least be friendly while we're together."

When he said that, her chest tingled. Maybe, maybe there was a possibility...

Stop. There's no possibility.

"So can I ask you to meet my friends? Is that allowed?" she blurted out. Sooner or later, she was going to have to run him by Kat and

Ashley. Sooner or later, she was going to tell them about this mistake she was making and hope they'd be able to beat some sense into her head.

Shrugging, Jamie agreed. "I'm okay with that."

"And are you okay with me fixing you dinner on Thursday? I just realized I cannot have sex on an empty stomach."

"I'd love it." Jamie licked back a wayward strand of hair that fell into her eye. "Haven't eaten anything home-cooked in forever."

"Don't get your hopes up. I'm no Martha Stewart," Bella warned. "I just want to try out my new recipes on you before I kill my friends with it."

"So I'm a lab experiment?" He drew her deeper into his chest.

"You'll have the privilege of tasting my cooking, so don't complain."

"And if it's terrible, hey, I love eating your pussy."

"Well, there's a backup option." She laughed.

Then cuddling, they fell asleep.

CHAPTER TWENTY

Bella couldn't stop herself from shooting texts to Jamie the next day. Sure, it was a very obsessive-compulsive girlfriend thing to do, but he didn't seem to mind. In fact, he was showing her a whole new side of him through this texting thing.

First, on Tuesday morning, he wrote her a puzzling one-liner.

Jamie: IWTOYWIM
Bella: Huh? What does that mean?
Jamie: Ask someone in your class. College kids know stuff like this.

Naïve as she was, she had then almost passed out in humiliation when her teaching assistant had told her what it meant (I will think of you when I masturbate.) She was probably going to be unable to look her TA in the eye for the rest of the semester.

Bella: Congratulations. Now my TA thinks I'm a nympho.
Jamie: Next time, maybe u should Google it. J
Bella: Good thing I like you or we'd be over.
Jamie: You like me? What do you like about me?
Bella: 1. Your sense of humor 2. That you give me chocolate after sex 3. That you wrote Love Me Like You Do
Jamie: Do you know what I like about you?

Bella: I don't want to know.

She was afraid he was going to say something cheesy and make her cringe.

Jamie: I'll tell you anyway. 1. Your body 2. Your brain 3. Your smile.

Bella: My brain's not no. 1?

Jamie: I'm a man. Your brain can never be no. 1.

Their texts had carried on all through the day, alternating between spicy, sweet, and mundane. Waiting for her phone to ping with his incoming text added new excitement to her life. Multiple times, she'd gotten distracted in class and stuttered when he'd written her a dirty text (which she was learning he was really good at) and embarrassed herself.

His last text for the day, though, was a very sweet,

Good night, angel.

Wednesday continued their thread of weird, inane conversations. She hadn't wanted to seem desperate, so she'd waited for 8 am before sending her first message for the day.

Bella: What r u doing?

Jamie: Arm cardio.

Bella: Oh. Didn't know u were into exercise.

Jamie: Not that kind of arm cardio.

Confused and suspecting he was playing with her, she'd Googled that. And she was right on the money.

Bella: Will you stop with the masturbation references? L

Jamie: Can't. It's way too amusing watching u fall for them every time. J

Nevertheless, she'd ended up smiling and that smile had helped her sail through a rough morning. At lunch hour, she checked her phone again.

Bella: Did you finish your arm cardio?

Jamie: Yes. I'm writing now.

Bella: What r u writing?

Jamie: An episode for a TV show.

Bella: About?

Jamie: Alligators mutating into ninjas and taking over the world.

Bella: WTF? How can you accept such a silly idea?

Jamie: It's the mark of an educated mind to be able to entertain a thought without accepting it. J

It took her scarcely a second to identify where that line had come from.

Bella: Quoting Aristotle? When did you become this smooth?

Jamie: Since I had sex with a professor last night. I swear I've gotten smarter since I slept with you.

Bella: Intelligence doesn't spread via sex. And u used a condom anyway.

Jamie: What about oral?

Bella: Oh, shut up.

Jamie: Hey, it's called giving head. Head is where your brain is, brain is where intelligence comes from. See the connection?

Bella: Where do u get these weird ideas from?

Jamie: Writer's mind.

Some of their conversations that day were downright ridiculous (and Jamie adamantly refused to admit that there wasn't a link between oral sex and intelligence) but they made her giggle like she hadn't in weeks. Jamie really had a way with words and the best part was, she got his sense of humor. And he got hers.

At the end of the day, he sent her another lovely *Good night, Angel* text.

As she sunk her head into her pillow, Bella realized she could get used to this. Used to being on cloud nine all day. Used to waiting for Jamie's texts. Used to laughing. Used to talking about totally random weird stuff. Used to sending heart emojis. Used to feeling loved.

She stopped cold at that thought.

Jamie didn't love her. He never would. In two months, he was moving back to LA, and then there would be no texts, no fun sex, no smiley emojis, nothing. After January, she'd be back to her old life. One without unhealthy addictions and empty illusions. But this relationship with Jamie was becoming less and less about sex and more about communication and sharing. He wasn't like her mother's lovers who made her bend to their schedule, who fed her a glimpse of affection at intervals they desired. Jamie respected her desires. He came over when she wanted him to. He texted her back instead of making her wait anxiously.

When was the last time she'd felt this level of emotional connection with a man?

She was treading a dangerous line here. And all she could wonder was what'd happen if she ended up falling on the wrong side.

He was waiting by the entrance of her faculty building on Thursday when she finished. Fifteen minutes early.

"You're either unemployed or your phone's broken." Bella hurriedly removed her glasses and dumped them into her purse. She'd already let him see her in her geeky avatar once, she wasn't letting it happen again. "I texted you that I'd buy groceries and be at your place by seven."

"Couldn't wait that long." Boldly, he dropped a kiss on her lips. "And it's better to buy groceries together. I'm allergic to a lot of stuff you don't know about."

She intertwined her fingers with his. "Like what?"

"Mushrooms, Brussels sprouts, kale—"

"Kale? Nobody's allergic to kale."

"I am. The last time I ate kale, I ended up firing my agent. Kale puts me in a bad mood."

She grunted. "That's not an allergy."

They argued about the legitimacy of his kale allergy all the way to the Trader Joe's on Union Square, which was predictably exploding with people and long lines on a weekday evening. Their stop there, even factoring in the time spent standing in the long line and hunting for something Jamie both liked and was not allergic to, was short.

Again, she made him carry the bags. A girl had to give her man a free workout sometimes.

"When we met on Tinder, I didn't imagine I'd end up like this," he said, as they cut across W 71st street, heading towards his place.

"How can I forget that? I'll probably be telling our grandchildren that story. How I met you and you freaked me out—" Her motormouth caught up with her brain a minute too late.

"You'll have to wait till they're eighteen to give them the full story, though. Can't leave out all the orgasms you had. That's the best part. The climax, so to speak."

"Is it just me, or are you getting cockier by the day?" Gliding over the awkwardness, she pointed to an ad with Megan Fox on it. "Look at her. She's so gorgeous."

Jamie spared a brief glance, but he didn't seem to be impressed. What man had such a lukewarm response to Megan Fox?

"I'm envious of her." Hastening her pace as the light turned green, Bella huddled closer to Jamie when the crowd of people around them attempted to cross the street at the same time.

"She probably wishes she was as smart as you. Then she wouldn't have to stand around in her underwear, wondering how she's going to remain beautiful for the rest of her life and keep getting work opportunities. She could be sitting in a warm office, eating what she wants, and sending saucy texts."

"She wouldn't trade her beauty for a boring life." Bella clamped her hands around shopping bags.

"If she's sensible, she will." He locked his arm around her and gave her some hot mouth action. In broad daylight. And she couldn't even find the willpower to scold him. "Who wouldn't want to have these delicious, sinful curves?" His hands stroked her inner thighs. "Or this sun-streaked hair, that dazzling smile, that sexy brain, and those endless blue eyes?"

Corresponding with the words, his fingers traveled to those parts of her. Goose pimples peppered her skin. Under his reverent stroking, she felt special. The kind of special that being in love was like. Except she wasn't in love.

"That's enough. You're going to give poor Megan Fox envy." Deliberately, she batted away his arm and kept some distance from him for the rest of the way.

Emotionally, though, it was difficult to keep her distance from Jamie. He just had a way of getting under her skin and into those parts of her that she never allowed anybody else to see.

Dinner wasn't an elaborate affair. With her limited cooking skill and Jamie's even more limited patience, they made a quick lo mein and scarfed it down quicker. Then, it was time to wait for the food to digest while watching TV, before they moved to the dessert—sex.

Actually, they might not get all the way there, because Aunt Flo had paid her a visit this morning. Blood-soaked tampons were not going to ever be part of her sex life with Jamie.

"Hey, I want to watch *Ultimate Power*." Angry that Jamie skipped over ABC, Bella snatched the remote from him.

"What? How are you still watching that show after the horrible conclusion last season?" Jamie tried to wrestle the remote from her control.

"I still like where it's going." A stand of hair blew into her eyes, and she lost the remote to Jamie.

Brushing away the hair from her eye, he said, "Come on. I don't want to watch murder and politics. Let's watch football."

"I can't watch men fight each other over a ball after I've just eaten."

"Bella..." Vexation crept into Jamie's tone.

The debate over what to watch raged for a few more minutes. In the end, they both lost to Masterchef, because a win, either way, would have been unfair, so it seemed only fair to settle for something both of them hated.

"It's a good thing we'll never get married. At least I won't have to fight for TV time with you for the rest of my life." Kneading her full belly, Bella fired empty breaths at the ceiling.

He raised his fingers in a figure of two. "We could buy two television sets. That'd solve the problem."

Bella's heart jumped inside her chest. Even a little hint like this from him, that he was open to a life together, was enough to get her excited and wishful.

Stop building castles in the air. He's leaving for LA next year.

The geographical distance was something she couldn't argue with. Deciding that they didn't want to watch Masterchef anymore, they settled for talking.

"Are you gonna be in New York for Christmas?" Bella asked.

"Yeah. Grant hosts a great Christmas party every year that I wouldn't miss for anything. You're invited, by the way." Jamie went to the kitchen to switch off the lights, and she saw him turn on his sound system.

"I'll be there—" All those words didn't make it out of her throat, because her voice froze midway.

That riff, that beat, that voice. Hell, it was Bryan's song that was playing.

You're my sunshine, you're all the stars in the sky.

She groped for something to turn it off, but she couldn't find anything. He'd written that song for her, which made it more personal and also more painful to hear it.

"Can you shut that? I don't want to listen to it," she shouted, as recollections of all the time he'd sung this song over her skin overtook her.

Tapping his feet and clicking his fingers, Jamie was humming along. "What's wrong with it? I happen to like this song."

"Jamie, turn it off. Please." The extra squeeze she added on the 'please' probably did the trick. He pressed a button, and Bryan was out of her world.

"Thanks." It was just a burst of air, unvoiced.

Placing his solid hand on the small of her back, Jamie regarded her with consternation. "That's an extreme reaction to a song."

When it came to Bryan, all her reactions were extreme.

Bella swallowed enough saliva to replace the lost lubrication in her throat. "Can I talk to you about something?"

"Sure." Jamie easing his hand down her back made it easier for her to talk.

"I know we've had sex only a couple of times, but...if we're going to be seeing each other in the future, even if only for sex, I have to make this clear..." As she thought of Bryan again, she knew she couldn't falter now. "You can't cheat on me. Even if we're only having a fling. It'll have to be just me and you."

Jamie fired a quick nod. "Got it. We're exclusive. I thought we were, anyway."

"And it's non-negotiable. My last boyfriend cheated on me, and I'm still recovering from it." Rolling her fingers into fists, she pressed them on her thighs.

"Did that song remind you of him?" Tender now, he planted a kiss at the top of her head.

Bella buried her head between her cupped palms. "Yeah. He wrote that song."

There, she'd admitted it.

Jamie's jaw was unhinged. "No shit. Bryan Singer was your ex-boyfriend?"

She was so angry, she bit her tongue as she hissed out the words. "For five years. Lived with him for two of those. The media didn't suspect because he was pretending to date his lyricist. But he was with me. Or at least I thought he was."

"He lied to you." That wasn't a question.

"Yeah. And I found that out through the news. It was the most embarrassing moment of my life. I was broken for years after that. I..." Overflowing emotion buried her voice. "I loved Bryan so much. I thought we were going to be together forever."

Jamie caressed the back of her head. "I want to say I'm sorry for what happened, but I'm not. Because if that hadn't happened you wouldn't be here with me, and I'm not sorry about that."

His touch reached her jaw. In his eyes, an invitation glittered. Bella didn't wait. She moved in to close the distance. Their lips fused together. Literally fused, because, for one magical minute, she didn't know which ones were hers and which were his. And she didn't care. She was at her most vulnerable, most broken, and she needed his warmth to make her feel better.

"Do you still hate when I kiss you?" Bella asked.

Jamie shook his head. "No. I think I've grown used to it. As long as you don't try to take my money or use me to advance in your career, I'll be able to get over my ex-girlfriend. Eventually."

He gave her a hint of his tongue, but then changed his mind and kept it sweet. Bella appreciated that. While she'd love to get passionate, she was still a little raw. After kissing some more, she told him more about her relationship with Bryan. She'd shared details of her and Bryan with Ashley and Kat before but sharing it with Jamie was totally different.

At around nine, Bella decided to head back home, though Jamie insisted that she stay the night. Usually, she liked being around people, but sometimes, she just needed to be alone with her thoughts.

"Goodnight, angel," he said when he finally let her go.

Hearing him say that made her feel like she never wanted to let him go. And that was the moment she realized she had fallen for him.

CHAPTER TWENTY-ONE

Dusting off his 'writing' laptop, which had lain neglected for months in his closet, Jamie slid on a pair of reading glasses. On his nose, their weight made him self-conscious. He couldn't read without glasses. Big deal. Bella couldn't, either. And she looked pretty sexy with them on.

The clock's hands marched slowly. He was waiting for it to strike 10:01.

10:01 PM was the lucky hour. Every project he'd started at 10:01AM had become a success.

After the lukewarm audience response to *Troubled Domesticity* and ABC's subsequent decision to cancel the show, Jamie needed every ounce of luck for his next endeavor. More than luck, actually, because his next project was something that had a 99.99% probability of failure.

After guzzling cans of beer and taking a drunken oath, he'd finally decided to write the sequel to *Love Me Like You Do*.

Love Me Like You Do Part 2.

For Bella.

Yeah, screw him. He was writing a whole script and staking his career on a woman he couldn't even define his relationship with. And if this movie never got produced—which it most likely wouldn't—he was going to give her the script as a birthday present. She had inspired and motivated him with her unflagging praise of his work.

December 19th. He had a deadline already.

Imagining the glee on her face when he gave her the script, he put himself in a positive frame of mind. Writing a script was a laborious endeavor at its best, and he'd need all the motivation he could get.

White sheets printed with black letters—the scene-by-scene, act-by-act outline he'd written yesterday, slept right beside his laptop on the worn-out surface of the desk. A water bottle, three Mars bars, and sound-canceling headphones sat to the right—his tools.

A little ping from the built-in speakers of his laptop pushed him into action. Digits on at the bottom of his computer screen read 10:01 am.

Time to put his foot to the pedal and the pedal to the metal.

He was doing this. Alright.

Pummeling the keyboard, Jamie threw any words that entered his mind on the page. The flow of the story was so furious, it pulled him into the deep night, begging him to finish this scene, this line. Squeezing his watery eyes, Jamie willed his cramping fingers to soldier on, all while imagining sharing his work with Bella, anticipating her reaction. Her surprise. Her joy.

As the last of the words left his fingertips, and he started making typos in every other sentence, he knew fatigue had set in. It was time to wind down. Surveying his work, he glowed at his productivity.

He'd written an entire act in a day. Not bad at all.

When he shut down his MacBook Pro, he was still bubbling with energy. He wanted to tell someone about it. Reaching for his smartphone, Bella's name was the first that came to his mind.

Over the weeks, he'd figured that she was a night owl, too. She often sent him late-night messages. He decided to try his luck.

Jamie: High as a kite right now. He wrote.

Bella: How many lines did u snort?

Jamie: None, but I finished an act of a new script.

Bella: Gr8. Do u wanna talk about it?

Jamie: Not yet. But I'll tell you soon.

Actually, he was so excited he had to restrain himself from telling her. He wouldn't ruin her birthday surprise.

Bella: Can't wait.

Jamie: What r u doing?

Bella: Vegging out on the couch.

Jamie: Doing what?

Bella: Vegging out, didn't I say?

After a second, another blue text bubble appeared on his screen.

Bella: Wish I was productive like u.

Jamie: Ur amazing already. Don't give the rest of us a complex by being productive, too.

Bella: Ur so good for my ego J.

He considered for a beat before he wrote the next thing.

Jamie: Can I take you out this Sunday?

Bella: U better.

Another message.

Bella: Uv been ignoring me all week.

Jamie: Sorry. Been busy. I'll make up for it.

Bella: Txt me the location. I'm going to bed now. Gotta work tomorrow.

As if on cue, his phone vibrated with his agent's call. The hour was late, even factoring in the coast-to-coast time difference, so it must be something important.

Jamie: Goodnight, angel.

He wrote and spent just another minute staring at the blank whiteness, waiting for a blue bubble.

Bella: Goodnight, cokehead.

That was all he needed to hear.

He got Patricia's call before it went to his answering machine. "Patricia. Haven't heard from you in so long. How're things at the agency?"

"Busy. Listen, I have great news for you. Actually, this opportunity came unexpectedly, but I thought you'd be interested. One of the screenwriters I used to represent is now the head of the cinematic arts department at USC. He just called me, saying he wants you as adjunct faculty for their screenwriting program. Would you be interested?"

He didn't have to think. "Definitely."

Before he'd left for New York, he'd asked Patricia to put out feelers at universities that had openings. As amazing as writing was, he wanted to give back to the community in some way. What better way than to nurture the new generation of talented writers? The only exciting and meaningful thing in his life—this fling with Bella—would be gone soon. Jamie wanted something to take her place. A new purpose. A new adventure. An adjunct gig would give him that.

"The salary's decent, and the dean was dropping hints on the phone that he might convert you to associate professor in a few years. Plus, since you're part-time, you'll have a lot of time to work on scripts."

"Sounds perfect." With *Troubled Domesticity* done, Jamie had no reason to stay in New York any longer. LA was better for his career. It was where he'd lived most of his professional life and most of his youth. "And I've been missing California sunshine recently."

"East coast weather getting to you?" Patricia's neighing laugh came through the line.

"Never liked the cold."

"And the forecast says it'll get worse in November. My sympathies are with you." Putting him on hold, she barked out instructions to someone. Judging from the whining tone that followed, it was probably her children. "I'll let the dean know that you're interested. You'll have to fly down sometime next month for an interview."

"No problem."

"Good. I'll see you soon, then. Bye."

Jamie rejoiced for a minute before he realized the implications of what he'd agreed to. If everything worked out, he'd leave New York forever.

He'd leave Bella forever. That thought scared him more than it should have.

He didn't want to let go of her yet. There was something between them—it was only budding, but it deserved a chance to bloom. Jamie couldn't remember the last time he'd been so happy in the company of a woman or lusted after her so badly. She was perfect.

Sexually, he was hooked on her. Emotionally, he was addicted. Physically, she was the most perfect thing he'd ever touched.

But there was a part inside him that knew he couldn't be her 'The

One.' She wanted a different sort of man. A man didn't have so many issues. A man who could trust her, let her in, opened up to her and stop seeing her as a walking shadow of his ex-girlfriend, even though they looked nothing like each other.

So how could he give up his chance for a better life in LA for her sake, when he could never be the man she wanted?

CHAPTER TWENTY-TWO

The internet broke on Wednesday.

And it wasn't Kim Kardashian's butt pics that did it this time. It was Bryan Singer's announcement that he'd decided to call off his wedding with Nicole. The superstar couple of the century was no more.

Pictures upon pictures of a tear-stricken Nicole paraded in front of Bella's eyes as she scrolled down TMZ.com, while Bryan looked like the unfeeling asshole that he was.

According to the ever-reliable internet media, Nicole was 'devastated by the split' that she 'hadn't seen coming in a million years.' One of her close friends said that she still loved Bryan and was clinging to the hope that he would come back to her.

Bella had to crack a laugh at that one. Bryan Singer never went back to a woman. Never.

He came back to you that night. He begged you to take him back.

He must've been stoned. Drugged. Or just feeling crazy. Clear-headed Bryan wouldn't have said that. It must've been a mistake because predictably, there had been no follow-through. No phone call, no email, nothing. If he wanted to, he could get a hold of her email address easily. It was on NYU's website. But the fact that he hadn't bothered to do that said a lot about his seriousness.

Reading further, she encountered something that slowed her heartbeat.

Bryan has confirmed through his blog, Facebook, and Twitter that his reason for calling off the marriage is that he is in love with another woman. He has described this woman as someone he fell in love with eight years ago and has been in love with ever since. In his own words... 'I let her go because I was a fool because I didn't know how to handle my feelings for her like a man. Recently, I ran into her again, and that's when I knew I couldn't marry Nicole. Not when I still had a chance to be with the love of my life. Nicole is a great girl, but she's not my sunshine.'

Blood sloshed around Bella's head. Sunshine. That was her nickname.

Goodness...he couldn't mean her. How could she be the reason Bryan had called off his wedding with the gorgeous Nicole? Had he really meant what he'd said to her that night at the bar?

I want you back. And I'll give up everything I have to keep you this time.

No, it was crazy. She might've been the girl he'd dated the longest, but she couldn't possibly compare to all his beautiful model girlfriends. And she'd made her distaste for him clear that night she'd run into him at the club.

The sharp ring of her phone sliced through her muddled feelings.

"Dr. Bella Hopkins," she answered, putting a lid on her frenzied thoughts.

"Hey, sunshine." A rich baritone, raspy, and entirely too familiar licked at her ear.

All her muscles hardened.

"Bryan, why are you calling me?" she croaked, unable to push spit down her throat because Bryan's voice had shocked her food pipe into closing.

"I finally broke things off with Nicole. I'm free now...no, I'm yours now. Take me back, sunshine."

Heart-melting as he sounded, she couldn't trust him. This was the guy who'd commercialized heart-melting, after all. And how dare he think he could erase everything he'd done to her with a simple I'm yours? An emotional scar such as hers wouldn't disappear with half-hearted apologies.

"I don't want you," Bella muttered through clenched teeth.

"You will, once I explain everything. Hear me out. I'm sorry for what happened that night. I was too drunk. I know I behaved like a jackass when we were together, but I never wanted to hurt you." A breath was drawn. "Give me a chance, sunshine. I'll make it better for you. I'll tell you everything you've ever wanted to know."

Closing her fingers tighter around the receiver in anticipation, she flared her nostrils. Letting him control her again flew in the face of everything she knew and had learned, but God help her because she couldn't resist the devil. Not when he whispered right into her ear.

"Talk." She didn't feel the vibration of those words in her throat.

"I know you're mad about what happened. I'm mad at myself, too. I was controlling and demeaning." He sniffed. What an actor. "But I didn't do that because I hated you. All those times I said you looked ugly in short skirts…I was just scared of other men noticing how beautiful you were. I hated imagining their eyes on you. I was terrified you'd leave me. I wanted you all to myself. I know, it was immature, but I loved you so much, I couldn't think rationally."

Loved me so much? Her inner voice screamed. How dare the asshat drag love into this? He'd never loved her, not for a teeny-tiny second. It had always been her in love. Alone.

"Ha. If you loved me so much, why did you cheat on me?"

Bryan could feed her all the BS he wanted, but let him try and explain this one.

"I'm sorry. That was a dick move." His voice was fervent, shaking. "I never wanted to do it."

"I'm curious. How do you stick your penis in someone's vagina without wanting to?" Rage burned at the pit of her stomach. Tempted to pull her hair out at the pathetic excuse, she sipped some water to calm herself down.

Bryan Singer would not get to her ever again.

"Wait—" He grew louder, afraid that she might slam the phone down—which she rightfully should have done. "That didn't come out the way I intended. The truth is, I was falling for you so hard that I wanted to give up touring to stay with you. That scared me. I didn't want you to mean so much that I'd give up my dreams for your sake. So I fucked Carina to prove to myself that you didn't have that kind of hold over me."

"What?" Disbelief groaned inside her head. Good thing he wasn't here, or she'd have clocked him in the face for that excuse.

Eight years. She'd waited eight years to hear this? That he'd cheated on her because he was scared he loved her too much?

Emotions boiled and bubbled inside her.

You bastard, do you expect me to buy this? Do you have any idea how devastated I was when you cheated on me? Do you know that my friends had to break into my house because I stopped eating, sleeping, and talking to them? Do you know I had to see a shrink for two years? Do you have any idea how many hours I spent crying every time your voice played on the radio when your picture showed up in a magazine I was reading? Every time I saw you with another woman, my heart ripped into shreds.

Those words remained in her head. Saying them would be admitting how much he'd once meant to her, and she wasn't going to give him that knowledge. So instead, she said, "I can't forgive you."

"I know I wounded you, but I also know I'm the only one who can heal you. We need each other, sunshine. Let's give us another shot."

"I don't need you. I need to stay away from you." Drying her stupid, weak little tears with the back of her hand, Bella shut her eyes and grounded herself. Breathe. Deep. Think of Jamie.

"Give me one more chance. Please. I've changed. Let's meet somewhere. I don't want to talk of our future over the phone."

"What future—"

"I want to marry you." This time, his voice held firm. Unnervingly firm. "I want you to be my wife. I want you to move to my house in LA and be with me. We'll be a happy family, sunshine. Isn't that what you always wanted? You know we have a connection. You can't break it so easily."

Chills cascaded through her body, fast and furious. Bella wished she could've said they were spooky chills. But they weren't.

Yes. It's what I always wanted. But I don't want that anymore.

"But not with you," she barked out, a little disoriented. Of course, there would never be any stability with Bryan because he'd find the next pretty thing and she'd be drying the ink on her divorce papers. He was promising her the illusion of security but real security came from being loved, being cared for. Bryan wasn't capable of such deep emotional investment in anyone, even himself. He'd be nice when he wanted to and forget about her after that.

Bryan choked. "Why not with me? You know I'm perfect for you. Don't you remember what we once had? It was good, baby. It was so good."

Yes. It had been good. Once upon a time, before the cheating had started, it had been good. Once upon a time, his lack of intellectual depth, his lack of integrity, and his deception hadn't mattered and all she'd cared for was how he'd lifted her out of her horrible home environment, how he'd given her the kind of love that her mother had never been capable of giving. Back then, it seemed like the world. But she knew better now.

"But it didn't last, Bryan." She managed to say the sensible thing.

"It'll last this time. I swear I'll make you happy this time. I've changed, sunshine. I'm man enough to love you now." Hoarse, he continued to beg, that sex-god voice of his dripping into her ears like honey. "Meet me. Just once. I'll convince you I'm serious."

Feeling her heart rattling against her ribcage, Bella screwed her eyes shut. She knew it was a bad idea, but she so badly wanted to hear his apology and then humiliate him as he had humiliated her.

Why couldn't she meet him? She wouldn't lose anything by giving him a chance to explain. Besides, Bryan sounded apologetic enough.

A flicker of exhilaration shot across her body. The promise of having him, of having anyone want to stay with her was addictive.

She'd had enough of waking up in the morning to a spiraling sense of doom. To a vague sort of emptiness in her chest, the constant churn of anxiety in her head. She was sick of living in permanent anxiety and hopelessness.

But she had Jamie now. And even if they were only together for three months, he gave her something to hold onto. She couldn't do this to him.

"Okay. Let's meet." Bella forced an airy whisper from the depths of her throat. Every syllable trembled, but she found the courage to stay the course.

"Do you mean it?" He sounded surprised.

"Yes. I'm willing to listen to your apology. Hell, I deserve an apology from you after the ridiculous act you pulled at the club that night."

They ironed out the logistics of their meeting and then his voice disappeared. Sitting in her ordinary room, she wondered if that had been a dream.

Not that what had happened had seemed dream-like at all. In her dreams, she wouldn't be meeting Bryan. That encounter in his car weeks ago had been bad enough. Maybe she needed to hear his apology and see that he meant it. Maybe once she saw that he really knew how much he'd hurt her, she'd be satisfied. Her anger would go. Her animosity would go. Her mistrust toward men would go.

And once she wasn't angry with him anymore, maybe she'd forgive Jamie, too, and stop seeing him as an extension of Bryan. Stop seeing Bryan's mistakes reflected in him.

Because underneath that playboy exterior, she was beginning to realize that Jamie was genuine. He was funny, caring, and warm. He showered her with the kind of love and affection that she'd thirsted for all her life. He had boundaries and he respected his time and hers; he wasn't unhealthy like Bryan. Despite her protestations, she was beginning to connect with him on more than a physical level.

"Shit."

Bella realized with a start that she was in love with Jamie. He'd fed her soul the very drug it'd been seeking all throughout. He'd given her attention, and respect and admiration, and understanding. He'd made her world brighter in such a subtle way that she hadn't even noticed until now how much she looked forward to their interactions. How much they gave her life.

But he would withdraw all of that soon. Because like everyone else, he thought she didn't deserve it.

CHAPTER TWENTY-THREE

Damn the elevator!

Grant bounded down the stairs of the emergency exit. The elevator in the studio building was taking longer than it should, and he couldn't be bothered to wait. Plus, he was athletic enough to manage the workout.

He was joining his friends for drinks at The Sky, a nearby bar and he didn't want to be late. They were all busy men, who had short lunch breaks. As soon as he opened the exit door, he passed Eve. They brushed each other. Rather, their clothes brushed. But the was effect was as intense as if their bodies had touched. Instantly, he felt ten times more alive. Though he was running late, he pulled her into the emergency exit.

"How's your day been so far?" he asked.

"Stressful." She waved a bunch of papers in his face.

He enclosed her face with his hands. "Let me make it better, then."

He sunk his lips into hers. They kissed slowly, passionately, with just a hint of tongue.

"Better?"

"Yes." Producing a tissue, she wiped lipstick smudges from his mouth. "But don't do that at work again. I don't want people to think less of me. I still have some professionalism left in me."

"You also have some uptightness left in you." He slapped the side of her thighs. "See you at seven."

There were five men in suits around the table they usually occupied at The Sky—his five closest acquaintances, five men he respected and trusted. Paul, his best friend, was missing, but then Paul had never fit into this crowd. He was a committed family man and these men weren't.

"Ordered you your usual," Donald, the balding CEO of a talent agency, said, gaze pointed at a bottle of whiskey.

"Thanks." Grant poured himself a glass. "What's everybody been up to?"

"The usual. Business." Vladimir dropped his head. "I heard you took your VP of Legal up to your Montana lodge."

His eyes were judgmental.

It made Grant feel like he'd done something criminal. He squirmed in his skin. "She didn't get a promotion this year. She was upset."

"So let her be upset. You're her boss, not her therapist."

"I can't let her be upset; I need to preserve the few female employees I have in upper management." He studied the glass of whiskey under his nose.

"There are rumors you have a thing for her." Ice clinked against the edge of Vladimir's glass.

"What?" Office gossip could beat tabloids any day.

"Right. It's ridiculous. I mean, you, with an old woman like her? You'd never stoop so low when you're surrounded by bombshells all day. Whoever started such a rumor had to be drunk."

All the men around the table guffawed at the joke.

Grant formulated a fake smile, discomfort creeping up to him.

With Eve, he simply didn't know where he was headed. She excited him like the first taste of alcohol excited a fifteen-year-old. They had great chemistry. They had a great conversation. They had great everything. But she wasn't good for him. And she wasn't what he should want. Desiring her threatened his comfort, his ego, his identity, his values. She was changing him, and he didn't want to be changed.

Fifty-two wasn't the age a man decided to toss aside the life he'd been living. It wasn't the age when he suddenly started believing in love and altering his standards. To be with her, he'd have to change. He'd have to transform.

He was too old for change. He'd lived his debauched existence for too long. Even if it was becoming boring and repetitive, it was all he knew.

"We're heading to Lace tonight. You coming?" Donald slumped in his chair.

Lace was a gentleman's club which Grant often frequented with his friends on the nights he was bored.

"I have other plans." Guilt chewed him. He was picking dinner with an old woman over strippers? If his friends knew, they'd laugh at him.

"With the blonde intern?" Vladimir mentioned it as if he knew it for a fact.

Actually, his plans were with Eve, but Grant nodded along.

"Doesn't every man wish he could be you? Humping hot twentysomethings day and night," Vladimir added with an envious chuckle.

Grant couldn't explain why he flinched at that. In the past, words such as those had made him feel powerful, virile, desirable. They'd been medals he'd striven to collect, the pat on his back he'd sought. But now they sounded embarrassing and misguided.

"Long live Eddie Mans." Robin, the new President of Legal and Business Affairs, joined in. Donald pulled him a seat.

Grant felt slightly nostalgic at the reference. Eddie Mans, the unapologetic womanizer he'd played in his most famous movie. He was still playing that role off-screen.

"How's it being President?" Grant asked, shaking Robin's hand with gusto.

"Busy. Frustrating. I have the most bullheaded woman working under me."

"Eve Rosenberg?" Vladimir guessed.

"Who else?" Robin turned his eyes upward. "That woman has an opinion on everything. Nothing I do or say is right. The department's procedures are outdated; the company culture is too masculine, asking her to make coffee is discrimination...someone needs to tell her that the workplace is not the place to release all her anger."

Grant felt everybody's stares. They expected him to be that man—the one who told her to stop doing the job she was being paid to do and cater to the wills of the men she worked for.

Last month, he'd have cocked his head and said something equally ignorant like, "I tried. But a man can never win against a vagina," and they'd all have laughed at it and trivialized it.

But today, he bit on the rim of his glass and stayed silent.

A minute later, Grant realized he should've said something to defend her. Letting his friends put Eve down wasn't right. But what right did he have to talk about right?

He was spineless. A man who'd lived his whole life trying to please the audience, the critics, the press, his directors, his co-stars, his friends. His career and income had depended on being likable. Desirable. On fitting in with the people he was supposed to fit in with.

Men needed a place to belong. These were the people he belonged with. He had a certain way he needed to be if he wanted to continue being with these men. He couldn't break out of years and years of conditioning at fifty-two.

What was she doing to him, anyway? These men were his closest acquaintances, the only pals he could have a good time with, and now he was criticizing everything they said, feeling uncomfortable for no reason, questioning this way of life.

He couldn't let her take away his friend circle. Let her keep her opinions and stuff them up her ass. Vladimir was right. The entire scenario—he and her—was ridiculous.

Sure, they had a good time when they were together, but that was all he should be having with her. Not grand delusions of something more. It would serve him well to remember that he was *the* Eddie Mans —he had a life every man desired. And he shouldn't be throwing all that away for the sake of one woman.

Patting Robin's shoulder, he said, "Don't let her get to you."

Now if he could only follow that advice himself.

CHAPTER TWENTY-FOUR

Bella turned off the television, telling herself she wasn't going to watch *Love Me Like You Do* again. If she watched it, she'd be reminded of Jamie. And he wasn't here. He was in LA. For some stupid business trip. Rubbing her swollen eyelids, she picked up a fallen eyelash from over her cheekbone and blew it away.

The words crawling on the page of the book were starting to jumble. Information overload.

Snapping the thick tome shut, Bella discarded her glasses and propped her back over pillows on her bed.

It was ten-thirty pm. Too early to go to sleep.

She could text Jamie. But she didn't want to seem obsessive. Already, she'd texted him fifty times today. She wasn't his girlfriend, or an obsessive stalker, to be badgering him with so many messages.

At times like these—lonely, empty times—she longed for someone. A sweet word murmured against her cheek. Wit. Conversation. A snuggle. A man who would just be there for her.

As she spaced out, a heavy feeling nested in her chest. Her mind wandered to a familiar place—the future that didn't exist. She wanted to go places, do things—and not alone. The last couple of weeks had been unbelievable. Jamie's company had infused every second of her day with color.

But this—this was a reminder of what her life was going to go back to.

Desolation. Boredom. Unfulfilled longing.

If you'd only not been stupid to fall for him.

It was strange, wasn't it? She'd longed all these years for someone who'd love her the way she deserved to be loved, but now that person was here, it was the one thing she didn't want.

Unlike Kat and Ashley, she didn't have any family. There was no mother she could call. No sister or brothers or cousins, either.

If she were to die right now, nobody would care. She meant nothing to anyone. Unlike most people, this wasn't the part of being single that scared her. The saddest thing would be to die without ever knowing what it was like to be loved. Without having had anybody look at her the way Alex looked at Kat or Andrew looked at Ashley.

She always invested her 100% into every relationship and was it too much to ask someone else to do the same? Why were people so afraid of investing themselves into anything? Oh, wait she knew the answer. Heartbreak.

Bella sighed.

With every tick of the clock, her meeting with Bryan inched closer.

And with every tick of the clock, her time with Jamie grew shorter.

Bryan looked almost sober when she took a seat opposite him in the private dining room at Charlie Bird. Well-versed in the art of being a celebrity girlfriend, she'd bundled herself in clothes until she was completely unrecognizable. It took her a while to crawl out of all those unwanted layers.

A frown pulled down Bryan's lips when he saw her sans the glasses and in nothing but jeans and a tee.

"What?"

"You didn't put on any makeup." He played with the table knife.

Irritation buzzed inside her. "And why the hell would I dress up for you? As it is, I'm doing you a favor by meeting you."

There. She'd said it. The words she should've said long ago.

"Don't be so prickly. I wasn't criticizing you." He leaned forward until his hotness was in her face.

He was handsome as fuck, but her heart refused to even cough. It trilled at its slow, steady pace, unaffected by the perfect male specimen in front of it.

A waiter, elegantly clothed, stepped in and placed a bowl of leaves in front of her. "Your green salad, ma'am."

"I didn't ask for this." Bella jerked her head up at Bryan, who nodded to the waiter.

"I ordered it for you. You'll like it." He set his palm to her back and slipped it down lower. Bella squirmed uncomfortably. His hands were the wrong size. The wrong fit. The wrong texture. The wrong color. The wrong person's. "And it's good for you."

Popping a forkful of greens into her mouth, she speared Bryan with a sharp look. "I hope this isn't the main course."

"I ordered juice, too, just in case." With a proud grin, he rubbed his thumb pad across her cheek. Her gut squeezed —not in a good way.

"Juice and handful of leaves cannot be my lunch. I need to eat more than that." She pushed some water down her throat.

"Sunshine, you need to lose weight if you want to have kids. You're already over thirty. Being fat will only make it harder."

The asshole. He was up to old antics already. Why had she been stupid enough to meet him again?

"I never said I was having kids." Slamming a palm down, she glowered.

"But you've always wanted to." As his fingers threaded through hers, Bella felt a flutter in her stomach. "Imagine how cute our babies will be."

"I'd rather choke on my own spit than have your kids," Gathering her arms in front of her chest, Bella stared him down. "And back up a bit. Before we get to babies, don't you think you need to get to that apology you owe me?"

"I'm sorry about what happened." That heart-melting smile lighted up his face. "It's the stupidest thing I did. Breaking up with you. I don't even know what I was thinking. All I can say is I'm a completely different man now. Please take me back."

"Sorry, the ship's sailed."

"Bella, please," He scratched the table. "I...there's something I haven't told you yet." His eyes drew away from her and he raked a hand through his glossy hair. "The truth is I've been depressed since my engagement to Nicole. Like, clinically. I take meds for it. Actually, when we were together the first time, I was depressed then, too, I just didn't do anything about it. Fame is a strange thing—too much of it is just as scary as the lack of it."

"You were at the top of the charts when we were together," Bella curled a strand of hair around her finger. One year into their relationship, his second album had skyrocketed him to international fame and won him a Grammy. "You still are."

"I know, but that was the first time I'd enjoyed so much success. In so many ways, it was a curse. Suddenly, I was being invited to all these parties, women were offering to sleep with me, producers wanted to talk to me, everybody wanted a piece of me. I got carried away by it because it was all I'd ever wanted—to be recognized and acknowledged." He leaned in. "But that feeling didn't last. I started to get scared. What if I turned into a one-hit-wonder? What if all these people didn't care about me anymore? What if I went back to being a poor, broke artist? That drove me to desperation, and then I made poor choices. But I've been seeing a therapist about it, reflecting on my life. And...I'm sorry. What I did to you was horrible. That night in my car, too. I shouldn't have groped you. I was way too drunk to say or do anything sensible, but if I hadn't drunk, I wouldn't have had the courage to approach you."

Bella sighed. "Bryan, I want you to be honest here. One time in your entire life, just please tell the truth." She looked into his eyes so he wouldn't be able to lie. "Are you doing this just because you wanna sleep with me?"

"No, never." She'd thought she knew all his tricks. All his expressions. But she was genuinely moved by his apology. There was actual emotion on his face. "You're the only friend I ever had. You knew me before I was filthy rich and famous. I can tell you things I can't tell anybody else. You're the only one who knows who I am."

That I do, Bella thought.

"What about Nicole?"

"She thinks of me as this suave, put-together guy. Plus, nothing stays between her ears. Everything I tell her finds its way to her friends. If I tell her about my depression, it'll be all over the news tomorrow." A nostalgic smile lighted his face. "You'll never tell anyone, right?"

"Never." She might hate him, but she wasn't vindictive.

"I knew I was right to trust you. Do you know why I call you sunshine? Because when you're with me, there is light in my dark world."

Bella swallowed, tamping down the urge to vomit at his cheesiness. "How touching."

"Absolutely. You're so funny, so loyal. When we talk, when we make love, I know I'm safe. I feel like there's something worth living for. My feelings for you run deeper than you know. Even I didn't know how deep until I met you again."

Giving up on the tasteless salad, she sipped some of the juice the waiter brought around. "Will you cut the bullshit already, Bryan?"

"So...will you take me back, sunshine?"

"No."

"You gave your mother a second chance. Why not me? I've never hurt you as much as she did."

Bella's gaze fell to the orange juice. "You don't deserve it."

Bryan gave an impatient tongue click. "Why won't you just move to LA with me? We could see a therapist there, work on our relationship."

"Don't tell me what to do." Bella kept her voice low, struggling to suppress the savage note that anger injected into her tone. "And I can't move to LA. I have a job here."

"You don't need a job anymore. I'll take care of you." He tried to force-feed her some more of the green salad.

"Oh, I remember how *that* ended last time. No, thanks. I think I'm gonna hold onto my job," she snarled.

"You'll have to give something up if you want me." Shivers peppered her hand when he glided his over it.

"I don't want you," she retorted, temper getting the best of her.

"Okay, I get it." She was shocked when he acknowledged that she was right. He'd never done that before. "Being an artist is really flexible, so I could move to New York."

"I'm shocked. Have all the women in LA died from some incurable disease? Is that why you're so desperate?"

"There's nothing for me in LA anymore. I want you."

Smiling, she said, "Don't even try to pull wool over my eyes again, Bryan. I'm not stupid."

"It's taken me a long time to get to this point in life. I'm ready for responsibility now. I'm ready for you. I want to be the friend you've been to me."

She wouldn't lie, his words struck her. Just thinking that someone would be there for her, she felt a whole lot of relief. She could breathe easily. There would be someone to pick up the pieces after Jamie was gone. Because when Jamie was gone, she was certain all that was left of her heart was going to be tiny, little chunks.

Not that Bryan could ever fill that space, or even soothe her when she was like that.

His features assumed a serious expression. "I'm going to stay in your life from now on, sunshine. Always."

A year ago, she'd have thrown up at the thought of him always being in her life. Now, it soothed her fears. She wouldn't be alone. She wouldn't have to face that scary, empty, hopeless feeling that crept up every night. But this was only an illusion. She reminded herself of that. It wasn't hard to turn away from the illusion when you had seen the real thing.

"No." Nodding, Bella picked her next words carefully. "I don't want you or need you.

She might be feeling all sympathetic for him now, but she had to make sure she wasn't making impulsive decisions.

"Don't friend-zone me, sunshine."

"Friend-zone would imply we're friends. Which we are not. We are nothing and will be nothing."

She expected him to protest, to push her to go his way, but he considered and gave in. "Fine. We'll start as nothing. But I want more, Bella. I could never be happy with us just being strangers."

"All I'm willing to give you is a restraining order. And if you don't like that, well, I can always arrange a cake for you. Baked by me."

Bryan nodded. He had a resigned expression. "You're being so stubborn."

That was shorter than she'd anticipated. She didn't want to shorten her time with Jamie even by a day. In a single day with him, she lived an entire year.

"Why shouldn't I be?" Bella tipped her chin up. "I have a boyfriend now. I want to protect our relationship. And that means you have to go."

Guilt stabbed her the moment she thought of Jamie. Why was she sneaking around behind his back doing this? He'd never do something like this behind hers.

"Boyfriend?" Bryan looked puzzled. "Oh, you have someone else."

Extricating herself from the place, she piled the layers of clothing back on herself. "Don't call me unnecessarily just because I'm going to block your number. And next time you badger me, I'm seriously reporting this to the cops."

"So cruel," Bryan said, chest deflating.

"You don't know what cruelty is." Scowling at him, she followed it up with a glare. "And don't think you can weasel your way back into my life. I'm not forgiving you ever."

"Baby—"

"Bye." She hurried out as fast as she could.

This could be the first time in her life that she actually felt calmer after talking to Bryan. He'd sounded alarmingly mature today, and sincere, too.

Bella plucked out a packet of peanuts from her purse and dumped some into her mouth. The sodium infiltrated her taste buds and calmed her down. When her phone vibrated in her pocket, she took it out to check if Jamie had sent her any messages. He'd sent her fifteen.

The latest one read,
Jamie: R u alive? Why aren't u replying?
Not bothering to scroll up to the other messages he'd sent, Bella typed a reply quickly.
Bella: Sorry.
Jamie: What r u doing now?
Bella: Eating penis.
Jamie: Is it good
Bella: Nah. Way too salty.
Jamie: You swallowed?
Bella: Of course. Why wouldn't I?
Jamie: Guess I won't have to use a condom next time u give me a BJ.
Bella: Huh?
Not immediately getting him, Bella scrolled up, and almost threw her phone away in humiliation when she saw what autocorrect had done. Her cheeks burned like lava.

Hell, she was so sick of autocorrect.
Bella: *PEANUTS. I was eating PEANUTS. The PEANUTS are salty. Damn, autocorrect.
Jamie: LMAO
Bella: Did I scare u?
Jamie: Nope. I was having pleasant visions of you swallowing cum.
Bella: Hey!
Jamie: Kidding.
Bella: I'm so sorry.
Jamie: Don't be. Autocorrect gets even the best of us.
Although that would go down as the worst autocorrect fiasco of her life, she was glad it had been him on the other end. He could make the worst moments seem better.

Another green text bubble (the color of his messages) slithered at the bottom of her screen as she melted into the crowd at the subway station.

Jamie: BTW what do I wear to dinner with your friends? I'm having trouble picking an outfit.

Bella: That's the first time a man's asked me that question.

Jamie: Too girly?

Bella: Just wear what you usually wear.

Jamie: I want to wear something different.

Bella: Ok, then wear a suit.

Jamie: See u at dinner.

As she flung the phone back in her purse, Bella felt the buzz in her heart die. She tried not to think about it. In two more months—one, now—she'd have to give up this sense of aliveness for something much more mundane.

She didn't delude herself. It was never going to be like this with anyone else. Never. And she was going to miss Jamie so much. Her heart nearly broke at the thought of being separated from him. One month suddenly seemed too short. She wanted a year, a few years, an eternity.

She wanted to be able to ask that from him, but she couldn't. She'd known what she was agreeing to when she'd agreed to it. She'd known what kind of man he was. A dangerous temptation. Still, she'd deceived herself into thinking that this relationship wouldn't break her. Now she was going to have to lie in the bed she'd made.

CHAPTER TWENTY-FIVE

"Glad you made it." Eve offered Grant a half-hearted hug and nothing more as she led him to her living room.

Grant wanted to feel her up, to kiss her senseless and then slide a dirty whisper into her ear, the way he usually did, but his mood soured when he saw both her daughters lounging on the couch.

"You didn't tell me *they* were going to be here." He wagged an accusing finger at the girls, who were so underdressed for the occasion, it was an insult to his ego.

"Alana's here for the weekend." Eve sounded a little worried.

As he swept into the living room, the two girls kept their noses buried in whatever they were doing. Grant stifled the urge to just turn back and walk out.

Here he was, legendary Hollywood star, multiple Oscar winner, and they couldn't be bothered to even push up their snooty little noses to greet him.

Clearing her throat, Eve tapped her feet, clearly embarrassed. "Girls. You remember Grant? My—"

"Your boyfriend. We know," Carla, whom he'd grown quite familiar with over the last few weeks, said, tapping the screen of her Nintendo 3DS with her stylus. Still no eye contact.

Alana flipped pages of a glossy magazine, pretending that none of this was happening.

"Be nice to him." Eve tapped his arm and pierced her children with a glare. "I need to finish roasting the potatoes and then we can have dinner."

Heading to the kitchen, she left him with her two disinterested daughters.

"And no playing on your DS or reading magazines when he's talking to you!" she yelled across the living room, but Alana and Carla pretended to be deaf.

Grant dropped on the couch and wedged himself between Carla and Alana. The fact that Eve trusted him enough to leave him alone with her daughters was a testament to how far they'd come.

Since September, they were growing closer and closer. They went on a lot of dates nowadays and sent each other lovey-dovey messages through work email. Every new detail he found out about excited him like a little boy.

Last week, she'd even taken another vacation with him to Los Angeles where he'd shown her his old Beverly Hills mansion and they'd strolled Rodeo Drive together. Then, they'd taken a detour to Stanford to visit her alma mater.

They were in the honeymoon phase. It wouldn't last. He knew it wouldn't. But it was good.

"How did it go with the sponsor?" Grant asked Carla, who had her nose buried and eyes glued to the blinking images on the small dual screen.

Somehow, Carla had gotten his number (probably from Eve's phone) along with the erroneous idea that he was a mentor of some sort because she called him every third day to ask for advice on her fledgling YouTube career.

"They said they'll pay me a thousand dollars for talking about the product. I'm so excited! My first endorsement." Her attention went back to her game. "Shoot! Mario died."

Grant regarded Eve, or rather her ass that stuck right up in the air as she bent to get potatoes from the oven. Arousal kicked him in the balls. Quite literally.

Frustration was a bitch. Sexual frustration was a bitch on crack. Grant tried to think why he hadn't taken Eve when he'd had an opening. Multiple openings. These days he rarely understood what he was doing around Eve. He cared for her. That was obvious. Beyond that, he had a jumble of confusing feelings surrounding her that he dared not try to untangle.

"What're you looking at?" Carla's round eyes peered from over her pink Nintendo 3DS.

"Your mother's ass," he twanged. "It's a damn fine ass."

A finger closed over Carla's lip. "Don't let her hear you say that. We're not supposed to use words like that at home."

Then he'd better not reveal anything else going on in his head.

He snuck a peek at the colorful animations twinkling on Carla's dual DS screen. "What're you playing?"

"Mario."

"What's it about? Does it have a storyline?" He didn't know too much about video games, but he could see a red and blue man sprite jumping around.

"You won't understand. It's complicated." Carla shrugged and closed one screen over the other.

Bringing her knees up to her chin, she hurled a glance at Eve in the kitchen. "By the way, when are you planning to marry her?"

That question caught him off-guard. Without a reason, his pulse raced.

"Sorry?" Grant rested his sweaty fingers over his pants.

Not once had he considered the idea of marrying Eve. Sure, he liked her. And since he'd never had sex with her, this was genuine affection. He wasn't confusing intense physical attraction with actual compatibility, as he'd done with Melanie.

But he was Grant Star, for crying out loud. Mr. Desirability. A sex symbol. He couldn't marry an old, unattractive woman. That would be like Hugh Hefner marrying a seventy-year-old grandma. It just wasn't right. What would people think of him? The media would laugh. His friends would laugh. His image, his appeal, would be ruined.

He wasn't going to lower himself to that level.

"We're just dating." The sudden urge to get up and stretch his feet overtook him. That odd tangle of emotions churned inside him again.

"Yeah. But at your age, people usually date with marriage in mind, not just for fun," Carla said.

At your age.

Even the kid thought he was old. Fifty-six was not old. Fifty-six was a good age for a man. Fifty-seven, on the other hand, was old. And Eve was fifty-seven.

"Not always," he said.

"You might want to tell my mom that," Alana spoke for the first time, looking up from her copy of *Scientific American*. "Because she's very serious about you. Why do you think she wanted you to meet us? We've never met any of her other boyfriends."

"Um…" Grant lost his voice.

"Dinner's ready," Eve informed loudly.

His hands were clammy and too many questions riddled his mind when he faced Eve.

"Coming." Alana bounced to her feet, and he tagged along with her.

Appraising the food on the table, he was hit by fear. Chicken and gravy. Roasted potatoes. Too homely. Too domestic. Too traditional.

Then, for some reason, Eve chose to sit next to him at the dining table, which didn't help him.

"The food looks good." His voice was flat.

"Thanks." When her daughters turned to look at the cake, she gave him a secret smile.

A smile that made laugh lines appear.

The imperfections on her face didn't even bother him anymore. He no longer looked at her thin lips and thought about lip fillers. Rather, he thought of licking them. And he wanted to run his hands over her lines, not erase them.

What was wrong with him? He shouldn't be thinking this way. He was Grant Star. He didn't look at wrinkles and think they were cute. How had she screwed him up so much?

He frowned.

"Something wrong?" Eve asked because he'd been staring.

He battled with words, before choosing the ones he knew would hurt her.

Stretching the skin on her cheeks with his thumb pads, he said, "You need to get botox, baby. You're looking like a prune."

Yeah, he was being an asshole, but it was the only way to preserve the man he was. The man he should be.

Eyes widening, she hissed. "Excuse me?"

"Pay some attention to your appearance, won't you? I don't want you looking like a fossil by next year." To add to the insult, he tossed in an annoying snigger.

Eve's fingers tightened around her fork.

"The potatoes are so delicious. Here, Grant, have some more. Isn't my mom a great cook?" Hyperactive, Alana transferred some potatoes to his plate, serving it with a hateful look.

The message was clear—stuff some of these into your mouth and shut up.

Eve returned to smiling. "So what were you discussing with them on the couch earlier?"

"Mario."

"I told you not to play that game all the time." Eve hurled a displeased look at her daughter.

Carla speared a potato with her fork. "Don't you think he should know I'm a video game addict if he's going to be my step-father in the future?"

Step-father? Grant coughed, then dunked water into his mouth, waiting for Eve to correct Carla, but she didn't.

So he did.

"I'm not going to be your step-father. I have no intention of adopting two annoying kids."

Taken aback, Eve blinked, but Carla smoothed over it. "Hey, we're not that bad. Once you get to know us, you'll like us. We grow on everyone."

Flashing a smile, she passed him the gravy.

"No, we don't," Alana cut. Her gaze darted between Eve and him. "He either wants us or he doesn't—"

"Why don't you tell him about Dartmouth?" shrill, Eve interrupted

Alana, "He's been asking me how you like college."

"Has he?" Alana directed at him, unconvinced. "Do you really want to know?"

"Not really. I didn't go to college. I don't think I'll understand anything."

At this, both her fists rained down on the table, shaking the plates and pots. "He didn't go to college. Mom, how can you be dating someone who didn't go to college? You always said that guys who didn't go to college were unrefined and stupid."

"Not always," Grant added.

He was proud of his beginnings, humble as they might be. And he didn't want anybody looking down on it.

"He's…different." Rubbing her cheeks, Eve closed her eyes. "And I've changed my mind about college since then."

Visibly perking up at this, Carla jumped on the chance. "Does that mean it's okay if I don't go to college?"

"No."

"But I can become a big star, too. Grant will help me. He's helped actresses make it big before. Haven't you?"

"Only the ones who slept with me." He meant for that to scare the girl away from using his influence. It wasn't true.

But Carla blanched. Alana cringed. Eve slapped her forehead.

Hell. That had come out too fast. He was used to making jokes like that. Most of the time, he was around adult men, who wouldn't bat an eyelid at that.

"You're just joking…right?" Carla asked, clinging onto optimism.

Unperturbed, Grant spooned food into his mouth. He tasted nothing, though. "Did you fall for it?"

Nobody believed him. Why were they all so uptight?

Tense, Eve fell silent. Alana cleared her throat. Carla chewed fast. An awkward pause ensued, broken only when Carla said, "The food's so good, Mom," for the fifth time.

"Yeah." Grant nodded along. "It's good, even if it's a little overcooked."

His ears picked up a long exhale. Then a slam of fists on the table.

"That's it. I've had enough of you insulting my mother. I think you two need to talk." Alana ejected herself from her chair abruptly, dropping her spoon on the plate with a clank. "Come on, Cee."

She forced her sister out of her chair. Bothered, Carla shot him a glance that said, 'You so screwed this up.'

"Sit down." Mustering all the strictness she could, Eve tried to keep the night from slipping into disaster territory, but Alana didn't look like she was about to be swayed.

"No, I can't watch this anymore." Searing him with a glare, she said, "You're obviously in love with someone who doesn't give a damn about you, Mom."

Her heavy footsteps, followed by Carla's, pounded the floor as they disappeared into their rooms and banged the doors shut. Dull sounds reverberated in the silent living room. Beats passed.

Resting her face between her cupped palms, Eve sighed. "I'd hoped you wouldn't ruin this."

"You're overreacting."

"No, I'm not. You've just embarrassed me in front of my children." He'd never heard her sound so furious. She was almost shouting. "I was right about you. You're a callous jerk. I can't believe I was stupid enough to love you."

Eve loved him. This stick-up-her-ass, demanding woman? How? Why?

"Now, don't make this—"

She stacked one palm over the other on the table and hissed.

"All you want is a pretty, Botoxed arm candy who's twenty years younger than you. I'm not that woman. I'll never be." Disappointment and regret poured out of her. "I always knew that. I just...hoped you would change. It's the stupidest thing, right? People never change."

"Don't blow this out of proportion. It was only a suggestion, for fuck's sake. And I said it nicely." He found himself raising his voice without intending to.

Eve went back to the chair and draped her arm over the back. Confrontation choked the air.

"You don't understand. My children mean everything to me. I want them to like you. I want them to accept you."

"Accept me for what?"

"For…" She gave up with a defeated breath. "Their father."

"I don't want to be their father!" he bellowed. "Nor do I don't want to marry you just so you'll let me inside your tight vagina. Do you know how ridiculous this situation is? I'm a legend in Hollywood, for Christ's sake. What am I even doing with you?"

That was the million-dollar question, wasn't it? He'd been asking himself that question every day. What was he doing with Eve? What was he doing to her? What was she doing to him?

He was still asking.

Horror cut across her face. "I-I had no idea you thought about me that way. I thought you l-liked me."

Grant balled his hands into fists. He wouldn't let her crushed expression get to him. He couldn't start pitying her. Or realizing how much he loved her now.

It was too late. She wasn't the right sort of woman for him, anyway. Their worlds were different. And he was too confused by all the new emotions to be able to make any good decisions.

"Just because we had a few months together doesn't mean I like you. I've kissed more women than you've met in your life. And trust me, most of them were better than you."

Okay, maybe that had been below the belt. But this was a battle. He couldn't be nice to her.

Gripping her head, she put her forehead on the table. "Fine. So that's how it is. But I never misled you about what I wanted. Why did you think you could do it?"

This was the part that frustrated and baffled him the most. His inexplicable attraction to her. He couldn't explain by any rational means why he'd thought it a good idea to date Eve. Or why he still thought she was worth clinging on to.

He'd changed so much he didn't recognize himself. He was a different man. He didn't want to be a different man. He didn't want to be a man at all. He wanted to be a sex symbol. A legend. An icon. The eternal ladies' man.

"I thought you'd change your mind once you got to know me. Be charmed and give in. But you're never going to let anybody inside you."

Two below the belt now.

Shriveling back in her chair, her head sunk low. "And here I thought you actually had some maturity in you. You're not twenty. Why are you still judging women by their appearance?"

His head suddenly throbbed with a headache. A bad feeling cramped his gut, but all the damage was done, and he didn't want to admit that he'd been too harsh.

"Stop PMSing." He hurled her a scowl.

"Sure. Accuse me of PMSing. That's what you always do whenever a woman says something you don't like." Pulling her hair out of the bun she'd tied it up in, she let it settle in loose waves over her neck and shoulders.

Plucking out sound from his vocal cords was hard. Even when he managed to say something, it wasn't the apology it should've been. "If you'd had sex with me the first time, it would never have come to this."

He would never have gotten this close to her. He'd never have fallen in love. He'd never be at her house. He'd never be hurting her.

His role was fixed—the debonair sex symbol. He wasn't going to start playing average Joe now.

"Is that what this is about? Did you never want anything more than sex from me?" Betrayal carried across her features.

"And now I don't even want that." Not that he was ever getting it now.

Eve let out a final, defeated breath. "I guess we should stop seeing each other, then."

This was the point of no return. Inevitability.

Grant conceded. "Obviously."

Thump. Thump. His feet slapped violently on the way out.

"I regret I ever loved you," Eve yelled over the gulf of empty space between them, and her cry was so broken, his heartstrings jerked. The words died into a whisper.

He didn't bother to reply. He focused on getting out. He could never belong with her. He should never belong with her.

Superstars like him didn't settle for ordinary. Superstars didn't want ordinary.

Even if the men inside them sometimes did.

CHAPTER TWENTY-SIX

Jamie knew something was wrong when he showed up at the restaurant he was supposed to meet Bella's friends at and he was the only person wearing a suit. Ducking his head, he made his way across the rustic interiors of the restaurant to the table where Bella was waving at him. Her face was the only thing that calmed his nerves and made all the stares he received worth it.

She wore a casual maroon dress that skimmed her knees and was a beautiful contrast to her tan skin. Light makeup enhanced her already beautiful features. If they'd been somewhere more private, he'd have made love to her tenderly.

"I didn't think you'd actually show up wearing a suit," she remarked when he slid into the chair adjacent to hers.

He kissed her cheek. "You look beautiful."

Scarlet suffused her cheeks.

"He's paying you compliments. That's a good sign." Kat, whom he'd met before, flashed him a smile and extended a pale, slender hand for a handshake. "Nice to meet you again, Jamie. I realize we didn't get off on the best foot, but I'm willing to change my mind about you. From what I hear, you haven't screwed up—yet."

There was another woman beside her, who looked markedly different. She was medium build, had a heart-shaped face and blonde hair. Next to Kat's bright red hair, Kate Moss-esque figure, and angular features, she looked almost girl-next-door.

"Hi. I'm Ashley." She held out her hand to him.

"Jamie."

"Would you believe she had a child two weeks ago?" Bella interjected, a hand flying to her mouth.

"Congratulations," Jamie said. "I wouldn't have been able to say that by looking at you."

Ashley sipped water demurely. "Thanks."

"See? I told you. You lost all the pregnancy weight already." Bella wiggled a finger at her. "He can't even tell you're a mother."

"I guess." Ashley's gaze flitted to her phone on the table. "Do you think I should call Andrew to check if Penelope is doing ok?"

"Stop stressing. He'll call you if he needs anything. Have some faith in him. He's the father of your child." Kat hooked an arm around Ashley's shoulder. "Relax."

"But what if—"

"Nothing will happen."

"Right." Apologetically, Ashley folded her napkin on the table into a flower. "It's a new mother thing. You constantly worry about your child."

Jamie picked up the paper flower. "That's some beautiful paper folding."

"Just a little something I learned back in school." Shrinking back into her seat, she rubbed her forehead.

They ordered drinks—two Pinot Noirs, one Rosé, and one orange juice—and decided to put off ordering food until later.

"So now that we have those out of the way, tell us a little about yourself. Bella's told us pretty much nothing about you except stuff we could've found online anyway." Bunching her hair, Ashley twisted it into a thin column and let it hang over her left shoulder.

"I'm not sure there's anything about me that can't be found online."

Kat tapped her knuckles against the table. "Come on. You're not that boring."

"Sadly, I am. There's no time for much in a writer's life except writing..." One of Bryan's songs drifted through the restaurant, and he had to immediately check Bella.

"What? Why're you staring at me?" His reaction made a slightly confused expression hover over her face.

"Nothing. Just wanted to make sure you're okay."

"Why wouldn't I be?" She was tapping her fork on the spoon, humming something that vaguely resembled the very song that was playing.

This one didn't seem to affect her at all. Maybe it had just been that particular song, then. Or something to do with that day.

"They're having a sale at Tiffany's this weekend," Ashley broke in, addressing him.

Jamie looked up at the waitress who brought him his drink and thanked her. "Are you planning to buy something?"

Kat sniffed. "Actually that was a tip for you. Buy an engagement ring for Bella while it's cheap."

"Guys!" Reddening, Bella rubbed her throat to control the series of coughs that blasted from her vocal cords. "Will you stop embarrassing me? We're not like that."

"Exactly. I'm leaving for LA in the new year," he corroborated with a nod.

Two sharp glances—one blazing green and one blazing blue—veered to Bella. "You didn't say anything about him leaving."

Like a deer caught in headlights, Bella blinked. "It...it doesn't matter. Jamie and I are just doing short-term."

Twin snorts erupted. "Short term."

Offended, Bella gave her head a shake. "What's wrong with short-term?"

"Nothing. Except I remember you crying on my shoulder and swearing that you were done with men who cannot invest themselves emotionally into loving someone." Kat's voice was charged with suspicion.

"Jamie can commit. He has committed to being with me until the new year. This is commitment, too." Muscles twitched around Bella's lips. Due to his proximity to her, Jamie could detect the bead of sweat rolling down the back of her neck.

Liar.

With a nervous laugh, she added, "I'm absolutely not going to fall in love with Jamie, so it doesn't matter. Why shouldn't we have a little fun? We're adults."

That laugh was too controlled to be believable. Her desperate body language said it all.

Fighting the impulse in him that told him to correct her, Jamie let it go. While he knew he could never be the one for her, he too, sometimes wished he could be. Unreal hopes were only human. She was entitled to hers as much as he was to his.

"Me neither." Jamie joined his palms under the table. "It wouldn't work out."

"You know, with the show not being renewed and stuff...well, long-distance will never work for me." Eyes shifting around nervously, Bella turned the pages of the menu card. "Oh, look at this. Don't loaded nachos sound delicious? I'm hungry. Let's get some food. Excuse me!"

"These chicken fajitas sound interesting..."

Kat buried her nose in her menu as a waitress hurried to note their orders.

Apologetic, Ashley looked at him from across the table and whispered, "Sorry about the show."

"It happens." Jamie gave a shrug.

"Loved it, by the way. Watched every episode. You did a great job on it."

"I'm happy to hear that." It meant a lot to him that she'd liked it.

A stretch of silence followed as Ashley's phone beeped and she checked it. Jamie used it to empty his glass and sneak some secret glances at Bella. She wasn't far behind herself, looking his way a few times when she thought he wasn't looking.

Sometimes, living without her seemed like an impossibility. He'd never have picked her out if he'd seen her at a bar or out on the street, but now that he'd been with her, he couldn't envision himself with anyone else.

No woman would ever get his sense of humor like her. No woman would write him silly messages, cry when she watched his debut movie for the millionth time, and cook him store-bought stir-fry.

No woman would ever be her.

She was pure magic.

And he wanted to be under her spell forever.

CHAPTER TWENTY-SEVEN

"You shouldn't be calling me," Grant said when Carla called him a week after Eve and his fallout.

"You shouldn't be answering my calls, either. But you are."

"Okay, kiddo. What'd you want?" he asked, gruffly.

"Relax. It's not about my mom. It's about me." She sneezed. "I want you to appear on my YouTube channel as a guest. You cool with that?"

Grant grunted. Carla Rosenberg. Ever the mercenary YouTuber.

"No, I'm not cool with that."

"Hey, come on. We can record this Saturday at my house. My mom will be gone."

"Lemme remind you what happened the last time I was at your house." He used the strictest tone in his arsenal. "Your mom and I broke up."

"Dude, you think I didn't know? Trust me, by now, the entire neighborhood knows." He heard sounds of traffic from Carla's end. She must be out. "She'll forgive you. I know she will. She really loves you."

"I said terrible things to her. If she's a smart woman—which she undoubtedly is, since she works for me—she won't forgive."

He heard her shrug. "I've called her worse. Being a parent, she probably understands how easy it is to say mean things to people without meaning to. When emotions are involved, words slip out before you know what you've said."

"Those words didn't just slip out," he protested.

"You meant them?"

"I wanted to. I tried to." He dropped his voice lower. "I want to."

"But you don't."

"No."

"That's a relief. I was getting worried that I'd have to put up with mom watching your movies all night for the rest of my senior year. No offense, but you have an annoying accent."

A mixture of hope and pride leaped in his chest. "She watches my movies?"

"After I've gone to sleep."

He faked nonchalance, even though his heart was humming a different tune. "Well, what can I say? They're good movies."

"They must be. She cries a lot while watching them."

"I don't remember having acted in any tragedies."

"Don't be dense. You know it's your face that's making her cry."

Grant chuckled. "And here I thought I was handsome."

"Get out of the movie star fantasy, dude. That was a long time ago. You're old now."

That snapped at his heart like a rubber band. Was she attacking his face? "I didn't age on-screen..." He dropped his argument. "But you're right. I'm not Eddie Mans anymore."

If he had snapped out of that fantasy, that role sooner, he'd never have hurt Eve. But he'd immaturely clung to his former glory, his shallow ego.

"You know, she always watches closely when you kiss the actress on screen. I think she thinks that if she sees you with enough other women, she'll remember what a disgusting pervert you are." She blew out a breath. "It's taking time."

"Healing takes time."

"Are you going to let her heal?"

He swallowed the regret in his throat. He owed at least that much to her. "Yes."

"Bad answer."

Grant jerked. "What?"

"When people heal, they go back to being who they used to be. I don't want her to go back to being who she was. She was boring, uptight, and miserable, and after she forgets about you she'll be boring, uptight, and miserable once more. She'll never again smile like a maniac when no one's watching. She'll never overstretch her cooking abilities to make us something fancy for dinner. She won't be happy, period."

"You're being dramatic. Eve still has her job. She still has you. That's plenty of happiness."

Carla drew a shaky breath. "What about you? Do you want to go back to being who you were?"

Who had he been? A people pleaser. A hedonist. A consummate womanizer. A man with no soul.

"I know you're only fifteen, but even you should be able to see how mismatched your mother and I are."

"Really? I thought you matched pretty well."

"Oh, please." He snorted. "And let's not forget that she's never going to forgive me."

"You're both too old to hold grudges for long."

"Will you stop calling me old? I'm not old. I'm middle-aged."

"Same difference to a teen," Carla said. "Anyway, I need to get back home soon. Let's talk about my YouTube video now."

"Not this week." Grant scratched his earlobe.

"But you'll do it?"

"Only because I feel responsible for leading you down the YouTuber path."

"And because you'll get to see my mom again."

"Maybe."

"Adults," Carla said. He could sense her rolling her eyes. "They're so obvious."

CHAPTER TWENTY-EIGHT

Clambering to the top of the stairs of his father's townhouse, Jamie paused briefly before knocking on Grant's study. Today was the first time in weeks he'd made time to meet with Grant. Between his awkward schedule and Grant's, there had been no opportunity to get together, but he owed his father at least one visit per financial quarter, so here he was.

Grant might forget him if he didn't manage to remind his father that he had a son at regular intervals.

The door was ajar, and through the slit of space, Jamie spotted Grant's head bent over documents, his glasses sitting low on his chiseled nose.

No alcohol or woman at his side. Judging from the way Grant's attention didn't flicker despite the rap on his door, he must have been seriously absorbed in whatever he was reading.

About to push through the door, Jamie got distracted when his phone buzzed with a message.

Bella: Where r u?
Jamie: With my father.
Bella: Oh, OK.
Jamie: Did u want something?

Bella: Nothing. Come by my apartment later.
Jamie: Why?
Bella: No guy asks why when a woman invites him to her apartment.
A smile slid up his lips.
Jamie: Will be there.
Bella: I'll keep my pussy warm.
Damn it. Why did she have to write that?

Now, he wouldn't be able to keep his mind on anything but getting to her as fast as he could. She was both a curse and a blessing that way. The last time they'd made love was still in his mind, though it had been five days ago.

Made love.

They'd not fucked. They'd not had sex. They'd made love.

He was still feeling it now. It would be days before he heard back from NYU about the job, but by this point, he didn't care. Whatever happened with the position, he wasn't going to leave New York. No way. He wasn't leaving his heart behind here.

Yeah, the winters were crap, and the summers worse, but he could survive. Grant had adapted, after so many years of living on the opposite coast. He could, too.

Gingerly, he tiptoed in, careful not to startle Grant. Concentration unbroken, Grant continued doing what he was doing.

He'd always regarded Grant as a sort of friend-father figure, but now, as the dim lamplight laid bare, the smattering of deep lines on the old man's skin, he could finally see that Grant was no longer the young, heroic figure he'd once been. Gray hair clung to his temples, scattered into the cap of dark brown at the crown of his head. Ejecting a frustrated hiss, Grant dropped the pen in his hand and tossed it over his head.

Then when he spotted Jamie's form, surprise forced his eyes wide.

"J, I'm so happy to see you." For a startled second, Jamie stayed put where he was, unsure what to make of the ashen hue of Grant's face. "I was just thinking about you."

"Did something happen?" Jamie threw a surveying look around his father's study. No bra. No lace panties. Not even lipstick marks on Grant's collarbone. "Why're you drinking so early in the morning?"

"I'm having woman problems." Grant clapped his legs together under the imposing rosewood desk.

"Woman problems," Jamie repeated, in disbelief.

"Her name's Eve. And before you make assumptions, let me tell you that she's neither young, nor blonde, but I'm very serious about her."

Unexpectedly, Grant broke out his prized A.H. Hirsch Reserve sixteen-year-old bourbon from the cabinet bookended between two legs of his desk. Glass clamored before he set another crystal glass on the table. Tawny liquid eased into it, drop by precious drop, followed by ice cubes Grant procured from the mini-fridge in the room.

"She's the one who works at Star Studios, isn't she?" Circling the glass, Jamie felt the coolness of condensing ice against the inside of his palm.

"Mmmm. Although I think she might quit soon."

Jamie folded his legs and collapsed onto a mauve wing chair diagonally opposite Grant. "She's very different from your usual type."

Not that there was anything wrong with that. Heaven knew Grant needed someone mature and sensible by his side instead of another bimbo.

"Hence the problems." The intensity in Grant's eyes sharpened. He let a cool sip of bourbon run down his throat. "She has kids. Two of them."

"So do you. One." Removing the whiskey from his hand, Jamie set it down on a carved table adjacent to the chair. "Is that the problem? Her kids?"

"Part of it." Absently, Grant fingered the papers on his desk. "J, do you know the feeling of loving someone who's out of your league, but the world thinks she's not?"

"Eve's not out of your league," Jamie reassured.

"See, that's where you and the rest of the world are wrong." Screwing his eyes shut, Grant hung his head. "She's totally out of my league. I don't know how to impress a woman like her. The regular rules don't apply. She has her own rules. Damn, she's frustrating."

Grant sounded really frustrated.

"Why does she matter so much?"

A low groan vibrated in his father's throat. "You know, there may have been countless women in my life, but I never loved any of them. I thought I loved your mother, but she was only an ego trip for me, a youthful infatuation. She made me feel desirable, virile, important. But now, at this age, I finally realize that loving someone isn't about self-importance or power."

Jamie tipped his chin down. "You're really serious about this woman."

Grant's breath whistled. "Dead serious. I'm fighting with myself over her. I'm fighting with who I want to be, who I used to be, and who I can never be. I hope I win, though, because if I don't, she will. And if she wins, she'll bail."

"Sounds complicated."

Grant rubbed his lined forehead. "I hate being in my head these days. It was always a simple place, but now it's worse than a battlefield."

In other words, Grant was experiencing the angst of being in love. Must be a novel experience for him. Jamie couldn't tell him that he was experiencing the same thing. His heart was torn between pursuing what he had going on with Bella and leaving it all for his old life. An empty life haunted by regrets of the past, where distrust and were his constant companions. But it was the familiar path, and what he had with Bella was...not. He thought he'd been in love before with his ex-girlfriend, but after listening to Grant, he realized that he'd just been addicted to being important to her. He wanted to solve all her problems, to have her look at him like he'd hung the moon. And she'd been just like his mother. She knew what kind of man he was, and she took advantage of him.

"What if she's like Mom? What if she's just in it for your money and fame?" Jamie asked, and it was his own fears that he was voicing.

"She's not your mother," Grant emphasized. "She has lived independently all her life and achieved success on her own terms. She has enough money to not need anything from me. Honestly, that's what makes this so hard. I can't seduce her with my wealth and fame. She wants my heart."

That line struck a chord with Jamie. Bella, too, had lived all her life independently. She wasn't like his ex-girlfriend, who depended on validation and the continual support of other people to do anything. And she, too, wanted his heart. Did he have one to give?

"Aren't you afraid of giving your heart to her?" Jamie asked now, quietly. This is possibly the most intimate conversation he'd ever had with Grant, and most of that could be attributed to how drunk Grant was. But he was beginning to realize that he wasn't so different from his father. They both had spent decades falling for the same type of woman, the dependent type because those women never demanded anything more than their money. Never demanded them to open up their hearts and change their fucked up beliefs. But true love demanded openness and vulnerability. And true love was worth having, even at that cost.

"Even if I'm afraid of it, that won't make what I feel for her go away." Grant groaned. "At my age, I've made a lot of mistakes and recovered from them, too. Even if this doesn't go the way I hope, I can recover from it. But I'll never be able to live with myself if I don't at least try."

"You could return to the women you had. They always made you feel good." Terrible advice, but what else did one say when one was attempting to do the same?

"Women don't help anymore. Whiskey does, though." Grant smiled at his glass. "Buy me a bottle next time you come. When'll that be? Next year?"

Jamie stood. "I've decided to stay in New York for a while longer."

"That's wonderful, J. I'm really pleased to hear that." There was genuine joy in Grant's tone. "Did you find something here?"

Jamie lowered his head. "Yeah."

He'd found love.

"Mr. Jamie Star." The interviewer, a man in a stern gray pinstripe suit shook hands with him.

Jamie brushed him a courteous smile, then waited for him to sit. "Hello, sir."

After his teaching demo, he was exhausted, but his long day of interviews was only beginning. He had hours to go before he was done meeting all the faculty and students he was supposed to meet today. Then, there would be the obligatory department dinner, where he'd have to schmooze and laugh some more.

"I'm Charlie Rubin, the head of screenwriting in the Department of Dramatic Writing." The interviewer turned his head to Jamie.

"Pleasure to meet you, sir." Smiling nervously, Jamie straightened his posture.

"So, Jamie, tell me about why you want to teach at Tisch School of the Arts? What draws you to us?"

The fact that my girlfriend teaches philosophy in the building down the street.

Really, Bella was the only reason he was interviewing at NYU. He already had an offer from USC after going down there and meeting the faculty last week. The terms were good, the money wasn't bad for a teaching gig, and the job was his. He should be celebrating and packing his bags.

But some part of him didn't want to leave New York. Didn't wanted to leave Bella. She'd become way too important to him over the last few months. So important that the very thought of having to live without her in LA was depressing. Although he'd sworn not to get long-term with her, he was now starting to imagine a future with her.

Together. In New York.

So he'd been grateful when an open position for an adjunct professor for film writing had been advertised at NYU last month. Wouldn't it be perfect if they could both go to work together, spending their morning commute staring into each other's loving eyes rather than the subway crowd? And there was always the potential for sex during lunch break. Or just meeting each other and having lunch together. Even small things like that mattered.

When Charlie looked at his watch, Jamie realized he'd been spacing out for too long. He rattled off the answer he'd meticulously researched and memorized for the interview.

"That's great." Charlie nodded, but his manner of nodding didn't give any clues to what was going on inside his head. "What would you change about the screenwriting course that we currently run, if you were to teach it?"

Jamie swallowed, trying to clear the lump sitting in his throat. This wasn't a tough question and he knew what to say. But suddenly, his nerves shook him.

What if he messed this up? What if he had to leave Bella forever? What if he never heard her voice again? What if, next March, he saw that she'd updated her Facebook status to engaged? What if he got a wedding invitation by mail next September? What if she married, and he became nothing more than a memory to her?

His heart sunk at that last one. He couldn't bear being nothing to her. She was everything to him. He didn't want her getting married to someone else. He didn't want some other man to be holding her hand, kiss her, make love to her. He didn't want another man to take his place in her life.

Because he loved her too much to let her go.

CHAPTER TWENTY-NINE

Grant didn't stay late at work very often. But today was one of those days when he had to.

Since he'd missed dinner, his stomach was jumpy, so he headed to the break room—which took him a while to find since he never went there.

As he pushed the door open, he spied Eve sitting on the counter beside the sink, nursing a cup of coffee. When she saw him, she ended up spilling coffee on herself.

"Sorry. Didn't mean to startle you." He'd have left her alone, but he really needed something for his hunger. Doing his best to make it quick, he pushed the buttons like they were on fire.

Behind him, she quietened. The stillness made her presence inescapable.

Since last week, things had gone back to normal at the office—as normal as they could be while he still loved her. He'd expected Eve to snap at him twice as much as normal, but she'd become completely detached, like she didn't see him anymore, didn't recognize who he was, who he had been to her. Grant wished he could be that detached because everywhere he looked, he only saw her.

"It's nine. Why haven't you gone home yet?" he asked, restlessly tapping the machine. Her presence making him charged.

"I had work to do." She crossed the room, hips swaying seductively. He cursed her mentally. "I should get to it."

It was damn hard to break his gaze from her. She looked so fucking beautiful, it was like stabbing his sore heart with sharp toothpicks. How had he ever thought her ugly? He must've been hallucinating.

He knew for a fact by now that he'd made a terrible, stupid mistake that night.

It had been his ego talking that night. It had been his ego talking the entire time. He didn't want to lose his place in the world, didn't want to lose the shallow feeling of superiority that he felt over other men because he was still desirable to younger women.

The entire week, he'd been trying to find the perfect words to apologize, a grand gesture to revert things to the way they had been. But no words were good enough, no gestures grand enough to apologize for the horrible, mean things he'd said to her.

He could either keep his ego, his shallow sense of desirability, and live in the emptiness he'd been living in. Or he could swallow his pride, accept that he was no longer Eddie Mans, and reach for something more. Something new. Something scary. Something lasting.

"Shoot!" he mumbled, realizing that his candy bar was stuck in the machine.

"It does that from time to time." Coming close to him Eve checked the machine, pushed a few buttons, and waited for a miracle to happen. "Here. It's working now."

The vending machine made a whirring sound and spat out his candy bar. She held it out to him.

"Thanks," he muttered.

The proximity to her made sweat bead on his skin. The coconut scent from her hair tempted him. Her eyes shone like jewels in the darkness. He itched to reach out his hands and stroke her skin.

If things had been different, they could've been cuddling in the corner of some bar, kissing like careless teens.

"How've you been?" he asked because he wanted to know.

"Okay." That coffee mug was still in her hand. She brought it to her lips. "You?"

"Same as usual."

It was awkward pretending to be colleagues again, when every stolen glance, every extra-long exhale indicated that there was more.

"I was an ass that day," he rasped. Not the pretty apology he'd been hoping for, but it was a start. "I'm sorry."

"As long as you know." Coffee gurgled in her mouth. She didn't betray any emotion.

"Eve, I—"

"Don't apologize for being honest. I always suspected you thought of me that way. I wanted to believe you didn't, but thanks for waking me up from that dream." For the first time that week, she met his eyes head-on and he wished she hadn't. "You told me in Montana that a man gets tired of illusions. A woman gets tired of illusions, too."

His throat clenched so tight, Grant was momentarily rendered speechless. "I still want you, baby."

"You think I can't tell? You look at my ass fifteen times a day." A little laugh stumbled out of him. Was he that obvious? "When are you planning on stopping the sexual harassment?"

"When I stop finding you desirable." Desperation swayed his voice.

She bracketed her head with her hands. "I swear; you flip-flop more than Donald Trump. First, you tell me that I'm an aging dinosaur and I need to get Botox, and now you find this aging dinosaur desirable. Pick your side."

He saw her heels hover dangerously close to his foot.

"You have no idea how much I regret what I said that day. It wasn't my finest hour. Just ignore that whole night. I was being…I don't know what I was being."

"You need to do better than that if you want me to take you seriously."

"That was my ego talking. I couldn't admit that I'd fallen for a woman who didn't live up to my standards—or rather, Grant Star's standards." His voice was frayed. "I've been a celebrity, a sex symbol for so long, I forgot there was actually a man beneath the mask. I forgot I had needs and desires that are not the desires the world expects me to have. They're so new, they even confuse me."

Eve blinked, and he sensed a softening of her expression.

"I won't ask you to change yourself again. Never. I love you as you are."

Her neck curved. She strode towards the door.

Blocking her path, Grant planted his hand on the blade of her hip. "Eve, please talk to me. I want to make things right. Tell me what to do. What's the price you want me to pay so we can forget about Saturday night?"

Her fists clenched. "You can't afford it."

"Try me. I'm rich. I have money stashed away in places you don't know."

Slitting her eyes, she growled, "This is not about money."

"If you want me to grovel in front of the board and declare that I'm a sexist bastard, I'll grovel. If you want me to write you one thousand words of apology every day, I will. Just say it."

"Leave me alone."

"That isn't an option."

"I don't want to see you again."

"Not fair. You're all I see these days."

A vexed sigh parted her lips. "What would get you to stop chasing after me, Grant?" Her gaze fell on his chest. "Wait, I already know the answer to that."

She paused as if considering. Placing her coffee mug on the counter, she smiled. He didn't like that smile. It was too suggestive. It did too many things to his heart.

"This is what you want, isn't it? This is what you've always wanted from me." Dexterously, she unknotted his tie. Unbuttoned his shirt. Caressed his chest. Suckled on his shoulder. He went steel hard.

Grant wanted to be honorable. As honorable as an aroused man could be, anyway. "You're letting me off easy."

"No, I'm letting you go. And I'm letting you let me go." His cock had been twitching, but when her hands reached down there and stroked it, it went hard as steel. "In your own words, all you've ever wanted from me is sex. Once you get that, you'll lose interest in me. That's why I'm giving it to you. To free us both from each other."

"It's not that simple."

Lord, she was good. Her hands were magic, drawing pleasure from the core of him. She stole his senses with her touch, and they responded to her manipulation much better than they responded to his commands.

"It is." She shimmied out of her skirt. "I won't forgive you, but I'll fuck with you."

"Did you say fuck?"

She speared his chest with a pointed nail. "So what?"

"Nothing. I just never expected you to say the word." His hand met her soft, round, ass. Grant froze.

Don't let her do it. Be a man. Get her forgiveness first. Oh fuck...

He went still when she smoothed his pants down. He tried to grip her hands with whatever weak self-control he had—tried being the keyword here.

It was like striking a matchstick to the side of the matchbox and praying for no fire.

Since he wasn't a religious man, his prayers weren't answered. It caught fire.

"To hell with it all," Grant murmured.

Let guilt slay him tomorrow. Tonight, he was going to make love to the woman he loved. The only woman he loved.

Not being in the mood to fuss with buttons, he tore her shirt. Unhooking her bra, he let her breasts pour out and then fondled the bare globes. They panted to his touch; soft, beautiful, hot. Her perfectly hard nipples were puckered, calling out to be sucked. He pinched them between his fingers, gave her a little taste of pain, before erasing it with his tongue.

She had succeeded in stripping him down to nothing but briefs. When he discarded his briefs, she gasped. "You manscape?"

"Gotta keep all the twenty-year-olds going down on me happy." Grant grinned sardonically. "And we should close the door."

His body was already holding the door closed. Bending a hand backward, he turned the lock. Click!

Now that was taken care of, he had no reason to hold back. Ripping her panties, Grant skimmed her clit. Eve's lips crashed on his and she bit him hard. Every time he flicked her, he felt her teeth dig deeper into his lips. Maybe he bled. He couldn't tell. He was too engrossed in the moisture growing under his fingers. It wasn't as much as he was used to, though. Still, he dared to circle her entrance with a finger.

"Tell me if it hurts." His finger thrust in and her magnificent softness clamped around it.

Sliding her tongue in and out of his mouth, she stopped to draw a breath and said, "It hurts so bad, I might come."

"I'm serious. This is uncharted territory for me. I've never..." He fought the embarrassment. "...never done this with a woman over thirty-five. You, honey, are definitely menopausal."

"Wait a second." Eve peeled herself away from him and bent down under the sink. An instant later, she was holding up a tube of K-Y Jelly. "That'll help."

Cocking an eyebrow, he inquired, "Why is there lube under the sink?"

She slapped his chest. "We're not the first people having sex in the break room."

"Lord, I love my employees." His laughter was so throaty, it vibrated between the walls.

"Here." She handed him the tube, mortified.

"No. You do it. I'll watch. I've fantasized about this. Seeing you stick a finger up your uptight ass."

She blinked. Swallowed. Grew a little tense. "I...I'm not sure..."

He didn't immediately understand her hesitation. But when she became squeamish, he figured it out. "Sweet Jesus. You've never touched yourself before."

A furious blush bloomed on her cheeks. "I grew up in the sixties, Grant."

"You're almost sixty, too. It's time you learned some self-love, no?"

"Teach me." Her eyes shimmered with fear. She sounded so vulnerable, like a young girl, who was scared of doing something improper.

She was such an interesting contradiction. Grant felt privileged to peel back one more layer of her.

"With my expert instruction, you'll be getting yourself off in no time," he boasted.

Instructing her to go and sit on the counter, where she'd be on a higher surface and he'd be able to see her clearly, he started barking out his orders.

"Go harder. Two fingers."

"Isn't one finger enough—"

"Follow instructions."

It turned him on to watch her red-tipped fingers ride over the seam of her intimate folds and make it wetter. But what turned him on, even more, was the stunning expression on her face, as she discovered herself for the first time.

His cock panted with need. He was desperate to enter, to finally penetrate the impenetrable Eve Rosenberg. But he had to make sure she was okay first. After all, this was a new experience for him, too.

"Three, now," he called out.

"You're a tyrant." Sticking her tongue out like a petulant child, Eve refused to obey.

"Come on," he pushed.

A faraway look crawled up on her face. "Grant, I find myself having stupid thoughts these days."

"Such as?" Grant laid his chin on the inside of his palm, expecting her to narrate a sexual fantasy. It should be interesting to get into her mind.

"I imagine a life where I'm your lover. One of the many you have. I've been judging your kind of life too harshly. Maybe being a little more open won't kill me."

"Eve, you're mad."

Sniffing, she said, "Evidently."

"And, for the record, I sleep with only one intern at a time."

Her fingers stopped wriggling inside her vagina and she drew them out. "That's enough watching. My hands are aching."

His mouth went dry. His cock made the decision. "Get ready, then."

Fishing out a condom, he spotted her flush when he slipped it on.

"You were carrying condoms?" She knocked her heel against a cabinet.

"Stop being a judgmental, woman. I practice safe sex."

Pulling her off the counter, he allowed her to suck in one quick breath before plunging into her. She yelped, her chin meeting his shoulder, her nails knifing his back. Her breath all but disappeared.

"It hurts?" Grant brushed back her hair, which was clinging to her damp face.

"No, I was surprised, that's all. I haven't been filled in a long time. I forgot what that feels like." Angling her hips, she tried to get him deeper inside her.

He pulled in and out, wild, unapologetic stroke after wild, unapologetic stroke. For the most part, she adjusted to his rhythm and accommodated. He should be going easy, but he didn't want to. He didn't know if he'd ever get an opportunity to hold her again. He had to take everything today.

"Sex in your fifties is so much nicer." Her voice was tired, but he heard the note of anticipation in it.

"The fact that you're having sex with me probably helps."

"I'm sure it does." She laughed. Her stomach clenched at that laugh and sent him shooting like a rocket.

He'd imaged this moment a hundred times in his head—the moment when he came inside Eve—but when he finally tumbled over the edge, it triggered something completely unexpected.

Tears.

CHAPTER THIRTY

Candles. Tens of them. Lit up and curving around the room in curly rows.

That was the first thing Bella guessed Jamie would see when he trundled into her studio.

And she was right.

"Why—what the fuck are so many candles doing here?"

Suspiciously, he sniffed the air, which was laced with the scent of sandalwood. Terrified blue eyes roamed over the expanse of her redecorated living room, which had been sprinkled with roses and lit with dozens of aromatic candles.

When they came to a stop on her body, she swore he lost so much air from his lungs that his chest looked concave.

"Holy fuck."

Not the greatest compliment, but it would do.

The candle's glow flickered over the outline of the tight lump in his throat, which grew bigger as he studied what she was wearing.

Bella counted the fact that he didn't raise an eyebrow at what she was wearing as a nod to her taste. His taste, actually.

After all, he'd been the one who'd purchased this slinky black, see-through bodysuit.

Allowing her own gaze to roam suggestively over her barely concealed flesh, she bit her lip as the tips of her rosy nipples budded. "I found it in your cupboard while looking for aspirin the other day. Thought I'd use it."

There was a twitch in Jamie's jaw. "And you're not going to ask me who I bought that for?"

"I know who you bought it for." Seductively throwing her hips side to side, Bella glided to him and twined her fingers with his. Then she sketched a wet line across his smoothly shaved neck with the tip of her tongue. "36D. It fits perfectly."

His uncomfortable pucker slid right off his face, replaced by a wash of color. Pulling at his spikes of hair, he hissed out a breath. "I should've known you were the nosy type."

"You didn't?" Working his buttons, Bella untucked his shirt, her impatient breaths playing against his chest.

"No, I forgot all about it. But I'm glad you found it." Jamie grinned.

Tucking one finger under the flimsy neckline, he eased it down between her breasts. Skimmed her taut bud. Then skittered down to the other aching bud between her legs and nipped it.

The thin slip of mesh shivered under his probing. So did Bella's pulse.

"You look ravishing." His voice rung with passion as he placed his hand on the small of her back.

I feel safe around you, she wanted to say, but that would give him the wrong idea, so she swallowed her words.

Exerting great willpower, Bella led his hand away.

"Lie down on the bed," she instructed, almost pushing him along.

Today was for his pleasure only.

She didn't intend to take anything from him tonight. Only give everything that she could.

"Why?" Two thick, bushy eyebrows moved up in puzzlement.

Her groomed nails, painted red for the occasion, dug into his biceps. "I'm going to give you a massage."

Over the last few weeks, he'd been working on his computer constantly, churning out some script or the other. Often, she'd caught him complaining about muscle pain and pinching his shoulders. So she'd decided to help him out a bit.

"A massage," Jamie articulated, in terse tones.

"Yes. A massage." Bella stripped him gradually—dealing with his belt buckle, peeling away his jeans, then everything underneath. Until he was buck naked.

"What kind of massage is this?" Jamie questioned, angling his chin up as he stepped away from the puddle his clothes had formed on the ground.

"You'll know." Making him lie belly-down on her bed, Bella brought up the blankets to cover the lower half of his body, while she concentrated on the upper half.

Anointing her hands with aromatic oil, she pressed the heels of her palms in circles on both sides of his spine and spread it generously.

His body sighed in relaxation under her kneading fingertips, growing limp. Easing muscles allowed her to plow into them a little deeper.

"Why did you suddenly decide I need a massage, anyway? Not that I'm complaining." He elongated his arms to either side of him, stretching.

"You've been whining about neck pain all week." Patting two fists into the network of knotty muscles under his glass-smooth skin, Bella put her back into it.

"You were listening to that?" Briefly, she spotted the tension in his jaw. Then it faded. "You know, you'd be a good girlfriend. You're so caring."

He tossed it out casually, but it hit her somewhere deep. Her fingers lost their gusto and drifted around tepidly for a bit. Bella felt her throat close. The hard bud of longing inside her itched.

Impervious to the change in her mood, Jamie bolted his eyes shut and sighed softly against the layers of bedding under him. "Yeah, baby. Right there."

Moments later, she found the air in her lungs again. "How does it feel?"

Chin sinking into a deep valley in the pillow, he said, "Good. But it'd feel better if you were straddling my back and pressing your hard nipples into me."

Slapping him for his insolence, Bella continued poking into his skin with her fingertips. "If I do that, I might fracture your hip bone."

His head bobbed up sharply. "Did you just slap me?"

"Um...sorry—"

"Do it again." Folding his hands back, he struck himself on the spot where she had.

"Huh?"

He licked his lips in a sensual gesture. "Do it again. I liked it."

She stilled. "This is a massage. Not foreplay."

That one moment of her hands away from him was all Jamie needed to turn around to the front and flash her a willpower-destroying smile. "It could be both."

A current of desire clouded her mind. His mouth beckoned. Before she knew it, he was pulling her close and she was swinging her legs down either side of his hips, swooping low to his lips. Her eyes drifted shut.

I want to be someone to you. That thought popped out of nowhere, but soon became swallowed up by the ferocious heat of the kiss.

Sensation touched every nerve ending on her lips when his tongue struck them. Under her, his steel-hard erection was starting to creep up and scrape against the skin of her inner thighs.

Torrid kiss after torrid kiss, they went at each other like starved beasts, unwilling to let go of the intimate contact. They traded tongues, moans, and breaths. Tingling heat flowed from him to her, snaking its way down to her moistening core, which purred with longing and dampness.

His hand found its way to her folds, and he pushed the line of mesh covering her slick wetness to the side.

Instead of snapping awake when he skated over the rim of her inner lips, Bella surrendered to him completely. He was that once place in the world where she felt completely safe. Completely wanted.

Snatching a single crimson rose from the ones she'd put at the bedside, Jamie trailed it over her nipples and abdomen and tickled her exposed pussy with it.

The clear blue pools of his eyes regarded her with a challenge.

Blue-eyed devil, she thought to herself as thrill spiked into her.

He continued to finger her, thrusting two fingers into her as his thumb pad played with her. Groaning and moaning, she attempted to perch on his shoulder bone to keep herself from tumbling back.

The pounding of an oncoming orgasm grew more inside her body. Blood rushed to her face, warming her cheeks and shortening her exhales. An unintended scream shot out of her throat, and at that instant, she came apart in every way she could.

Her voice disintegrated into whimpers. Her body into a zillion specks of stardust. Time halted to a single second—this second. The only reminder of reality was a whiff or two of sandalwood that she caught between shaky breaths.

The orgasm burned through her, hot and entirely satisfying. Her entire being luxuriated in the bliss. Folding her eyelids shut, Bella gave herself over to the powerful, all-consuming fall. And it was on his chest that she fell. His rock-solid comfortable chest.

"Love you," she murmured into his chest, without even realizing what she was saying.

Love him? He's leaving for LA in a month. You can't love another happily-never-after.

His arm was stretched over to the bedside, where he was flicking buttons on his phone screen.

Pulling herself off his chest, Bella clubbed him in the head with a pillow. "You're typing texts in the middle of our cuddle?"

"Ouch. Hey. Don't." He cupped the bottom of her head and yanked her back as she charged for a head-butt. "I wasn't messaging. I was checking my recording."

An evil grin fell on his lips and the sound of her aroused, pitchy scream enveloped the room.

Bella colored. "Oh, God. You did not."

"Wanna hear it again?"

"No. Never." Reaching, Bella tried to steal his iPhone from him.

Jamie didn't give it up, though. "But I do. I want to hear that sexy cry every morning and every night. Actually, I think I might make it my new ringtone."

"You. Will. Not. Delete it this instant. Delete. Do you have any idea what'll happen if someone finds out about it? Sex tapes get leaked online all the time. My career as a respectable academic will be ruined if this finds its way onto the internet."

"Nobody will be able to tell it's you." Spooning by her side, Jamie winked. "After all…I'm the only one who's made you come like this."

More embarrassment flooded her. "Delete."

Jamie paused for a heartbeat. "Ok. But only if you promise me one thing."

She carried a warning glower in her eyes as she said, "I'm not in a negotiating mood."

"Then get into one." Jamie dangled the phone in front of her eyes. "Because otherwise, you can forget about me deleting this."

If she was a dragon, she'd be breathing fire from her nostrils. "Are you threatening me?"

"I believe I am."

Hell. That cocky tone. She couldn't win against that cocky tone. Ever.

She flailed her oil-soaked hands against his ribs. "Fine. What do you want me to promise?"

"Remember that apartment in Brooklyn we saw together? The one owned by my friend."

"How could I forget that?"

"It was incredibly sweet of you to give up on that because you wanted to kiss me without any expectations. Trust me when I say this, but that's the most selfless thing anyone has ever done for me." He waited for her to catch up. "I know how much that house meant to you. I know how much your dream of being a homeowner means to you. It isn't fair for me to take your dreams away, not for the sake of one kiss."

"I don't regret it," Bella said.

"I'm glad you don't. But I do. Thanks to being with you, I've overcome my heartbreak. So there's no reason to hold yourself back on my account. I want you to promise me that you'll consider that house again. That you'll buy it if that's what you want."

"I can't—"

"You can. I'm telling you to. I've set up a meeting with Gage for this weekend, so meet him and finalize the deal."

"Jamie, why are you doing this?"

"You've changed my life in more ways than you can imagine," Jamie said. "Please. Let me change your life in the only way I know how to. Give me this chance."

Bella dropped her shoulders. She should've refused. And she would've if it had only been a house. But it was the place where she'd first kissed Jamie. And she wanted to own that piece of memory forever. It was greedy to want so much of him, but she knew there was no other way to hold onto what they had apart from this small opportunity that Jamie was giving her. Did he know that, too? Did he want her to remember him, too? Had his feelings, too, grown beyond infatuation into something that kept him up at night?

"Alright," she said slowly. "I'll consider it. The price is still the same?"

Jamie nodded, a smile pushing into his cheeks. "And now that we have an agreement, I'll delete this file. God knows I'll miss your voice."

CHAPTER THIRTY-ONE

When Eve slid into his office on Monday evening, Grant's heart almost dropped out of his chest. Grant's heart contracted painfully as she strode towards his desk. She didn't look happy. For both their sakes, he hoped she wouldn't tell him that she wanted to leave. Because he couldn't bear it.

He missed her. He missed her laughter against his cheek, her sarcastic wisecracks, her warmth, her flushed skin under his hands. He missed kissing her, taking trips with her, expanding his horizons with her. He missed the light in his life that she brought.

So when she'd let him have her on Friday, he'd taken the offer without debate. But he was realizing the error of his ways now. In taking her, he'd confirmed everything she held true about him—namely, that all he wanted from her was sex.

But that wasn't the case anymore. He wanted more from her. He wanted her forgiveness, to start with. He wanted their relationship back.

"What's the matter?" His heart thundered.

He'd been worried all weekend about today. That hot interlude they'd shared still made him tingle. He'd never have pegged Eve as the sexually spontaneous type, but the woman was so full of surprises.

She'd blown his mind, but she'd also shown him her vulnerable side. He liked seeing that part of her more than anything else.

"I had to give you this." She pressed an envelope onto his desk. Dread filled his gut.

"I didn't ask for any documents," Grant said, more breathless than he'd like to have been.

"This is my letter of resignation." Three grenades couldn't have put a crack in her poker face.

"Eve, sit down. Let's talk." Grant held his voice steady—a tough feat when she was shaking him from inside.

"There's nothing to talk about. I've already made my decision."

He groaned. He didn't need her being difficult again. As it was, he'd been nursing too many glasses of Jack Daniels in the darkness of his room this weekend and he was not completely recovered.

Taking a step back, she held his gaze for longer than he was accustomed to. A spark flickered between them. Died just as quickly.

"Baby, sit down," he pleaded. "We need to talk about what happened Friday night."

Her amber eyes exploded into the color of fire. "Friday night never happened."

Grant clicked his tongue. Being difficult was probably embedded in her DNA.

Drawing to his feet, he went over to her side and sandwiched her hands between his. "It most definitely did." His top buttons were open, so he only had to tug his shirt to the side to show the faint bruises coloring his neck. "Proof."

She blew out a groan. "That's not why I'm quitting."

"That's exactly why you're quitting. It's written all over your face." Cocking a brow, he tossed her letter into the cylindrical metal dustbin at the base of his desk. "But I can't let you go."

"How can you let me stay at the company after what happened yesterday? I can't even look at myself in the mirror anymore. Who was I? What was I doing?" Her honey eyes were stormy—full of hurt and rage. "I acted so unprofessionally. I was half-afraid you were going to threaten to sue me for harassment today."

"Catch me suing anyone for sexual harassment." Grant guffawed.

"But I'd like you to explain why you suddenly decided it was a good idea to seduce me in the break room."

"Because I was hopped up on coffee and I'd left my brain in a bin somewhere, obviously." She coiled her fingers into a tight fist.

"The real reason, please," he insisted.

"Fine. I wanted to fuck you. No, I needed to. Do you think you're the only one who has been longing for sex since we started dating? I've yearned for it twice as much as you. But I can't own my sexuality the way you can, and I didn't want to get hurt, so I kept it to myself." She downcast her eyes. "I hate that side of me. It's embarrassing, at this age."

"I like that side of you. It's beautiful, exciting, and turns me on." Grant cased her face with his hands. Immediately, goosebumps rose on her skin.

She frowned. "I can't do this, Grant. It's not good for me. You're not good for me."

"Orgasms keep you young, didn't you know?"

Rolling her eyes, she tipped her head back. "You know what the funny thing is? I almost believe all the lies you tell me. You're an arrogant, misogynistic bastard, and somehow, I keep finding ways to rationalize everything you do. When I'm with you, I lose all my senses. You have that effect on a lot of women. As much as I'd like to think I'm above your charm, I'm not. I'm just another woman who succumbed to you."

"No, you're the woman who made me succumb to you."

Her skin warmed under him. Chewing her lip, she said, "I'm quitting."

"You can't. Carla goes to school here." Grant tried to play the child card.

"I'm moving to another company, not another city."

"I'm not letting you go."

"You don't have a reason to reject my resignation."

Even though she was furious, she didn't withdraw her hand from between his. So she still wanted him. Good.

"Oh, I have a very good reason." Pulling her by his arm, Grant lined up their chests. "I'm in love with you."

He expected her to cry, to jump in joy at his declaration of love.

Instead, she went off like an angry firework. "Love? Do you even know what love is? Do you know it means to love someone forever? It means accepting the fact that they'll grow old, ugly, sick, irritable, weak, stupid, and dependent at some point. It means accepting their faults, their weaknesses, their humanness, not trying to Botox them away."

"Eve, I—" He tried to interrupt, but she put a finger on his lips.

"All you care about is looking good. Being powerful. Preserving your image. Having a pretty face hanging on your arm. Well, I'm not young enough, or beautiful enough, or sexually competent enough to keep your kind of love."

Disappointment squeezed out of her voice and pierced him where he was weakest.

She was right. She was so right. He didn't know what love was. Because no one had shown it to him before.

"I won't cheat on you. I was faithful to my wife." He did his best movie star voice, the one that melted women's hearts.

Eve pouted. "It's not your faithfulness I worry about. I just don't want you to wake up someday and grimace at the age spots and sagging breasts next to you. I don't want to feel inadequate and insecure because I can't meet your unrealistic expectations."

"I can't make you believe me, but I'll tell you this," Grant said. "Since we started going out, I've changed. I may have been very critical of every flaw on your face in the beginning, but slowly, I began to adore them. My concept of beauty became deeper. I hated it, though. You were what I wasn't supposed to find beautiful, but I did."

Eve wasn't giving up. "It's not only about my appearance. I'm very different from the kind of woman you're used to. I can't have sex-on-demand like a thirty-something, nor am I going to be able to fulfill your very traditional expectations of what a woman my age is supposed to do." She blinked like she was going through a list in her head.

"You've already defied all my expectations, so let's just say I'm prepared."

She carried on like he'd not spoken at all. "I'll still be working, obviously, but I'm quitting this job because—"

"No."

"I can't stay. Even if I stay with you, I can't stay here. It would be too awkward. I think I'll finally start the business I've been planning on starting."

"I'll hire you," Grant promised. "And I'm glad you said you'll stay with me."

"I didn't say that."

"Do you still love me?"

He expected her to shirk away and be wishy-washy, but she said, "Sadly, I do."

He took a deep breath. "I love you, too. It took me a while to realize but...but that's because I've never been in love before. Not like this." He gave her hand a squeeze. "Eve, believe me when I say this because it truly comes from my heart. Even when you have twice as many lines on your face, and you're half a minute from death, I'll love you."

Eve's face relaxed, but she was still in fighting mode. "This is not over, yet. I want you to make amends to my daughters about what you said to them."

"I already did."

"Really?" Speechless, her jaw unhinged itself.

"Oh yeah. And I'll do anything else you want me to do. I'll jump any hoops you put me through because you are worth it. You're more than worth it." He walked towards her. "Someday, I'm gonna look back and think, how in the hell did I ever find a woman like you? How did I find someone who could make a man out of me?"

"And I'm gonna look back and think how I found a man who could coax the woman out of me."

They exchanged a brief, emotional gaze before the heat of the moment sealed their lips together in a perfect, sensual union. Warm. Pure. And beautiful.

CHAPTER THIRTY-TWO

Deadline days made every writer nervous. But this deadline day might just be the easiest in his life.

As Jamie trailed Bella to her apartment, after dinner with her friends, he gripped the gift in his hand tighter. He'd held out giving her his gift, because the right occasion hadn't popped up, and he wanted her to be in a place where she could read leisurely.

Trekking up the stairs, she opened the door with him behind her. The flap of heat from the radiator felt heavenly after freezing out in the December cold.

"Right now, I wanna give a big hug to whoever invented heaters." Unwrapping her red scarf from around her neck, Bella tossed it on the couch. Her coat went on the coat stand next. "It's a lifesaver."

"It's colder than usual out there." Jamie dropped his jacket, too, stripping down to his cardigan.

Sneaking a glance at the green wrapped rectangular box in his hand, Bella raised an eyebrow. "You've been carrying that around forever. Are you actually going to give it to me or not?"

"Sorry. I was waiting for the perfect moment. Happy birthday, angel. Congratulations on turning thirty-five." He added a long, hot kiss to the gift.

"Turning thirty-five is not such a great feeling for a single woman, you know." Bella tumbled onto the couch.

"At the risk of sounding cliché, I'm gonna tell you that age doesn't matter."

Frisking the package, Bella put a puzzled frown on her face. "What's in it? A book?"

"Open and see."

Tearing it open impatiently, Bella lost her balance and tottered when she saw the title on the front of the spiral-bound book. "*Love Me Like You Do Part 2?*"

Tears clung to her lashes as she flipped the pages and made an attempt to read the words through wet eyes. "Oh my goodness—you made them get married."

"You wanted me to." He kneeled down beside her.

He was itching to pull out the second surprise he'd planned for her. But he wanted to wait for the right moment. The timing was crucial before he told her that he was planning to stay with her in New York. "Should I pour you some wine while you read?"

"Wait—" Leaving the script on the couch, Bella tucked him between her warm, cozy arms. "Thank you. I'm speechless—I don't know what to say. Nobody's ever done something so special for me before."

"You're a special woman, so you deserve something special," he said. "I hope you like the story, though."

"If you wrote it, I'll definitely like it. I've not liked anything you wrote. I'm your biggest crazy fangirl, remember?"

Their first awkward coffee at Grumpy Coffee and Bakery flowed into his mind, and he released a smile. That felt like so long ago. It'd only been six months since then. Six months in which they'd gone from enemies to professional acquaintances to friends to lovers. Looking back, it was unbelievable how serendipitous their meeting on Tinder had been.

It was even more fiction-like than any rom-com meet-cute he'd ever written. Maybe they'd always been meant to be.

"Do you remember what I told you when we first met at the coffee shop?" Their faces were close now, the tips of their noses brushing.

"That you wanted my body? I was totally weirded out by that." Her breath carried traces of sugar and cinnamon from the cinnamon roll she'd consumed earlier. It wafted over his skin.

"No, I told you that you were the one I'd been looking for." He gulped, his fingers skating down a smooth strand of her hair.

This is the moment. Do it.

"Mmmm. Yeah. You did say something like that. What about it now?"

Jamie dug his hands into his pocket. The moment was here.

"I meant it."

I'm going to stay with you, Bella.

The words sounded clear and decisive in his head, but when he tried to get them out, he was interrupted by Bella's mobile ringtone. "Sorry, it's my real estate agent. Gotta get this one."

"You decided to buy the condo?" he asked.

Bella nodded. "I couldn't resist. And Gage was very sweet to me. He explained everything and said I can move in next month. I got my real estate agent to check the contract and everything out. I'll sign tomorrow if he gives me the okay."

Bella muttered "Hello," and Jamie smiled, busying himself with pouring wine. Well, he was glad she had got what she wanted. Now that there was a possibility that he might be visiting her more often, he was even more excited for her to move in there. He crossed his fingers that everything might go smoothly.

But that bubble was popped quickly when Bella's face turned to a ghostly white in front of his eyes.

"Oh, I see...I have to reconsider this...I'll call you,"

Then all of a sudden it hit Jamie. He'd forgotten about that completely. The fact that he was paying half the price. That was supposed to be a secret. He'd thought he could convince her to work with his real estate agent who'd keep that information from her. But between his interviews and screenwriting, there had been no time to do that.

"Jamie." Bella's voice was cold as ice. "You lied to me. You said I could buy the house with my own money, that it'd be mine, but it was never going to be mine, was it?"

"I can explain." Hurriedly, Jamie sprung to his feet.

"Start explaining, then." The script lay open and ignored. Bella's attention was completely on him now. "Was this your plan from the beginning?"

"I wanted to help you out."

"I'm not a charity for you to donate to!" Bella screamed. "I didn't ask for your help. I wanted to buy this house on my own. With my own money. I wanted something that would belong only to me, that nobody could take from me."

"It would belong only to you," Jamie assured. "I paid the difference to Gage already. Once your down payment is cleared, the house will be all yours. It will belong only to you."

"But as long as I live there, I'll never be able to forget that you'd paid for half of it. I'd feel like a leech living there. I would never be able to cut my ties with you completely. This isn't what I wanted." Her voice was low and breathy.

Jamie tried to put a hand on her shoulder, but she shrugged him off. "Baby, it isn't a big deal."

"It's a big deal for me! I don't want to become like my mother."

"What's that supposed to mean?" He had heard that her mother was abusive, but this and that didn't seem connected in any way. Was there something he'd missed?

"My mother was a co-dependent woman." Tears glinted at Bella's eyes. He'd made her cry. He felt like shit. "She always lived off the charity of men whose love was unstable. One day, they'd move her into a mansion and profess their love, the next month, they wanted her to move out so they could move their new mistress in."

Jamie stopped. Didn't that sound just like him? A man professing his love and buying her a house? But she had to know, she had to see that he wasn't like that. He *really* loved her.

"Bella, I don't see you like that," he said. "I won't ask you to move out. I can't. As I said, it'll be your house—"

Bella interrupted him before he could say anything more. Her emotions were spinning out of control. She was cracking her knuckles angrily, and Jamie had no idea about how to defuse the situation he'd set off.

"That's what you say now," she said. "But you'll change your mind once you see other women. What am I to you, anyway? You sure you won't regret dropping five hundred thousand on a three-month fuck buddy?"

"You're not just a fuck buddy." Jamie gathered all his courage and put them behind his words. "I think...I've fallen in love with you."

"You *think*?" Scorn dripped from her voice, though she was taken aback by his confession, too. "And what'll happen when you *think* otherwise?"

"I won't think otherwise."

"I don't trust you," Bella replied, instantly.

It cut him deep. Jamie knew he hadn't started out being the most reliable person, but couldn't she see that he was not a jerk at least?

"If you respected me, you'd have told me the truth and let me decide instead of giving me false hope. But you wanted me to feel indebted to you, didn't you? Like your past girlfriends. Maybe that's why you bought them things. So they'd always feel like they owed you something."

"Bella, that's unfair," Jamie said.

"Is it?" She exhaled. "I mean, can't you see it, Jamie? How this will change everything? Say you suddenly show up a few months later and beg me for a hookup, how can I refuse? How can I refuse the guy who bought me a whole damn apartment? I'll always be your kept woman like my mother was."

He hadn't considered that angle.

"I'm sorry." Jamie raised a shoulder blade, expecting Bella to calm down. "I didn't think that far. But trust me, I had no intention of controlling you or using you for sex."

"I told you when we started this that I wanted you to end things cleanly in January."

That hit Jamie like a truck slamming into his face. He realized he hadn't told her about the job interview and everything else.

"And if I don't want to?" he asked.

Bella's eyes widened in shock. Horror. Crap. That had come out all wrong like he was expecting her to continue their sexual relationship.

"I will end it, then," Bella said, clasping her hands. "In fact, I'll end it right now."

"Bella?" It bled to drag her name out of his throat. The pained, horrified expression she wore didn't help one bit. "Let's not do this."

He tried to close the gap between them. She didn't let him, shifting further away from his grasp. "No, Jamie. I can't do this anymore. It was wonderful, but I realize now that I was stupid. I'm not the sort of woman who can do these types of relationships without getting hurt."

"Don't be angry at me, Bella. I didn't want to hurt you…I didn't know this would hurt you. Let's take everything back? Start over again. I'll look for a new house—"

"It doesn't matter. You're leaving anyway. I just realized how stupid I was, for having a three-month affair with you. In the end, I've ended up like my mother."

"You're not—"

"Have a great Christmas. I think it's better if we don't meet again." She waved and turned back as if she'd never said anything. And he could tell from the way she held her shoulders that she wasn't going to talk anymore. Even if he confessed now, it wouldn't make any difference. Bella needed time to process everything, and even then, there was no guarantee she'd forgive him.

Jamie didn't know how he kept his feet on the ground. He just somehow did. And somehow, he even managed to drag them away from her.

Distant. Cold.

He realized she didn't love him. She'd never said she loved him. She still didn't.

"Goodnight." He turned on his heel, not sure she'd heard that.

CHAPTER THIRTY-THREE

Even as tears streamed down her face in rivulets, Bella refused to give in to the urge to run after Jamie, crush him in an embrace, and profess her love to him. What would she say to him, anyway? What could she say that wouldn't make her sound pathetic? She could tell him she loved him, but she couldn't command him to love her back in the same way or stay with her forever. He had said he loved her. And that had given her so much hope. But it was clear from his actions that love didn't mean the same thing to the two of them.

It was meant to happen, Bella reasoned. If not today, then ten days later.

She knew he didn't want messy entanglements. He had his writing. He could hook up with anyone anytime. That was the life he wanted—simple, commitment-free.

She couldn't tell him to give up his career in LA to stay here with her, and she couldn't quit her job to move either, especially if he didn't want her there.

The worst part of loving one-sidedly was the helplessness. Watching him walk away and not being able to say anything convincing to make him stay. No matter how badly she wanted him, there was only one way for this to work—him loving her back and agreeing to stay in New York. That was as likely to happen as a blue moon.

Growing smaller, his form disappeared from the street outside her window, along with all the hope in her body.

Discomfort would fade, she consoled herself. Time would erase memories. One day, she'd forget his face, his voice, his presence. One day she'd forget that she'd ever loved.

Drying the tears plugged into her eyes, Bella took a brave step inside her bedroom. His script was still at her home. She couldn't find the courage to throw it away.

So she ended up reading it through the night.

The next morning, her head felt clearer. She even managed to get up at the time she usually did, and make breakfast and dress up for work, before remembering that the winter break had already started. Just a week ago, she had been full of excitement to spend her vacation time with Jamie, the last few days before he vanished forever. She'd wanted to make them magical. Special.

But now there was nothing but empty, boring days to look forward to. She thought of calling someone to unload her agony on them but didn't want to bother Ashley with her problems. Ashley must be busy with her newborn daughter. Given the hour, Kat must be at work, too, so she sat around on her couch in her work clothes and stared at the ceiling, firing sigh after empty sigh at it.

Before she knew it, the pain that she'd stuffed into a cage inside her heart burst through its bars. She started crying. It wasn't a pretty kind of crying, with little sniffles and one streak of tears. This was all-out sobbing. Weeping. She even fell off the couch. It was that intense.

Stop, she yelled at herself. *Don't become like her.*

She may have broken up with Jamie, but she wasn't going to let it affect her life. She wasn't going to wallow in the misery like her mother. She was stronger than that. Last night, that had seemed doable. But today, she was stunned by the realization of how deeply she had loved him. Why was she always falling for unavailable men? This was her problem. This was why she could never have any happiness.

Her brain, being the torture chamber that it was, replayed all her happy moments with Jamie. The script he'd written for her sat on the coffee table like a giant elephant in her living room. When she'd reached the end yesterday, she'd been so happy. But now, she wanted to burn the darned thing. Because it was a reminder of what she wanted to forget.

It was also giving her self-doubt. She remembered how many times Jamie had apologized last night, the way he'd seemed genuinely surprised at her anger. She might have been too harsh on him. But she was just protecting her heart, right? She had to protect her heart. If she let him walk all over her like Bryan, she could never come back from it.

When Bella had exhausted all her tears, she finally called her estate agent and told him she didn't want to buy the house. He sputtered into a series of coughs. She was certain she'd ruined his morning coffee with her phone call.

"You're passing on an apartment this fine?" he screamed into her ear. "You've been hunting for a house like a possessed woman all year and now you're throwing away your golden opportunity?"

"I can't afford it," Bella replied.

"Why not? Someone else paid half of it. It's well within your budget now. And the owner is keen to sell it to you. You just need to sign a bunch of papers and it'll be yours. You're at the finish line."

Bella heaved an exasperated breath. "I told you. I want to buy the apartment on my own."

"You could always pay this..." The real estate agent shuffled papers in the background. "Jamie Star...the money he put in. He hasn't asked for the house to be transferred to him or asked for any part of the property, from what I can see."

"As I said, I don't have that kind of money."

"Bella, this is a free house." The agent's voice was testy now. "If you sign the papers, he cannot legally claim the house as his. There's nothing here he could use against you to take the house from you."

"I'll still feel indebted to him, though," Bella said. "I don't know what he was thinking. We're not really friends. I have no idea why he would even do this." Unless he wanted to keep her at his beck and call forever. Something ugly twisted inside Bella's heart at that thought.

That kind of manipulation wasn't something the Jamie she'd known would be capable of. He was confused, sure. He was scared, sure. But he wasn't controlling. He'd been flaky, but he'd never been mean or possessive or controlling.

But what if that was a front? What if under that façade of niceness, he was just like the men in her mother's life? The thought knocked the ground from under her feet. And she knew this was her fear speaking. It was casting an illusion over the reality, distorting the Jamie she knew into someone else. She knew him. She'd heard him. She'd been with him. She'd had sex with him. He wasn't that kind of person.

"Listen, this is my advice as a professional," her agent's voice continued to buzz in her ears. "Why don't you cool off for a few days? Think this over again. You might see things differently in a week or two. You really have nothing to lose here."

"I've already thought it over," Bella snapped, irritated. "I don't want this house. I can't depend on a man's charity. I have more self-respect than that."

"It's not charity." The agent cleared his throat. "He must really love you. Don't see a lot of men buying their girlfriend apartments, not even the rich ones. Trust me, I've been in this business for a long time."

"He doesn't love me," Bella protested, even as she started to remember Jamie telling her that he did last night. He'd written the script for her; he'd said he loved her...maybe he wanted to say more. But she'd never given him the chance.

"Then why would he go so far for you?" the agent said. "There's a limit to charity, too."

She'd never imagined she'd be getting scolded by her real estate agent. But maybe the guy knew her better than anyone. He knew her most desperate dreams and desires. He knew what kind of future she wanted to build. And while she didn't trust anyone's opinion but her own, objectively, what he said did make sense.

Her mother's lovers had never bought her houses. They'd just let her stay at theirs, always under the threat of eviction. The house was always theirs. She was always theirs. A possession.

Jamie hadn't done that. He'd wanted the house to be hers. Not only that, he'd wanted them to be equals. He could've easily paid all the money, but he'd wanted this to belong to both of them. And he'd left the final decision up to her. If she took this house, it could only be under one condition. She wanted him with it.

"Okay. Give me a few days. I have to do a few things. I'll call you back with my decision next week."

"I'm glad you're being objective about this," the agent said, then he disconnected.

Finding Jamie's number (which she thankfully hadn't deleted yesterday in a fit of rage), Bella typed furiously.

There's something I forgot to tell you and I need to say it now. I'm going to your apartment. Please be there.

Bella didn't expect a reply. Jamie would be too raw to reply. If he wasn't getting stoned somewhere, that is.

Thirty messages and hours later, Bella was outside Jamie's apartment, freezing into an ice sculpture. Jamie was not at home. Her calls went unanswered. No matter how many times she buzzed, nobody answered.

Bella understood that he needed time to get over what had happened. But she was afraid that if she gave him too much time, he'd get over her.

Bella: I'm waiting outside. Please come before I get frostbite. P.S. I love you.

Moments later, he replied.

Jamie: I didn't ask you to come.

Bella: I want to apologize for what happened. Talk to me.

Jamie: Can't talk now.

Bella: I'm not going anywhere. If you won't talk to me, at least let me see you're OK.

She expected him to answer curtly, but seconds later, he sent a photo of him with another woman. His hand was slung over her bare shoulder. Silicone boobs spilled from the V of her halter neck. Jealousy and possessiveness dug their talons into her.

Jamie: I'm OK. Great, actually. Made a new friend.

Her first instinct was to revert to her usual mental narrative. *I attract cheaters, he's a loser, he cheated on me, etc.* But she had come here deciding to trust him. And, upon closer inspection, she realized Jamie's hair was shorter in the photo. It must be an old pic. She wasn't possessive, but she hated seeing him with another woman.

Bella: You moved on fast.

She hadn't wanted to write that in a message. She'd wanted to tell him face to face. But desperate times called for desperate measures.

Jamie: Go home.

That was the last message from him.

CHAPTER THIRTY-FOUR

She'd buzzed his apartment fifteen times. Bella Hopkins was one hell of a persistent woman. Didn't she know how to give up?

"Bella, get the message. I don't want to see you right now," Jamie yelled into his home security system.

"I'm sorry, Jamie," came a familiar voice. "I know I was unfair to you yesterday. Please. Just let me in. I want to apologize."

Jamie checked the picture on the tiny screen. His control was slipping from him already. But he didn't care. He wanted so much to hold her in his arms. He'd known she'd see sense if he gave her time, and she'd come through for him. She hadn't taken his heart and run away with it. She had sorted out her emotions like a boss and she wasn't the type to blame her mistakes on other people. He admired her so much at this moment. If it had been him, it'd have taken him a lot longer to get to this point.

But right now, he really couldn't see her. After last night, he had gotten drunk as a fish. He smelled of alcohol and sweat from dancing at the club, and if she saw him now, he was sure she'd change her mind and go back home.

But when she said, "Just hear me out," once more, he caved.

"What's your deal? Why're you here at nine-fucking-am?" Jamie barked, as she glided into his apartment, smelling like a fresh meadow of flowers.

He really, really hadn't wanted to see her at his doorstep before he'd had a chance to shower. But when did the world ever follow his commands? At least he'd brushed his teeth.

"You smell." Bella pinched her nose, gagging. Sleep deprivation had her eyes looking like a panda's, but somehow, she still managed to make his heart drum. Damn her.

"That's a great way to earn my forgiveness. Insult me," he said, snarky.

He staggered back when she slipped her head under his chin. It was too easy to allow her warm, hard skull to press on his chest. Hope boomed through his alcohol-dulled senses.

Her tear-soaked lashes slanted up. It had been scarcely twenty-four hours since he'd seen her blue eyes, but they seemed so different. "I'm sorry for what happened. I never meant to hurt you. I just had a lot of experience with men who try to control women by taking care of them when I was young. I thought you were like them."

"I told you I wasn't."

"Yes. I believe you now." The tip of her nose rubbed his ribs through his thin sweatshirt "Also, I want to tell you that I love you, too. I'm sure of it. You meant it when you said it, too, right?"

"Of course I did." Jamie embraced her and damn, it felt so good to be able to hold her like this, to have his body pressed against hers. They belonged together.

"I'm sorry for not trusting you. My childhood keeps interfering with my relationships. You'll have to be patient with me. I promise I'll eventually see sense."

"It's alright, Bella. Don't be so hard on yourself." Dragging a hand through his hair, he stifled the spectrum of emotions bubbling inside him. "Can I tell you something ridiculous I did last week?"

"Did you finally follow my recipe and bake a revenge cake?"

"No, but I go a job in New York. At your university. I'll be teaching screenwriting there part-time starting this summer." Better make this clear right now.

"Jamie...why?" Bella's eyes were filled with tears. Fat drops rolled down her cheeks. "I always thought you were flaky, but you've been making more effort than me to make this work. I judged you wrongly. I'm so sorry."

He smoothed his hand over her hair, relishing the silky feel of them beneath his fingers. This was heaven. "I love you. Of course, I'll make an effort. It's the least I can do."

She trembles in his arms. "I don't even know what to say...I'm speechless. Wait, no, you can't do that. You can't stay in New York. Your career's in Hollywood. I don't want you to sacrifice your career for me."

"I'm not sacrificing anything. Scripts have long development processes. I don't have to be at the set all the time. I could come and go, depending on whether I have work or not. There's no reason for me to hang around in LA all the time."

"I love you so much." She had tears in her eyes.

"I love you, too." He rested his head on hers. "And I should have said it earlier, but I was scared, too. I didn't think you loved me back, because you were already talking about us breaking up."

"But now you know I do."

"Thank you." Her arms tightened around him. They let the silence wash over them for a few minutes, wanting nothing more than to be enveloped in each other's warmth. Jamie wished the moment would never end. "I was thinking this morning...since you paid for the house, too, if I buy it, I want you to move in with me. Of course, only if you want to."

"Is that really what you want?" Jamie asked, surprised at her sudden request. He hadn't considered moving in with her so quickly, but when she said it, something clicked in his heart. It felt right. He had no doubts or reservations left.

"Yes, it's really what I want." She rid herself of her sweater. Under it, she wore the T-shirt Rosie had given her. It read Miss Gorgeous. "All morning I've been thinking about how much I've been living in the past. My mother is dead and gone, but her shadow constantly haunts my life. I feel like if I don't change now, I'll forever be a person trapped in the past." A small pause later, she added, "I'm glad I met you. You may not realize it, but you've helped me become a better person."

"Same here, angel." Jamie planted a kiss on top of her head. "I was being controlled by my own fears and heartbreaks, and I felt so powerless, I wanted to control everything around me. But I surrendered to you, to our love, and my life has changed because of that."

Suddenly, realization dawned on him. He wasn't scared of heartbreak anymore. More importantly, he wasn't scared of having his heart broken by her. Because she was the woman he'd chosen. And even if it didn't work out, their time together would always remain magical. He wouldn't regret this. He would always cherish this.

Taking off her scarf, shoes, and gloves, Bella set them on his couch. Her eyes met his in a pleading gaze. "I'm only human. I'm flawed. I can't make all the right choices all the time. Sometimes, I act out of fear. I hurt the people I love without meaning to."

Fiddling with her jeans, she popped the top button open. Instant lust speared into him.

"I take it we're moving onto the eighteen-plus part of your apology now?" he said, with a disapproving glare.

"Pretty much."

"As much as I want to make love to you, I cannot be so horrible as to do that while I'm smelling like this." The end of his eyebrow lifted to a sharp point. "I'll take a shower and be back."

Smoothing her jeans down her legs, she struggled for a bit before they came off. His heart pitter-pattered against his ribs. "Let's take that shower together."

He cupped her face. "I think I'll enjoy being able to see you and hold you whenever I want."

"Not as much as me." Bella swallowed.

Finally, her fingers tucked under the bottom of her T-shirt, and she lifted it over the top of her head. Jamie's lungs contracted at the sight of her in just a beige T-shirt bra. Her tits strained against the tight hold of the cups until she unhooked her bra. Throwing it on the floor, she let her breasts pour over his chest freely. Jamie got an instant hard-on.

Something solid pushed into the side of his thigh. Her knee.

She removed the last piece of clothing on her—her cotton panties.

Visually cataloging every detail of her body—the angry swell of her breasts, her lush, pouty lips, the dangerous curve of her hips, her big booty—Jamie got harder. And then it became a battle. A battle to not kiss her. To not touch her and feel those heavenly hips glide under his hands. To not cup her huge breasts and tease her nipples into aching desperation.

And this wasn't a battle he wanted to win. Jamie shrugged out of his clothes, leading her to the shower. The huge rainfall showerhead rained thick streams of water over both their heads. A warm current sizzled between them, shocking him with the feeling of something special. Bella broke her gaze from his neck and planted it on his eyes.

Her hand encircled his wrist before he had the opportunity to move. She descended onto his lips, and their lips coupled.

While he'd expected this kiss to be special, the fireworks that exploded in his brain were phenomenal. She pressed her boobs into his chest and there was something so right about her skin on his. All the words, the zingers, the clever, witty one-liners in his vocabulary failed him in that instant. There were no words, no turn of phrase clever enough to describe something so pure and deep.

Withdrawing from her mouth, he worshipped her curves with his fingers, taking greedy handfuls of her flesh, suckling it, stroking it, sliding his tongue over it. There was no way he could have enough of her. Not in an eternity.

"Jamie, can I ask you to promise me something?"

"Mmmm." He groaned between her legs.

"Promise that you'll always..." Lacing her hands between spikes of his hair, she shivered. "Love me like you do."

"I will always. Promise."

EPILOGUE

On the eighth of March, Jamie attended a wedding. Decked in grand décor, the gardens outside had been groomed to look like a miniature version of heaven. White, cream and beige reflected the couple who'd be celebrating their marriage here on this day.

No, that couple didn't include him.

It was Grant and Eve.

Jamie pressed his chest to stifle the powerful emotion that rose up to his throat. He doubted he'd feel as happy at his own marriage as he felt today. When Grant had told him that he was planning to get married, Jamie hadn't expected it to happen so soon. Actually, it wouldn't have happened this soon if Bella hadn't been willing to let Eve use her venue reservation.

And Eve was the last woman he'd have imagined his dad ending up with. She wasn't tight, blonde, or twenty. But she was the right woman. If she could turn Grant from a commitment-phobic, I'll-bang-anything-with-a-pulse player to committed family man overnight, she must be.

Grant was a different man these days. Kind, loving, and warm—the father Jamie remembered from his childhood.

All he wanted to do was hang around Eve and her girls. Even now, they were giggling over some private joke, in their happy little bubble, blissfully ignorant of all the guests.

It was impossible to be in their presence and not feel the love.

"Have this one, it's really good." His internal gushing went up in smoke at the sound of Bella's voice. Mouth stuffed with canapes, she tried to feed him some.

Bella's pastel dress draped over her unabashedly curvy figure, which he'd grown to love more, over the last few months. Big round pearls sat on her earlobes. Her jaw moved constantly, as she chewed.

"I'm okay." He wasn't feeling like eating.

"These are the best canapes I've ever had," she mused. "Hi!" Waving to Carla and Alana—his new step-sisters, Bella grinned.

Jamie had met them a few months ago. They were a lot younger than him, but he'd found some common ground with them, which was a good start.

"Hi." Carla came over, while Alana continued to chat with her boyfriend. Spotting the canape in Bella's hand, she said, "They're so good, aren't they?"

Bella licked her lips. "The best."

"I better grab some more." Giving Jamie a pat on the back, she vanished. "Catch you later."

"She's nice." Bella gave an approving nod in her direction. "And funny, too. She was making me laugh all through the ceremony."

"Figures. She's a comedian."

"And a good one."

Jamie went ahead and hooked an arm around her waist. "Are you sad to see you're not there?"

He gave a pointed look in Grant and Eve's direction.

"Why would I want to be there when I can be here with you?" Clapping her baby blue eyes on him, she dropped her eyelids.

"And how does it feel to have moved into your own house?" he asked.

"Even better than I expected." She whistled. "Though the second bedroom does feel a little empty. It's lacking a certain...someone."

"I'm glad to hear that." He took her hand and kissed it.

Jamie lost his grip on Bella as a camera click popped into his ear.

Of course, this being Grant Star's wedding reception, there were bound to be photographers. Grant had sold the photographic rights to *People* magazine, who'd sent some of their photographers to capture the big day.

The best man, one of Grant's colleagues, sounded a spoon on his glass, ready to toast to the new couple. "Well, I think I'll start the speeches before Grant decides to do something rash."

Jamie could understand why he'd say that. The way Grant was making eyes at Eve could make a fifteen-year-old blush.

"Good afternoon, ladies and gentlemen. I'm Paul, Grant's best friend. Actually, Grant's only friend, which explains why I'm the best man." Nervously, he wiped an imaginary bead of sweat.

Somebody chuckled at that.

"Grant's always had a way with the ladies." He shot Grant a cheesy grin. "Although not with this particular lady. Not until recently. Personally, I always thought they'd make a great couple. And it's cliché to say this, but I was right, wasn't I?"

"He was," Jamie said to Bella, laughing.

"By the way, I'd like to thank everyone for making it to the reception of this wonderful couple. This is a truly special day." Stroking his white beard, Paul paused. "And now, I'm going to have to tell you all about the time when Grant saved my life..."

A yawn drifted out of Bella's throat.

"Didn't sleep last night?" He cascaded his hand down her flowing hair.

"You didn't let me. You were snoring all night."

Pinching his eyebrows together, Jamie protested. "I don't snore."

She clicked her tongue. "You so do."

"Shhhh," Jamie said. Paul was still talking.

"Having been married for over thirty years, I have some advice to dispense about marriage. Yeah, I can see all those eye rolls. Bear with me for another minute." He faced the couple. "I'm sure you're both old enough to have become wise. Still, I'm not sure age has had the same sobering effect on Grant as it has had on the rest of us, so I have to advise."

The noise died down as the seriousness of the moment intensified.

"You're both embarking on the most amazing and meaningful journey of your life. At times, things will be tough, and at those times you must remember why you loved each other in the first place. Be each other's best friend. Love each other. Overcome trials instead of being overcome by them. Love is precious. Who knows whether you'll find it again. To sum it up in a quote by Lao Tzu, being loved by someone gives you strength while loving someone gives you courage. And now that's out of the way...."

Grant squeezed her fingers sympathetically, and it struck Jamie that this was the first time he'd seen his father be so warm to a woman.

Paul raised his glass in the air. "Here's to a lifetime of happiness for Grant and Eve."

Applause resounded, followed by champagne glasses hitting teeth.

Entwining their fingers, Bella and Jamie toasted.

To love, friendship, and forever.

ACKNOWLEDGMENTS

This book was made possible by the contributions and support of many talented people. I would like to thank Liv Shredder in particular, for her great comments and feedback, which helped improve the manuscript. I also owe a debt of gratitude to Chelsea Kuhel for editing and proofreading this book. A big thank you to my sister for always supporting me.

As always, I welcome comments, suggestions and feedback at alicemilleromance@gmail.com

If you want information on new releases, sales, and early previews, sign up to my newsletter.

ALSO BY SASHA CLINTON

You're Still the One

★★★★★ *If you like "The Notebook" you will definitely like this— Shredded Book Reviews*

★★★★★ *If you're a sucker for romance, this is the book for you— Amber R, Goodreads Reviewer*

Debut author Sasha Clinton weaves a raw, powerful tale of second chances, forgiveness, and finding love in the unlikeliest of places...

"We're like figures trapped in a snow globe, frozen in the snow, incapable of walking away from each other."

I was twenty-two, unemployed, and fresh out of college when a handsome stranger offered me his umbrella on a rainy night in New York.

His name was Andrew Smith, and six months later, I married him.

A year later, my life shattered into pieces when he divorced me.

Now, at thirty, I'm an editor at a large publishing house and Andrew is a billionaire. We inhabit different worlds. Except he has suddenly decided to write a book about his life. Worst part? My boss wants me to work with him on that book.

The more time I spend in Andrew's proximity, the more I start to remember why I fell in love with him. He's intense, charming, sexy as sin. As secrets from our past are dragged out into the open and old misunderstandings are cleared up, there seems to be no reason to not give our love another chance.

But can I fall in love again with the man who once broke my heart?

In my Arms Tonight

★★★★★*A great story with fantastic characters...this is one series you don't want to miss—Kirstie, Goodreads Reviewer*

★★★★★ *Sheer reading pleasure. Thank you Sasha for a story that will keep me revisiting, just because it's that good—Bianca E, Goodreads Reviewer*

Author Sasha Clinton returns with an emotional romance about what happens when a woman who hides her true self behind a mask meets a man just like her...

We're all monsters hiding behind pretty masks. I learned this the hard way, when my father, a respected lawyer, turned out to be sleeping with underage girls in his spare time.

As a reporter, I make my living digging up scandals and exposing the true faces of respected men.

I don't trust anyone. Especially not politicians.

Dark, sexy, ambitious, and older than me, US Representative Alex Summer is the sort of person I should stay far, far away from.

But he helps me out on the subway one night and our lives become intertwined after that. I'm drawn to him like a moth to a flame. I want is to see the monster under his mask. I want to show him mine.

I know Alex is hiding dark secrets behind his flawless face but guess what?

So am I.

Henry & Me

★★★★★ I adored this cleverly amusing book from start to finish—DJ Sakata, Goodreads reviewer

★★★★★ I suggest 1-clicking it now, sitting back and simply enjoying this fun, flirty yet meaningful story about Max, Henry and a really great supporting cast!—Barbara, Goodreads reviewer

Author Sasha Clinton returns with a hilarious new rom-com about what happens when an inept, out-of-work actress is forced to work for the guy she brutally rejected in college...

My name is Maxima Anderson and there are three things I regret in life: being mean to Henry Stone, moving to Hollywood for my acting career, and choosing to become Henry's housekeeper. The third's the worst, though, because I suck at housework. I'm pretty sure Henry hired me because he knows this, too, and wants to see me make a fool of myself while he savors my misery.

Did I mention he's a millionaire and he's paying me a ridiculous amount of money to do a bad job at housekeeping?

But things aren't going according to his plan. Or mine. Because I'm beginning to realize that under his stony façade, Henry has a golden heart. And he's gotten so much cuter since college. Our chemistry sizzles hotter than my burnt pancakes, and his sweet words corrode my resistances faster than bleach corrodes the lime scale in his bathtub. And if I don't do something about it, I might end up falling for the guy I hurt once...and hurt him again.

Printed in Great Britain
by Amazon